BETW
BRE

Also from Warner Books

BETWEEN THE LINES: THE CHILL FACTOR

BETWEEN THE LINES:
Breaking Point

DIANE PASCAL

WARNER
BOOKS

A *Warner* Book

First published in Great Britain in 1993 by Warner Books

Copyright © Diane Pascal 1993

Television Format and Series concept
Copyright © Island World Productions Limited 1992

The moral right of the author has been asserted.

A CIP catalogue record for this book
is available from the British Library.

ISBN 0 7515 0695 8

Photoset in North Wales by
Derek Doyle & Associates, Mold, Clwyd.
Printed and bound in Great Britain by
Clays Ltd, St Ives Plc

Warner Books
A Division of
Little, Brown and Company (UK) Limited
165 Great Dover Street
London SE1 4YA

BETWEEN THE LINES: BREAKING POINT

'I can still smell whitewash,' said Cope.

'Can't I just take you out for a meal and talk about—'

'Don't make me laugh, caveman!' she said with a broad smile, returning to her desk and snatching the mail from her pigeon-hole as she walked past. A blonde-haired colleague at the next desk looked up and smiled to herself. It was always good to see Molly in full swing, making mincemeat of men who thought they were important.

Tony Clark held her glare. 'You stand there behaving like a two-legged rottweiler and call me primitive?' Sharp talk never fazed Clark; like all powerful men he loved a challenge. A little public humiliation was quite a turn-on.

After a charged pause Cope said, 'You want to buy me a meal? Eight o'clock tomorrow, Frank's in the Docks Road.'

He had won, and he walked away without uttering a word to spoil his victory. But he didn't know Molly Cope.

'That's a.m., by the way,' she said, without looking up from the piece of paper she was studying. 'Eight a.m. Don't be late.' Clark slowed up. Damn her cunning! As he paused in front of the swing doors he heard her reading from the sheet she had torn from the teleprinter and gloating to her blonde colleague. She knew he was listening, and she was enjoying herself. 'How's this for a heading? "Police stop white man in car!" Now that *is* a scoop isn't it?' Molly Cope was young, black and angry.

1

It was drizzling that morning in New Brighton, a down-at-heel and weary district of Liverpool. In Westbury Street an irritable shopkeeper was pulling down the striped awning outside his shop with a hook on a long pole. There was no one else in the street. Several of the dozen shops were boarded up, including the coffee bar next to the post office, and most of the others hadn't opened yet. A solitary tree on the wide pavement struggled to brighten up the drab appearance of the red brick flats above the shops on one side of the street and the bingo hall on the other. A milk float loaded with green crates trundled past, and a motorbike approached from the other end of the street.

The bike stopped outside Dalglish's newsagency and sub-post office on the corner of Westbury Street. Two women were talking between the chipped postbox and the rack of newspapers displayed next to the post office door; the younger of the two was rocking a pushchair. The motorbike which drew up alongside them was small, perhaps 120cc, and its tall rider was wearing a leather jacket, black jeans and a dark blue helmet. Without taking the helmet off he pushed open the post office door.

A young boy was looking with wide eyes at the confectionary display at one end of the small shop. He

1

fingered several bars of chocolate, and while the elderly postmistress's back was turned he slipped a Caramel bar in a yellow wrapper into his pocket.

The postmistress was wearing a long waistcoat over a floral housecoat. She had knitted the waistcoat herself. She was serving a woman in her sixties in a grey anorak, and they were talking about the weather in the time-honoured British tradition. The postmistress had just handed over the woman's pension when the biker drew a silver gun from his jacket and brandished it dramatically in the air. The woman in the anorak gasped and leaned back against the counter, terrified. The biker pointed the gun at the floor in front of the young boy, who had turned to leave, indicating that he should lie down, which he did, sharpish, sweat breaking out immediately on his forehead and and under his thin arms. He lay there, clutching his Caramel until it started to melt, his breathing shallow. The biker went to the counter and pointed the gun at the postmistress. She knew what she had to do, and began fumbling around for cash. There wasn't a great deal of it; although there were a lot of people on 'social' in the district, most of them went to collect their money from the large post office next to the Co-op on the main road. Sometimes she wouldn't see more than a dozen punters in a morning in Dalglish's. She took the carrier bag that the biker stuffed under the counter and began filling it with twenties, tenners and fivers, her hands trembling.

A man in jeans and a hooded sweatshirt top entered the post office, nodding at the women who were still talking outside, moaning about the price of groceries, while the toddler in the pushchair gurgled. The man in jeans wanted a packet of Marlboro to kick-start the motor. Alarmed by the arrival of this newcomer, the biker turned round and punched him hard on the jaw, taking a good swing at it by pulling his arm right back

2

behind him first. The man fell to the ground, gripping the bridge of his nose as blood ran down his face and splashed his sweatshirt. The woman in the grey anorak was crying.

The biker was breathing so heavily that the perspex of his visor had steamed up. He jammed the carrier bag which the postmistress thrust under the counter into his jacket, ran out of the shop and got onto his bike just as the shrill alarm sounded. The two women had disappeared around the corner and into Jeffrey Street. The biker reversed, did a U-turn and sped away. The little boy lying on the floor had wet himself.

Several hours after the New Brighton robbery a navy-blue car screeched up outside an old-fashioned pub in a windblown street overlooking the Mersey. It was a grey kind of day. A mangy dog nosed at a plastic wrapper discarded on the broken tarmac. A crinkly-haired man in a suit stepped smartly out of the back of the car and into the pub, followed by his driver.

The first man was a detective inspector, and he had been to this pub before. It was not a social visit. He knew very well who hung out in there, and he wasn't afraid of confronting them. He walked straight through the main bar, through the smoke, the shrill laughter, the distorted pop music pumping out of the jukebox, the pool tables, the smell of best bitter, the sense of temporary escape – yes, he knew this scene all right. He had been working this beat too long to feel out of place in the suit. All the space in his mind was taken up with one thought: who had done that sub-post office? He had good reason to suspect the answer.

He stopped twenty feet away from a low table where four young men were sitting, drinking and laughing, in front of a barred window. One of them had built a little castle with beermats.

'You been a busy boy this morning, Dicks?' drawled Kendrick when he spotted his man. Silence fell like a portcullis. The young men looked at Kendrick standing in the opening between the bars, his chunky constable behind him. The current of bitterness between the two camps was palpable. Dicks was the tallest of the small group of drinkers. He had a thin, angular face, black hair and inscrutable blue eyes. He wasn't the kind of man anyone would be happy about meeting in a dark alley. Next to him sat a man with a semi-skinhead haircut. Dicks mustered every drop of contempt in his body and spat: 'Fishing with my friend, Mr Kendrick, *sir*.'

'I'll get you, Dicks,' said Kendrick.

'Will ya?' He feigned surprise. 'What for?'

'It's only a matter of time.'

The pair of them looked steadily at each other. They had been circling each other round the city for years, allowing grudges and hatred to ferment. Dicks raised his right arm and pointed two fingers at the detective's head in a mock shooting gesture. Slowly, and deliberately, he pulled the invisible trigger.

Late that night Kendrick took a confession from the tall twenty-four-year-old Liverpudlian with blue eyes in a starkly lit interview room in Egberth police station. The blue eyes were shining unnaturally, and the black hair looked as if it hadn't seen a comb for quite a while. Dicks was coming down off a basinful of marijuana and Ecstasy. It wasn't the first time he had been 'interviewed' by the law.

'Taped interview,' said the crinkly-haired man in a deadpan, firm voice. 'June the second, 1990. Twenty-three fifty-two hours. Present: Edward John Dicks and the arresting officers, Detective Inspector William Kendrick and Detective Constable James McPherson.

'I must remind you, Mr Dicks,' he continued slowly,

4

'that you are still under caution and that this interview is being recorded and may be used as evidence in a court of law. Do you understand that?'

'Yes, sir,' drawled Dicks.

'Did you,' said Kenrick deliberately, 'at about nine o'clock this morning, enter Westbury Street sub-post office armed with a pistol?'

'Yes sir, I did sir.'

'Tell us what happened.'

'Well I . . . er . . . I gave the lady behind the counter a bag . . .'

'That's right, Dicks. Carry on.'

'A carrier bag . . .'

2

Detective Inspector Harry Naylor fingered the two-year-old press cutting, the ubiquitous cigarette dangling in his other hand, its cylinder of ash trembling as the train juddered.

'And Dicks was charged that night?' asked Naylor's colleague, seated at the window.

'Yes,' replied a tall, pale-skinned red-haired woman sitting opposite. The single word was enough to reveal a melodious Scottish lilt.

'By Kendrick?'

She nodded. 'On four counts of armed robbery, all post offices, including the one at New Brighton that morning.'

Detective Superintendent Tony Clark, the man at the window, took the press cutting from Naylor, concentrating on what his sergeant was telling him and simultaneously running his silver pen down the single column of type on the press cutting, headlined DATE SET FOR DICKS APPEAL. In a second column his eye fell on a photograph of the smiling journalist who had uncovered the story.

Sergeant Maureen Connell, the redhead, handed her boss another photocopied press cutting over the train table, which the three of them had cluttered with files, notes and clippings, packets of cigarettes, soft-drinks cans and the usual detritus of long-distance train travel. The second cutting read SOUTH LANCS SERIOUS CRIME SQUAD: INVESTIGATION DEEPENS. Alongside the giant photograph of a senior policeman Clark clocked a small photograph of the same reporter, a striking young black woman called Molly Cope. 'Has Kendrick been involved in any of the other South Lancashire embarrassments?' he asked.

'Doesn't look like it,' said Connell. Clark drew a circle around Molly Cope's face. It was going to be important to pump her for all she knew. He looked up at the emerald-green blur of the fields rushing past as they left London behind. The story was familiar enough. The complainant has been arrested, and his statement had been doctored after he'd signed it to make it look like a confession. It could have been another triumph for ESDA – Electrostatic Deposition Analysis – if the notes from the case hadn't all gone AWOL.

Naylor stood up and looked around the carriage restlessly, scratching his head. It was always the same in this job – the beginning of a case was the most difficult. They had to ease themselves into it. But it would come. Naylor was a pro. 'Want a coffee, Maureen?'

'Cheers, Harry.'

'Guv?'

'Yeah, thanks Harry.' Naylor lurched off through the automatic doors and towards the restaurant car, his craggy face expressionless. He was in his mid-forties, had been in the force all his working life and had always worn his hair long at the back, a good inch over his collar. Except for a stint with the Flying Squad, he had served as a divisional CID man in a variety of police stations in London and the neighbouring counties. There weren't many men in blue who had cultivated such an impressive network of contacts in their years as a street-level policeman as Naylor. Straight, bent or with a slight kink in the middle,

Naylor knew them, and it wasn't surprising that he had developed a world-weary cynicism. He was good at his job, wouldn't tell anybody anything he didn't think they needed to know, and was a shrewd judge of human nature. He was a natural in the police investigations bureau.

'Three coffees please, mate,' he asked the waiter, a typically saturnine British Rail employee in a ridiculous red bow tie and waistcoat. As he poured tiny pots of UHT milk into the styrofoam cups Naylor wondered how his boss would fare with the turnip-top police chiefs of South Lancs. Probably OK. He liked Clark – with one or two reservations – and he reckoned that the three of them, Clark, Maureen and himself, made a good team. Naylor was Sancho Panza to Clark's Don Quixote. He went in ahead and decided how much Clark needed to know, or squared things up when Clark had left. Naylor fixed things, and he always fixed them right, whatever it took.

This job shouldn't be too much trouble, he reflected as he stirred the coffees. The South Lancs Serious Crime Squad was being investigated after a series of their cases had been blown out on appeal. The whole shooting match was under the supervision of a very senior police officer, and Clark and his team from the Complaints Investigation Bureau at New Scotland Yard had been rowed in to handle only a small part of the inquiry.

Naylor crushed his cigarette against the side of an empty styrofoam cup, picked up the plastic tray and set off back to his carriage. In the business of investigating complaints and allegations against the police, which was the CIB's remit, it was in many ways easier to work with an out-of-town force rather than your own. There wasn't quite the same sense of scoring an own goal, and there was less chance of investigating people who were friends or friends of friends. On the other hand, of

8

course, you didn't know the ropes quite so well and you didn't have the same background in the culture or the advantage of knowing the gossip about the characters involved.

Naylor was hoping that they wouldn't be up there in Liverpool for too long. Professional advantages and disadvantages apart, Naylor was a serious Cockney, and the truth was that he didn't really enjoy being out of London. He felt like a fish out of water if he didn't get back to his terraced house in Bethnal Green of a night and chat the day over with his wife, and – if he made it early enough – their two daughters and one son. It was in the back of his mind that since the arrival of his new boss at the CIB several months previously the job seemed to be hotting up; their elders and betters were putting them on increasingly important cases. Where was it leading? It was obvious to everyone that Clark was a career copper who'd be looking to shine as brightly as possible. This made Naylor very slightly uncomfortable. He had no aspirations of advancement. He wanted to do his job – which was to see justice done – as well as he could, and be allowed to lead his life outside of it in peace. He may have been one of life's rough diamonds, but even the most unpolished among them find their settings.

It was a particularly lively press conference – the liveliest in South Lancashire for some time. The hacks loved it: something was happening for once, and about fifty of them had turned up, spiral-bound notebooks or mini tape-recorders in their hands and white identification badges on their lapels. Two senior police officers in uniform and a man in a grey suit from the Police Complaints Authority were seated at a long table on a podium at one end of the echoing hall, facing rows of reporters and a posse of photographers as well as a television camera crew and two video cameramen.

9

In the middle of the triumvirate at the top table, Deputy Assistant Commissioner More, a tall, imposing man with a fringe of white hair around a bald pate, finished reading his statement amid the incessant clicks of camera shutters and the bright white glare of flash units.

'In the light of this,' he concluded into the small row of microphones, firmly but with a trace of weariness in his voice, 'the Metropolitan Police investigating team has been increased to a strength of sixteen officers and two civilians. We continue to work in close co-operation with, and under the supervision of, the Police Complaints Authority.'

He took off his glasses and folded his arms. Before his words had died away half of the audience had their hands up. But one young woman was ahead of the pack. She jumped to her feet and launched in.

'Molly Cope, *Liverpool Press*.'

'Yes, Miss Cope, we know,' said More sardonically. You've done enough damage already with your endless ferreting around in our business, he thought. Journalists like you are like dogs with bones – once they get them between their teeth they can't bloody well let go.

This woman was a born public speaker. With confidence and aplomb belying her twenty-seven years, Molly Cope stood demurely in her smart cherry-red jacket, white open-necked shirt and long white skirt and delivered her speech – without notes, of course. 'For nine months you have been investigating three hundred and twelve complaints and forty-two arrests. Three men have been released by the appeal court who between them spent seventeen years in prison that they shouldn't have.'

More looked away, and twisted the fingers of one hand around those of the other. 'Yet,' Cope went on emphatically, 'all we have to show for this waste of the public's time, money and, worst of all, liberty, is one officer retired on medical grounds, one cautioned and five suspended – on full pay. Not a criminal charge in sight. Meanwhile members of the public, like Teddy Dicks' – here a note of exasperation crept into her voice – 'who has now been in prison for over eighteen months waiting for—'

'Did you have a question, Miss Cope?' the Deputy Assistant Commissioner interrupted, his voice cold enough to freeze a bowl of hot water.

'Yes,' she replied, looking him in the eye. 'Which would you say was foremost in your minds whilst carrying out these investigations: the interest of the public, or the police force?'

More stared at her and composed his answer. Damn you, woman! he thought. The whole business had become a nightmare for More. He had arrived in Liverpool nine months previously from New Scotland Yard in order to sort out the South Lancs Serious Crime Squad. Troubles had been rumbling there for some time, and it got heavy when two men who had been convicted of a brutal offence were subsequently released on appeal and the detectives involved made to look right charlies in court. Questions had been asked, and a pall of failure had settled over the South Lancs squad.

More had been in the force for twenty years and he was well aware that bad smells did sometimes go away. At first he hadn't worried too much, but had worked hard to overcome the difficulties and rebuild the squad's credibility and public image. Before he had been promoted and moved to London two years previously he had been working in the south-west, and he was finding life up here in the north much tougher. There was quite simply more crime in Liverpool alone than there was in the whole of Cornwall and Devon put together, and he had never anticipated this level of

11

suspicion against the force in general. Yet there was something in More which rose to the occasion. He was made of stern stuff, and he had the balls to ride the big waves and the confidence to hold his head up and lead his team through.

But he did wish he didn't have Molly Cope to contend with.

3

Tony Clark sprawled over the double bed in the hotel room, his tie off and his pink shirt hanging out of his trousers. He was a man of average height and build, thirty-seven years old with a good physique, and he was very good-looking, with smooth, light brown hair, alluring blue eyes and a strong nose and chin. The deep red bedcover on which he lay was covered in notes, newspapers and a black briefcase. Above the bed two old-fashioned pink lamps cast a yellow glow over a reproduction oil painting of a vase of flowers. The Shaftesbury Hotel wasn't actually seedy; it was just a grade or two below mediocre.

Clark's mind was racing after the first day on the job. The complainant, it emerged, was a self-confessed professional villain with a long list of unchallenged convictions. Dicks was hardly likely to be a popular character in the police stations of Liverpool, and Clark could see that he and the other members of the Met CIB team were going to rate only slightly below Dicks in the popularity stakes within the force. It didn't worry him. He looked forward to setting up the team desks at Huskisson Street police station the following day and rolling up his sleeves to get on with the job.

His wife telephoned, and he gripped the receiver under his chin as they chatted. Sue was about to go off to work. She was on night shifts that week. She was a staff nurse at one of the leading London teaching hospitals. They had been married for two and a half years.

'All right darling . . . Yeah, sleep well . . . I'll see you soon,' he told her, and when he had replaced the handset he swivelled round to the bedside table and poured a slug of Scotch into a glass. It was his second of the night. The telephone rang again.

'Hello,' he said, his clipped tone indicating that he could do without another telephone call. 'Wha . . . Jenny! How the hell did you track me down? Jenny, it's over between us! I thought you understood that. Too many people know. It's over . . . Of course you can't come up here to see me . . . Jenny, if you did that I would never speak to you again . . . This place is crawling with Met—' There was a knock on the wall. 'Probably the Assistant Commissioner knocking now, he's in the room next door . . . Shit, there's another one,' he said as someone knocked on the door. 'Just a minute!' he shouted, and spoke in agitated, conspiratorial tones into the receiver. 'I'll ring you in a couple of weeks. Don't ring me . . . all right . . . bye.'

Clark slid off the bed and hurried over to the door, cradling the bottle of Scotch and his glass and breathing tense expletives to himself as he always did when he was stressed. He opened the door. It wasn't the Assistant Commissioner. It was his team, Naylor and Connell. That was a relief.

The pair of them barged in. Naylor, in shirt-sleeves, had a creased look about him, but Connell always looked cool and sophisticated. She might have been treated as one of the boys, but she always looked better than any of the boys did. That evening she was wearing a chocolate brown silk shirt and tapering cream slacks.

'You watching it too?' asked Naylor as he swept over to the television, switched it on and sat down on the edge of the bed.

14

'No,' said Clark, pleased that they were too preoccupied to notice his agitation.

'Oh, thought that's why you knocked – or perhaps it was the big boss who knocked.' The Assistant Commissioner had been hammering on everyone's wall to tell them to turn the telly on, quick.

Newsnight were running a piece on the press conference, and at that moment they were screening a clip of Molly Cope in full spate. More struggled to defend himself against her tongue-lashing with dignity. 'I am merely here to investigate criminal or disciplinary offences—'

'Amongst your fellow officers,' interjected Cope, with masterful stress on the word 'fellow'.

The programme cut back to the studio, where a dour presenter wearing a florid tie was grilling Deputy Chief Constable Trevor Dunning. 'Well, Mr Dunning,' began the presenter. 'The cry seems to be "Whitewash".'

Dunning braced himself. 'Inevitably. John More you saw there, who is leading the investigation, is an old friend and colleague of mine. He is a superb police officer and as determined as anyone to ensure that this country gets the police force it deserves. But he can't win. There's no question in my mind that any internal investigation of the police must be carried out by a wholly independent body.'

'Why doesn't the Police Complaints Authority fulfil that role?' interrupted the interviewer quickly.

'It was never intended to,' continued Dunning confidently. 'Investigations are still carried out by the police, sometimes with PCA supervision.'

'Isn't it Police Federation policy that their members should not meet members of the PCA?'

'Almost without exception the police and the PCA work extremely well together. I accept that some members of the police force will have to be dragged screaming and kicking into the Britain of the 1990s. But there are those of us who are determined that it will happen . . .'

The background to this interview was the release of the Edgbaston Two on appeal earlier that day. It was this that had provided a platform for the Deputy Chief Constable to call for radical reforms of legal procedure: initial police investigations to be under the control of a legal officer outside the force; a non-adversarial process of trial; the wholly independent investigation of complaints against the police. Dunning had gone to some length to proclaim that his remarks constituted purely personal views. He had first made them in an academic seminar context, but the media had got hold of them, and he was now obliged to see it through and explain himself. It wasn't turning out too badly. His views were being perceived as a manifesto for comprehensive reform – and he had his eye on the job of Metropolitan Commissioner.

'Impressive, isn't he?' commented Clark quietly as the three of them listened intently to the *Newsnight* interview.

'Dunning?' said Naylor. 'D'you think so?'

'Don't you?' asked Clark, genuinely surprised.

'I think he's a grey-suited, all things to all men politico. And I'll be buggered if he's going to drag me into the 1990s, screaming or otherwise.' Naylor stomped out of the room, leaving the door open.

'What's up with him?' asked Clark as he switched off the television and walked across the room, the Scotch bottle in his hand.

'He hates being away from home,' said Connell, who had been leaning against the wardrobe while the two men sat on the bed. 'I think he's missing some wee wifey's spotted dick.'

'Or vice versa.' It was a typical Clark one-liner. 'Nightcap?' he asked Connell, holding a glass in the air.

But she smiled wryly and went to the door. Nightcaps in hotel rooms were hardly her style.

Tony had notes to catch up on and documents to read. But he felt fraught, agitated and stressed, so he set the alarm for 6.30 and took a hot shower, another glass of Scotch balanced on the edge of the bath. The hot water and clouds of steam calmed him down. The telephone call from Jenny Dean had rattled him. He felt uneasy; he felt as if he hadn't behaved particularly well towards her, and he didn't like that. He thought he was basically a good guy – a good guy who liked to enjoy himself but didn't do anyone any harm. And, basically, he was right.

His affair with Jenny Dean had begun when they were both working at Mulberry Road station in south London. She was young, very pretty, very lithe – irresistible. Tony couldn't resist, anyway. Tony didn't usually even consider resisting if he wanted something badly. He had only been a detective superintendent for a couple of months when this Liverpool case had come up. When they had boarded him, as a successful detective chief inspector with a good reputation, he knew through the informal grapevine within the Met that he'd got the promotion long before he turned up at New Scotland Yard for his interview.

But he hadn't known where he was going to be posted, and while it was under discussion among his elders and betters, a small-time pusher and snout had led to Clark and his team at Mulberry Street being placed under covert investigation by the CIB – the team Clark was now a member of, which covered complaints of both disciplinary infringements and crime within the force. It had come as a nasty shock to Clark when he had discovered that he was being investigated. He was asked if he had been in the frame for alleged leaks to criminals which had blown out a series of Mulberry Street drugs busts. Like all coppers, he had bent the rules and gilded the lily in his time, but he wasn't *bad*. Not at all. It didn't make him feel any better when the CIB revealed that they knew he was having an affair with WPC Jenny Dean.

Clark was given the chance to wipe the slate clean by acting as an informant within his own nick. It meant more than one betrayal of trust, personal and professional. But if Clark was willing to get his hands dirty to put villains in the bin, he was willing to do the same to clean up Mulberry Street – and to safeguard his future career, of course.

The job had been done, and Clark looked for his reward: a posting to the Flying Squad as detective superintendent. He was in for another surprise. His promotion was going through all right, but his performance in the Mulberry Street operation had convinced the top brass that he could make his most effective contribution as an investigation officer within the CIB.

If Clark couldn't take a joke he wouldn't have joined the force. He decided to do the job in Complaints as best he could, knowing that it was a minefield and so keeping a wary eye out so as not to lose his legs. As his new CIB boss, Deakin, pointed out when Clark accepted the post, if he had shown positive enthusiasm for the work he wouldn't have been offered it.

Clark's new job frequently involved investigating people very much like himself, which could be perceived as either a strength or a weakness. In some cases they were people who were used to being deferred to, but holding the rank of assistant commissioner or the Queen's Police Medal didn't make you fireproof. While Clark was determined to do the best job he could, he was a career copper: he looked forward to life after the CIB, and there had already been moments when it had been hinted that pursuing a particular course of action was going to make him deeply unpopular with rank and file officers he hoped one day to command, or would make him an embarrassment to senior officers who would perhaps control his promotion prospects in the future. It wasn't that Clark always conformed when it came to the crunch: but he was a grown-up, and he worked hard to prevent the crunch coming.

He got out of the shower and rubbed himself down with a ratty hotel bath towel. The phone call from Jenny Dean kept coming back to him. It wasn't the first time he had cheated on his wife and in his heart he knew it wouldn't be the last. But that didn't mean he didn't love Sue; it didn't mean that at all. She meant more to him than anything else in the world. But did that really involve sexual fidelity forever and ever? Why should it?

Their relationship hadn't been too good lately. She was finding the long hours of his new job difficult to cope with. Tony found them difficult too, but he couldn't do anything about them. He wanted to make it work, to get on, and every time he made a commitment to Sue to make it home early, Deakin, his Chief Super and immediate boss, seemed to spring something urgent on him. There had been rows, between him and Sue. But what could he do?

Sue had got wind that he was having an affair, too, and there had been an ugly scene. What with one thing and another he had decided it had to end with Jenny — not least when she turned out to be involved in one of his cases, and it had threatened to turn nasty. He had thought she was going to go quietly, but obviously she wasn't.

With a stab of anxiety, he swallowed the rest of the Scotch in one gulp.

4

The taxi drew up in a wide cul-de-sac outside Huskisson Street police station, and Clark, Connell and Naylor stepped out into the fresh morning air. Connell glanced at Liverpool Cathedral beyond the bollards as they walked briskly towards the station. A policeman jumped into his car alongside them. With their briefcases swinging the three of them pushed open the navy-blue swing doors, and Clark led the way through the bustling hall.

'I thought they said he was coming here!' a shrill woman's voice rang out. 'Well, where is he? I can't keep coming back here. He's under age.' She was speaking to the duty sergeant over the counter of the reception desk. Various other scruffy individuals were loitering around, and a man in a stained gaberdine was asleep on a grey plastic chair. A snivelling toddler was picking his nose and pulling on the querulous woman's knitted skirt.

'There's no point in having a go at me about it,' said the sergeant.

'Excuse me,' said Clark, showing his ID to the irritated man. 'Detective Superintendent Clark. Assistant Commissioner More is expecting us.' The woman scowled. Who the bloody hell did he think he was? She had been kept waiting an hour before she had been seen to.

'Incident room, second floor, sir,' said the sergeant, and he pressed a buzzer to let the three of them into the heart of the station. By the time they reached the door, however, the buzzer had stopped and the door had relocked.

Clark exhaled deeply and returned to the sergeant, who had resumed his wrangling with the woman. 'Excuse me, sergeant . . .' he said, trying to control his voice.

'One moment, sir,' said the sergeant politely, and continued to deal with the woman. 'I've told you. We took a statement and released him. How should I know where he is now?'

As Clark was on the point of exploding a WPC came into the reception area and punched a code into the door lock. As she went through, Clark and the other two made to follow her.

'Can I help you, sir?' said the WPC innocently.

'We've come to see Assistant Commissioner More.'

'You'll have to see the sergeant at reception,' she said sweetly, and shut the door in his face.

'Arsehole,' said Clark. He was turning to go and give the duty sergeant a blast when he saw Naylor punching a code number into the door, which duly opened. Clark looked dumbfounded.

'Born crook,' said Connell with a smile.

'Aren't we all?' chirped Naylor.

They made their way along a corridor and up two flights of echoing stairs which smelled of turpentine. On the second floor they wandered down a corridor, feeling lost in an alien environment. Clark glanced into an office where a thickset man with crinkly hair wearing a dark grey suit looked up at him, surprised. It was Kendrick. Another man was writing at the opposite side of the desk.

'That's not it,' said Clark in a low, irritated voice as he strode on. 'Excuse me,' he said to a uniformed

21

policeman's back. 'Can you tell me where I can find the Met incident room, please?'

The man stopped, turned around and, with an ugly expression on his chubby face, asked Clark: 'Are you a detective?'

Clark nodded. 'Yeah.'

'Then you find it.'

Clark turned to the other two, a look of resignation on his face. Naylor smirked.

All three of them were used to this kind of treatment, of course. It was an occupational hazard. Working in the police complaints division was the lowest of the low as far as many coppers were concerned. The most golden of all the rules in the force was 'Don't grass on your own kind'. It was probably a tenet better observed in the police force than among criminals, in fact. Police culture depended on a complex web of loyalties and misunderstandings (it was also shot through with jealousies and resentments), and it was essential that when an officer shouted for help, his or her mates piled in without a second thought. If you expected them to do that for you, then you found yourself willing to watch their backs when they were in trouble. After all, doing something 'wrong' wasn't that unusual. And if it was some minor disciplinary offence – like transgressing the PACE codes of conduct – well, for God's *sake*. Occasionally, it was more serious an offence than that, and then, well, loyalty was loyalty, wasn't it?

It wasn't surprising. After all, if a civilian were to drink and drive, or lose his or her temper and hit someone, or let slip confidential information acquired in the course of his or her work, the consequences were unlikely to be catastrophic – a fine, maybe, or a ticking-off. A police officer would lose a career, and more than that, as he or she perceived it: the status which defined him or her as a human being.

It was in this context that Clark and his two side-kicks found themselves on the wrong side of a wall of strong dislike and bitter contempt at Huskisson Street. Everyone employed at the station knew of the troubles that had beset the Crime Squad, they all knew the implications of this bloody investigation, and they were closing ranks. Not much escaped them: they were expecting three more nerds from New Scotland Yard that day. Kendrick had known exactly who Clark was when he had looked into his office. But Clark didn't know yet who Kendrick was.

Just as the officer was snarling in Clark's face the Deputy Assistant Commissioner who had been verbally roughed up at the press conference stepped out of a door behind them. 'Ah, Clark,' More began. 'Hello. Welcome to Beirut.' The pair of them knew each other from New Scotland Yard, but they had never worked closely together. More held open the door into the incident room, and Naylor and Connell went in. More had wanted to nobble Clark alone straight away, and he spoke seriously to him as they walked along the corridor.

'I want you lot back in London in a couple of weeks. My gut feeling is that this Dicks character is hitching onto the bandwagon. None of the three officers involved had been implicated in any of the other shenanigans around here.' He stopped and turned to face Clark. 'Don't get me wrong, bent coppers I want in the bin, but I will not countenance a witch-hunt. Understood?'

'Understood, sir.'

'Right, carry on.' He opened a door and showed Clark an enormous office in which a bevy of uniformed officers were handling quantities of files and paperwork. Naylor, his jacket already off, and Connell were standing on either side of a group of tables pushed together in the middle of the room. The tables were piled high with bulging files, so high that they had to be pushed around, not lifted. More looked at Clark's face, studying his reaction. Clark looked daunted.

'Thank you, sir,' he said with a trace of irony as More held the door open for him.

'Well, consider yourself lucky,' said More ruefully. 'Most of us have been moving a pile like this every week for the best part of a year.'

By the middle of the afternoon the tables in the middle were in better order. Policemen and WPCs were working at adjacent desks, apparently oblivious to the new arrivals who had set up in such a wholesale fashion in the busy incident room. Connell had a neat pile of files next to her. She was studying one with a photograph stapled on the top sheet inside. The photograph was of the crinkly-haired man Clark had seen when he had first entered the station: Kendrick.

Connell had been summing up the nitty-gritty of the Dicks case – or what she had uncovered of it – to her boss. 'Dicks was arrested,' Connell reported, 'by Kendrick and McPherson at nine twenty-five p.m., taken to Egberth station and booked in by the duty sergeant, Sergeant Poynton, at ten p.m. He made a taped confession at eleven fifty-two p.m.'

Clark was sitting at a desk behind her, his sleeves pushed up, smoking a cigarette and looking troubled. A laptop computer was open in front of him. 'He made no complaint at the time?' he asked Connell.

'At the committal proceedings he mentioned being roughed up but he never made a formal complaint,' chipped in Naylor, who was sitting opposite Connell, also smoking, and looking fed up.

Clark looked down at a sheet of paper. 'This complaint, lodged by his new solicitor last week, mentions being roughed up but it also claims that he was high on drugs, deprived of food and water and denied his right to a solicitor. Any mention of those in the reports?'

'No,' said a weary Naylor. 'Not as far as I can see, anyway.'

'Is that the basis of his leave to appeal?' asked Connell, sipping cold coffee from a styrofoam cup.

'No, the local rag's found someone, an old friend of Dicks, who is willing to testify that he and Dicks were out of their minds on a combination of dope and Ecstasy at the time he was picked up. He says he would still have been bombed when he made his confession.'

'It's a bit hard to prove after two years, innit?' said Naylor, resting his temple on his fist and twirling a biro round in his other hand. 'I'm surprised they granted leave to appeal.'

'Any other force but South Lancs and they wouldn't have,' said Clark grimly. There was a pause. Adjacent typewriters clattered.

'So, where do we start, then?' asked Naylor, scratching his ear.

'I want you to talk to this new witness, er, Dicks' friend Clive whatever his name is,' Clark replied authoritatively.

'We're going to talk to Dicks.'

Connell nodded. They were off.

They managed to organise a pool car, but it was a struggle. Connell had been obliged to go as high as More to see to it that the matter was arranged and pushed through swiftly. 'Sorry to trouble you with this, sir,' she had said, 'but I seem to be encountering a bit of resistance.'

More had quite a soft spot for Connell, and had often paused in the carpeted corridors of his floor at New Scotland Yard, if he saw her, to indulge in a friendly chat. He chuckled. 'Resistance?' he said. 'You should count yourself lucky. I usually get hit by a range of ballistic missiles.'

They had eventually been handed the keys of a newish red Ford Granada which they found in the car park at the back of the station. Connell drove while Clark sorted through papers in his lap. She looked out at the Liverpool streets as she picked her way to the prison, reflecting that something about them reminded her of her native Aberdeen. She missed Scotland, and she liked visiting the north of England as it made her feel closer to home, and not just in the geographical sense. Mind you, she had been living in London ever since she graduated from Edinburgh University, where she read politics – and that was fifteen years ago.

When they reached the monolithic prison, a model of dour Victorian solidity, they parked in a side street and walked round to the entrance, where they flashed their IDs and were shepherded inside. They weren't quite so unpopular there. A prison guard led them up to a heavy metal grille. He unlocked the grille, then another, and escorted them through while another officer locked up behind, jangling a heavy set of keys. After following the first guard through a maze of cold and forbidding institutional corridors, Clark and Connell were shown into a high-ceilinged interview room. There was nothing in the room except a dozen formica tables with grey plastic chairs tucked under them, and the thin morning light shone through a row of high, barred windows. A blue-eyed man in his early twenties in a pale green open-necked shirt was already seated at a table next to a man in a suit and tie who was obviously his solicitor.

Clark and Connell sat down on the other side of the table and Connell placed a small tape-recorder on it. A prison guard stood like a grim statue at the other end of the room, his hands clasped behind his back. The detectives introduced themselves, and Clark asked the young man, Teddy Dicks, about Detective Inspector Bill Kendrick.

'He's a bastard, he's always had it in for me, harassing me.' Dicks looked aggressive.

'Did you never think of complaining?'

'Do me a favour, I've got form,' snarled Dicks in a rasping Liverpudlian accent. 'I stole me first Vauxhall when I was twelve. We complain and someone fills us in, boof.' He threw a right hook in Clark's direction, quick as lightning, his face twisted with bitterness and pain.

Clark blinked very slowly, registering displeasure but not fear. The solicitor remained impassive, sitting like a Buddha. 'What d'you think he's standing there for?' Dicks continued, nodding at the prison guard.

'I think we'll be all right, officer, thank you,' said Clark, and the man left. 'Right, Teddy, the day of your arrest.'

'Yeah.' He paused. 'You got a fag?' Clark took a packet of Silk Cut out of his pocket and put it on the table in front of Dicks, who took a cigarette, lit it and inhaled deeply, savouring the taste of tobacco. He resigned himself to going through his story. There was no point in being obstructive – in a way he and Clark were on the same team.

'We'd been in the pub, then we went to a mate's and three of us done some E.'

'How much?'

'A tab each. We had a good bit of blow 'n' all. I reckon it was that that did my head. When *Take the High Road* was over I went walkabout.'

'Alone?' interjected Clark.

'Yeah.'

'For fresh air?'

'Amongst other things.'

'Such as?'

'You ever done Ecstasy?' He knew the answer. Connell smiled. 'I fancied a bird. So I walked about a bit, then Kendrick came up to me.'

'Where was this?'

'New Brighton, Victoria Road.'

'At about four in the afternoon?'

'Yeah. Kendrick says nine o'clock. Lying bastard.'

'Then what?'

'He grabbed me and took me down the docks. I tell you I was freaked.'

Shortly before dusk a large red Granada drew up in a wet and deserted street on the docks, its windscreen wipers on slow speed to clear the fine rain. The high warehouse walls lining the street were stained with water and grime; it was a colourless, depressing scene bereft of human life. Clark got out of the passenger seat and left Connell in the vehicle. He wanted to walk around the docks area where Dicks alleged Kendrick had taken him and listen to the tape they had recorded of Dicks' version of events that morning. He needed to get the feel of this story. At the end of the street the water rippled slightly, like a wheatfield, in a cold evening breeze.

Clark pulled up his collar, walked into the first warehouse, its doors wide open, and switched on the tape-player as he wandered through the desolate building.

'Did he caution you?' he heard himself asking.

'He grabbed me arm and said, "Right you little shit, we're going to talk" – is that a caution?' crackled Dicks' voice. 'He took me down to the docks and smacked me one in the ribs. I went down like a bleeding sack. I thought he'd killed me. I couldn't breathe.'

'Kendrick's statement at the trial,' Clark had said to Dicks then, 'claimed that he followed you through the docks to a spot behind a deserted warehouse where

28

you removed the helmet, gloves and jacket you had used for the New Brighton job from their hiding-place. At which point he arrested you.'

'That's lies,' said Dicks sharply. 'They just produced the stuff later at the station and pretended it were all mine.'

'What about the hair in the helmet which Kendrick stated matched yours?'

'He probably took it off me head and put it in there. I mean, it's not exactly complicated, is it? Putting hair in a helmet?'

'At the docks,' Clark went on, ignoring Dicks' rhetoric, 'did Kendrick ask you questions?'

'No, he just told me he was going to solve his little problem of who'd done the post office jobs. He said they had to be down to someone and it was going to be me.'

'Then what happened?'

'We went through the docks to the water and he called his mate, McPherson,' Dicks continued, his voice hardening. 'Then they put me in their car and we drove, like hours. I watched the houses go by. They talked to me. Kendrick smacked me a few times.'

Clark held the tape-player closer to his ear as he strolled inside the derelict warehouse buildings, past the graffitoed columns and the huge cracked windowpanes, the split orange crates and splintered wood. It was a grim scene of industrial dereliction and decay.

Arriving back at the car not long afterwards, he sat sideways on the edge of the passenger seat, facing the road, lost in concentration as the dusk thickened into thick. 'Where did they take you?' his own voice continued. This was the second time Clark had listened to the tape. Connell had left him to it as he wandered round the empty warehouses – that was her job, unless he solicited her help. She knew that sometimes he

29

needed space. And anyway, she had welcomed the time to give some quiet reflection to this whole business herself. Now that he was playing the tape again as they sat in the car she was listening with interest.

'Egberth nick,' said Dicks.

'You knew it?' Clark asked him.

'Nah, never been there before . . . Anfield, Sobell, Huskisson Street – been to them all, but never Egberth, miles off me beaten track . . .'

'Egberth?' said Connell, getting out of the driver's seat and looking over the top of the car at Clark, who had also stood up. Clark nodded. She could read his mind. They shut the car doors and started driving.

By nine-thirty that night the pair of them had arrived at Egberth police station in another part of Liverpool. Connell reflected that she was going to know the city quite well by the time they were finished up there. An officer showed them along a busy corridor into a cell. The records had been checked, and they knew this was the right cell. This was where Dicks had been brought by Kendrick the night he was arrested. Clark and Connell had both seen plenty of cells in their time, but they glanced meaningfully at each other as they looked around: this was a grim one. Twenty feet long and eight wide, filthy tiled walls striped with the yellowing remains of leaks, one high, barred window, a blue plastic mattress on a wooden bed, a toilet pan with no seat, a bench and an appalling smell.

Connell sat down on the bench, switched on the tape-player and held it out in front of her. Dicks' voice echoed around the small, stifling room.

'I suppose we got there about six. Still light.'

'What sort of condition would you say you were in?'

'You kidding me? I was tired, high as a kite, scared, freaked, this big bastard's knocking the shit out of me. The whole place stank of piss and spew.' Clark, who had been pacing the cell, stopped and turned off the tape-player. They sat in silence for a moment in the chilly night air, imagining being tired, frightened and intimidated in that Godforsaken hole.

Some people would have said that Teddy Dicks never stood a chance, that he was one of those people dealt a duff hand at birth. He was the sixth child of an alcholic docker and his asthmatic wife. Teddy remembered his mother as a permanently exhausted figure wearing a pinny and pressing a hanky to her mouth. She had held the family together after a fashion – though nobody quite knew how, as even when her husband was working he drank most of the money. She died when Teddy was nine, and that was when things started going badly wrong.

Mr Dicks carried on much as before, refusing to acknowledge his responsibilities. An elder sister, fifteen when her mother died, had a stab at running the household, but she more or less gave up after about eighteen months because it was too difficult, without any money, anyway, and she married a boxer who later beat her up. A couple of aunts paraded in and out from time to time, trying to impose order and cooking the odd square meal, and a neighbour used to bring in a huge dish of bread pudding every Saturday. Teddy could remember that.

The boys ran wild. It was amazing, in retrospect, that social workers didn't have them all put into care; if it had been the nineties rather than the sixties they probably would have. Teddy was the youngest, and he grew up quickly, dragged into a premature adolescence by his brothers and sisters, who simply stationed him in the corner of a room while they did what they had to do rather than leave him on his own. Nevertheless, he spent a lot of time alone.

He always hated school, and responded to it by

naughtiness, and consequently every teacher he ever had hated him back. Most of the kids in his class and in his street were committed truants. If you asked Teddy Dicks who his role model was as a child he probably would have said Jason Squires, later jailed for setting fire to an old people's home he had unsuccessfully tried to rob and killing two residents.

He really never had a chance.

5

Back at the incident room at Huskisson Street even
later that night Clark and Connell sweated over Dicks'
information, sustained by a bottle of white wine. They
had picked up take-away pizzas on their way over from
Egberth, and had eaten them in the car. They were
both used to taking their food on the hoof. Clark had
dived into a local off-licence for the bottle, though he
had taken so long about it that Maureen had got out of
the car and joined him. She found him crouched
down, examining the bottom shelf. There wasn't
exactly a lot of choice in this off-licence: if you didn't
like Liebfraumilch or Lambrusco you were in trouble.
Clark eventually straightened up, triumphantly
holding aloft a dusty bottle of unspecified Bordeaux
white which must have been lingering at the back of
the shelf for years as it was priced £1.75.

A couple of police officers were working at the far
end of the incident room, sitting in pools of light from
their anglepoise lamps, and they turned their heads
when Clark opened the wine with the corkscrew he
kept in his briefcase. The station was blissfully quiet
after the chaos that reigned there all day long. The
wine was drinkable – just.

It was not, of course, the first time that Clark and
Connell had found themselves in such an intimate
situation. But there were no tensions between them –

33

those had been resolved in Clark's first few weeks at the CIB. Maureen was a beautiful woman, by anyone's standards. She was tall and slender, with that abundant wavy red hair, clear skin and a devastating smile, and despite her lively sense of humour and gracious manner there was a touch of the ice-queen about her, a trait which often drives men wild. She was single too; no one in the force, in fact, knew anything about her private life. Clark had made one or two discreet moves on her – he couldn't help it, it came as naturally to him as breathing – but she had let him know that it was no-go. She couldn't countenance the notion of an affair with a colleague, to start with, and would never be prepared to compromise her professional integrity. She had other reasons, too, but she kept those to herself. Connell enjoyed working with Clark: she liked to be around energy, brains and ambition, even if she did take a slightly detached view of her own career prospects. As for Clark, he was impressed and intrigued by Maureen: she was just the kind of gutsy, self-possessed lady he went for, and the fact that she could be a good colleague and a drinking mate without either blushing or fluttering her eyelashes at the endless innuendos only made her more intriguing. In short, it had worked out fine between them, and they enjoyed a comfortable, friendly and productive professional relationship.

Clark reckoned Dicks was telling the truth. They played the tape again. 'Well?' he asked Connell, sitting opposite him.

'I think you're right,' she replied.

'Listen to the confession tape again,' said Clark, fired up now. He thought he was onto something. He slipped in a new cassette and pressed the start button.

'Apart from the robbery at New Brighton this morning,' began the ponderous, slightly weary voice of Detective Inspector Bill Kendrick, 'were there any other robberies you wanted to tell us about?'

34

'Er ... yes, sir, er, three more.' It was definitely Dicks, but his voice was completely different.

'Shall we start with New Brighton?' Kendrick said.

'Yeah, er, New Brighton post office, yeah, I done that one.'

Clark leaned across and switched off the tape-player. 'Dicks sounds rough,' said Connell, lighting a cigarette.

'He does, doesn't he?' mused Clark.

'Mind you, it was midnight, he was scared, and he'd been drinking.' Connell tried to be fair to Kendrick.

'Then he shouldn't have been interviewed!'

'What's Kendrick meant to do, breathalyse him?'

'Mmmm. Maybe.' Clark made it all sound so easy.

She smiled, half in bitterness. 'Everyone knows that probably half the statements we take involve people who are over the legal drink-drive limit—'

'Then they shouldn't be interviewed. Not until they've seen a doctor or sobered up.' Clark swapped the tapes and switched on the machine again.

Connell thought her boss was being a tiny bit unrealistic. But she let it go.

By eleven the next morning Naylor had his man. He had found Dicks' friend at home at his mum's house in New Brighton watching television, and suggested that they take a stroll. Clive's mum had wrung her hands in her housecoat as they left the tiny two-up two-down; she had seen enough trouble in the family already. Both her sons had done time and her husband was a regular at the local nick for Saturday-night drunkenness.

Naylor walked Clive alongside boarded-up shops in the squalid Victoria Road where deprivation hung in the air like a pall of smoke. Clive was co-operating. He didn't have Dicks' vicious bitterness about him; but then, he wasn't in the nick, was he? He had a semi-skinhead haircut and was wearing a plaid shirt, unbuttoned, with a T-shirt and four tattoos underneath it. He walked with his hands deep in the pockets of his jeans.

'Totally boxed,' said Clive when Naylor asked him what kind of state Dicks had been in when Clive saw him on the day of the robbery. 'He like fell out of the squat, that one I pointed out to you in that street back there, and disappeared. I tell you, he was out of it, that was really strong gear. Then a couple of days later we hear he's being done for armed robbery, you know. I tell you, it stinks.'

'So d'you know the guy who arrested him?' asked Naylor as they walked.

'Kendrick? Oh yeah, we all know Kendrick. He had it in for us, you know, specially Dicksy. He'd been hassling us in the pub that lunchtime. He was always needling us, snooping about. Always seemed to know where we were. Right pain in the arse.'

'Oh, so you weren't surprised then when Dicksy was picked up that afternoon?'

'I'll tell you what surprised me – him confessing to the Bevington and New Brighton jobs. I mean, he couldn't hve done Bevington 'cos he was fishing that morning, but he definitely didn't do the New Brighton 'cos he was with me. There's no way he did it. No way. Yet he confessed to it. It stinks.'

They stopped outside a white brick building and Clive turned away, looking more than disgusted. A bag lady dragged herself past them, a dressing-gown tied on top of decrepit red duffel coat. She asked Naylor for twenty pence for a cup of tea. He only had a fifty, so he gave her that, but she didn't look particularly pleased. On the other side of the street a smart young black woman came out of a junk shop. She put a notebook into her briefcase as the shopkeeper, a porky man in his late fifties wearing a cream peaked cap, came to the door after her. There was an old-fashioned pram for sale by the door, and a line of old clothes hanging above it.

'So he didn't do the Bevington job and he definitely couldn't have done the New Brighton job?' said Naylor, making sure he'd got the story straight.

'Yeah,' said Clive.

'Did you testify to this at his trial?'

'Oh yeah!' said Clive with exaggerated mock sincerity. 'He's pleading guilty and I walk in and say he didn't do it? I thought he'd done a deal or something. I left it alone.'

The young woman coming out of the junk shop looked over and recognised Clive. They greeted each other, she with a wave and a bright smile, he with a friendly nod. Clive liked her: she was one of the few on their side. She walked off down the street jauntily, and Naylor realised it was Molly Cope, the journalist. He recognized her from the small photograph they ran next to her stories. She had got to Clive first.

At about the same time that Naylor was walking Clive's story out of him, Clark and Connell were back at the prison, this time in order to visit the doctor who had seen Dicks when he was brought in. The corridors there smelled of paint. They were shown into Dr Bedi's office.

Bedi, a West Indian, was in his thirties. He had a handsome face and a Che Guevara-style beard and moustache. He had been working at the prison for five years and was a highly respected member of the team. Even more to his credit, the prisoners liked him, too. He was articulate and co-operative, though Clark sensed that he was overworked and oppressed – he knew how much prison doctors had to cope with. The office was light, bright and airy, furnished with the usual apparatus of the consulting room, and Bedi was wearing his white coaat.

Connell picked up a back copy of the *Liverpool Press* on his desk; Bedi knew what they were after, and had spread out all the material he had in his files on Dicks. The newspaper carried a large photograph of Dicks, badly battered and sporting two black eyes.

'What were Dicks' injuries when you first saw him?' Clark began, after they had done the introductions.

Bedi consulted the notes he had recorded at the time. 'Bad bruising around left eye, faint bruising around right eye. Two cuts and some swelling on the bottom lip. One cut, almost an inch long, should have been stitched when the injury occurred,' said Bedi. 'By the time they got him to me it had started to heal of its own accord, so I left it.'

'So this was the day after he arrived in prison, two days after his arrest?' asked Clark, sitting on a stool and leaning against the white wall next to two neat clipboards hanging on hooks, a hospital photograph of Dicks in his hand.

'Yes.'

'How old were the injuries?'

'Well, this is not a matter of fact, merely opinion, but I felt at least a day old, probably two or three.' Bedi sat at his desk with his arms folded, speaking seriously and looking at Clark.

'Could have been self-inflicted?'

'Quite possible.'

'Could have happened since he arrived at the prison?'

'Less possible.'

'Is it true that you gave the newspaper the original photo?'

'Yes, with the governor's permission.' Bedi took the paper that Connell had put down on his desk and handed it to Clark, who compared it with the hospital photograph in his hand.

'Look at the black eyes,' said Clark, placing the two pictures in front of Bedi. 'These are different.'

'Yes,' said Bedi, pointing to one of the shots. 'The newspaper photos's been enhanced.' The wild and angry eyes stared back from both pictures, but in the newspaper the right eye was surrounded by dark rings, whereas in the hospital shot the left eye showed the severest injury – and even that wasn't as bad as the hideous bruising shown around the right eye in the paper.

Connell was surprised that neither Bedi nor Clark seemed to think it was a particularly big deal that a journalist or editor had seriously tampered with the photograph of a man convicted of a serious offence.

'Were you called at the trial?' Clark asked Bedi.

'No.'

Back in the incident room after a sandwich lunch, Clark carried two more bundles of files down to the already overburdened tables where Connell was working. He looked harassed; his sleeves were rolled up and a cigarette dangled from his lips. The room was noisy. As he approached the desk he picked out Connell's voice speaking on the phone. 'Definitely a silver gun . . . Thanks very much . . . Oh yes, we'll keep you informed.'

She replaced the receiver and looked up at Clark. 'Defence lawyers. They're convinced that Dicks didn't do the New Brighton job.'

'What are they going on?'

'The part of the statement covering New Brighton only amounts to fifty words. It could easily have been given to him by Kendrick. The eyewitnesses described a tall man with a dark blue helmet and a silver gun. The other three jobs were almost spot-on in their descriptions of Dicks, and in each case referred to a black helmet and a black gun.'

Clark took this news very seriously. He was onto Kendrick, there was no doubt about it. But could he prove it? Assistant Commissioner More's words were playing on his mind: 'I will not countenance a witch-hunt . . . ' He had to be very, very careful.

'Sir?' said Connell.

'Yes?'

'Who d'you think it was who tampered with that photograph, you know, the one with the enhanced black eye on the wrong side of Dicks' face?'

'Some journalist,' said Clark casually. 'Must be the kind of thing that goes on in newsrooms up and down the country all the time.'

Connell was as surprised at this cavalier attitude as she had been in Bedi's office. 'But it's an offence to pervert the course of justice, and trumping up brutality not only has a big impact on public opinion, it also gets used as evidence in courts of law.'

'Well, what do you suggest we do? Arrest every journalist who gets high on a story and gilds the lily?'

'There's gilding and gilding, sir, as you well know' – at this Clark looked up at her from his file in mock outrage – 'and I would have thought that there should be some kind of moral limit, and that they should know that they'll get canned if they step beyond it.'

'Dream on, Mo,' said Clark, finally putting down his file. 'You know what a delicate relationship exists between detectives – I make the distinction between us and the men and women in blue – and the press. We need each other. There's always been a strong sense that it's best not to rock the boat. I don't like it either. There's a lot of things in this world I don't like, but I can see why they exist, and I can also see that I'd need a very cogent reason for disturbing their equilibrium.'

Kendrick entered Huskisson Street station at six that evening, accompanied by Detective Constable McPherson, a burly man who resembled the Kray twins. Both were wearing suits and ties, and they were followed by a constable in uniform. As they walked through the corridor towards the club bar, McPherson was plainly agitated.

'Just relax, will you,' said Kendrick, slightly irritated by his junior's wobbly behaviour. 'I've told you – it's all sorted.'

'Shouldn't we—'

'Just do as you're told.'

They stopped at the door of the crowded bar and saw Connell, Clark and several others around a table, smoking and drinking between the snooker table and the bar itself.

'Jesus Christ,' said McPherson.

'Those Met bastards are everywhere,' said Kendrick. With that, Naylor appeared behind them. 'Excuse me,' he said, and they turned and let him through. Kendrick decided not to go into the club room after all, and McPherson followed him back out into the street, his flabby face pale. He was only twenty-six, but he looked much older, mainly because he was so solid. He was always taken for a bruiser, and if it was just a case of shoving a scrum-half out of the way on the rugby pitch, he was. It was probably only on account of his size that the careers master at school had suggested he try for the police. It certainly wasn't on account of his intellectual capacities, anyway. McPherson had been the kind of overweight child who used to get stones thrown at him in the playground. Risk was a word which didn't feature in his vocabulary, and he would have done almost anything in the world to avoid being put under the spotlight.

'Evening all,' chirruped Naylor as he arrived at the team table in front of a poster advertising beer headed 'Raise Cain'. He had been obliged to walk past the snooker table, and the uniformed copper about to take a shot had stopped and made a great show of waiting for Naylor to get out of his eye-line.

'Terribly sorry,' Naylor had said with mock politeness and a broad grin.

At the table Sergeant Hickey, one of the Met team up from London, was briefing Connell and Clerk. 'More than half the cases under investigation were brought to light by her,' he said, leaning on the back of his chair.

'Didn't she start off the whole shooting match in the first place?' asked Connell.

'More or less. She certainly relaunched the Dicks case.'

'She's either one sharp cookie, or she's got an insider,' said Clark, twiddling a beermat in his hand.

'Or both,' said Hickey. 'Drink, anyone?'

'Cheers, mate. Mine's a pint,' said Clark.

'Same,' said Naylor, loosening his tie.

'Mo?'

'Scotch on the rocks, please, with a dash of water.'

'Someone should see her,' said Clark, returning to the task in hand.

Naylor slid into the seat next to him. 'You talking about that girl from the *Liverpool Press*?'

'Yes,' said Clark.

'I did see her, today. Not to talk to, like. I was having a chat with that friend of Dicks' down at New Brighton and there she was.'

'Working?' asked Clark.

'Well, either that or she does market research in her spare time,' quipped Naylor. 'Cracking-looking bird, I'll give her that.' Clark's face froze for a second as he registered interest.

'Well, I think it's about time I had a chat with Ms Cope,' said Clark, making a meal of the way he pronounced 'Ms'.

'Don't you think it would be better if I did?' asked Connell provocatively. She knew how far she could go.

'No, no,' said Clark with a mischievous smile, picking

up his pint glass and draining it before Hickey got back with the next one. 'Better if it was me.'

6

Clark was spruced up and in the editorial offices of the
Press in about an hour. He was wearing a dark navy
suit, a pale blue shirt with a buttondown collar and a
navy tie with a discreet pattern. The offices were in a
large, modern building in the centre of the city, and as
he pushed his way around the revolving doors he
reflected that it was refreshing to be in a non-police
and non-criminal environment.

'Molly Cope, please,' he said to the receptionist.

'Her line's busy,' she said, after she had tried to call.
She looked at Clark. He seemed respectable enough.
'You can go on up if you like. Third floor. The lift's
over there.'

He smoothed down his hair and adjusted his tie in
the lift mirror, feeling confident. When he stepped out
onto the third floor there was only one way to turn,
and through a pair of swing doors he found himself in
the busy newsroom. He stared at the open-plan sprawl
of modern desks, word processors, pot plants and
partitions where journalists and secretaries were
embroiled in the latest stories.

'Excuse me,' he asked a young man hurrying past in
red braces with a fountain pen sticking out of his
mouth. 'Can you tell me where I could find Molly
Cope?' Without taking the pen out of his mouth the
young man pointed to a cluster of desks on a raised

44

platform. She was sitting behind a VDU wearing a sleeveless salmon-pink top with a black brooch and black trousers. Her long, wavy black hair was swept back in a loose pony tail, and she was concentrating.

'Ms Cope?' She glanced up at him standing over her. 'Detective Superintendent Tony Clark. I'm from the CIB, and I'm in Liverpool to look into the allegations surrounding the Terry Dicks case. I've been very impressed with your investigative work and I wonder if we could help each other out.'

'I'm not interested,' she said, and stood up. She looked at him icily.

Clark looked surprised. 'I just thought we could have a chat,' he said, standing in a weak position in the middle of the office.

'Did you?' She looked at him, picked up a piece of paper from her desk and walked away. 'I'm afraid I'm not interested in being lobbied by coppers.' She wouldn't have been interested in being lobbied by coppers at any time, but at seven-thirty in the evening with the news pages about to go down she was especially displeased to see Clark in the office.

She ripped a sheet out of the teleprinter as she swung past. Clark followed her. 'The CIB is a section of the police force based in New Scotland Yard and devoted entirely to the investigation of bent coppers. I don't like bent coppers, and I want any help I can get in nailing them,' he said, in an attempt to appeal to her obvious mistrust of his fellow officers.

'Good, very, very good,' she said, as if she didn't believe a word of it and couldn't care less. She looked up, finally, and sniffed the air. 'I can still smell whitewash.'

'Can't I just take you out for a meal and talk about—'

'Don't make me laugh, caveman!' she said with a broad smile, returning to her desk and snatching the mail from her pigeon-hole as she walked past. A blonde-haired colleague at the next desk looked up and smiled to herself. It was always good to see Molly in full swing, making mincemeat of men who thought they were important.

Clark held her glare. The colleague looked up. The stakes were raised. 'You stand there behaving like a two-legged rottweiler and call me primitive?' Sharp talk never fazed Clark; like all powerful men he loved a challenge. A little public humiliation was quite a turn-on.

After a charged pause Cope said, 'You want to buy me a meal? Eight o'clock tomorrow, Frank's in the Docks Road.'

He had won, and he walked away without uttering a word to spoil his victory. But he didn't know Molly Cope.

'That's a.m., by the way,' she said, without looking up from the piece of paper she was studying. 'Eight a.m. Don't be late.' Clark slowed up. Damn her cunning! As he paused in front of the swing doors he heard her reading from the sheet she had torn from the teleprinter and gloating to her blonde colleague. She knew he was listening, and she was enjoying herself. 'How's this for a heading? "Police stop white man in car!" Now that *is* a scoop isn't it?' Molly Cope was young, black and angry.

So there he was, standing in front of a ridiculous greasy spoon in the Docks Road. It occupied half of the ground floor of a solid Victorian building which had seen better days, and it was painted yellow. The buildings on either side had been pulled down, though the sites hadn't been redeveloped, and the ground was a scrubby wasteland, sprinkled with dented Coke cans, used condoms and spent glue tubes. A taxi had dropped him on the opposite side of the road, and Clark stood there in the sharp wind, trying to cross as the juggernauts thundered past. He felt irritated at Cope, and slightly sexually charged by yesterday's encounter.

She was already there when he arrived, sitting with a mug of tea. Her food was ordered, so Clark stood at the counter next to the industrial-sized tea urn and ordered from the woman in charge, a very large woman in a startlingly florid pinny. The local radio station was on, blaring out football news, and a couple of men were tucking into eggs, bacon and fried bread. 'Scrambled eggs, please,' said Clark, feeling conspicuous in his suit.

'One egg or two?' asked the woman in the pinny.

'How do you scramble one egg?' he asked her quietly. He wasn't looking for a confrontation – he had just never heard of anyone eating one scrambled egg. She wasn't amused.

'Two scrambled,' she shouted into the kitchen.

'Toasted?'

'Yes, please.'

'Two toasted.'

'Tea?'

'Yes, please, not too—' she swept off to the kitchen. '—milky.'

He sat down opposite Cope when he had got his tea and looked at her over the congealed sauce bottles.

'Like it?' she asked, raising her eyebrows to indicate that she meant the café.

'Not particularly,' he said, trying to disarm her. She had tried to shock him by getting him to go there. She wasn't going to win that game.

'I do. It's unpretentious and honest.' Her tone was defiant.

'Then I don't know what either of us is doing here.' He lit a cigarette.

She looked stern – like a schoolteacher. Her hair was only half pulled back, and she looked very beautiful.

47

She genuinely liked Frank's, and had been calling in for breakfast since her university days. Now it was on the route between her one-bedroomed flat in a wonderful art deco-style thirties block and the *Press* offices, so it suited her nicely. And Molly Cope had made a rule a long, long time ago never to go out of her way for a man.

'What do you want?' she asked him curtly.

'I want to know three things. Firstly, how bent is the South Lancs Serious Crime Squad?'

'Very,' she said, without a second's hesitation.

'Two, if we caught a self-confessed mass-murderer would it be possible, in the present climate, and all right with you, for us to put him away?'

'No.'

'No?' He was shocked.

'It's not your job to put him away, it's the court's job.'

He studied the table.

'You had a third question?'

'Can I speak to your insider?' He sipped his tea.

'I don't have an insider,' she said sharply.

'And if you did?'

She chuckled. 'And if I did, I wouldn't tell you.'

'You have an insider because you have unearthed more evidence—'

She interrupted him irritably. '—than the entire Metropolitan Police investigating team? Where there's a will there's a way.'

Clark shook his head and pointed at her, sure he was right. 'You've got an insider.'

'Woman's intuition.'

'Sexist bollocks.'

She smiled at him; it was only a little smile, but it was the first one. Continuing quickly while he felt he was gaining her confidence, he jumped in. 'Why do you dislike us so much?'

'Because during the West Midlands investigation

48

and this one you have not put a single policeman away.'

'It's not our job, it's the court's job.'

The woman in the apron appeared with two plates of scrambled eggs and toast. 'Two scrambled eggs,' she said unnecessarily. Cope started to cover hers with brown sauce and Clark looked at what she was doing, only half concealing his surprise. She kept pouring. He picked up his briefcase, snapped it open and took out half a bottle of Marks and Spencer's champagne and a plastic bottle of freshly squeezed orange juice, the thick, fashionable and expensive kind. The idea had come to him the previous night when he was leaving the *Press* building, smarting slightly that she had caught him with her eight a.m. trick. He had jumped into a cab and asked to be taken to the nearest M & S. He had got there at five to eight, just before it closed, and he had been looking forward to this moment ever since.

He started opening the orange juice first, as if it were all totally normal. She didn't know how to react; she felt that he was gaining on her. He smiled. 'It's a joke,' he said.

'I know,' she said, smiling naturally in her surprise. 'It's a good joke.' She looked into his eyes and felt very strange. *Damn you!* she thought. *I really do like you.*

Clark slammed the car into reverse and parked in the Huskisson Street car park. The digital clock on the dashboard said 9.38. He was late, and cursed under his breath. He grabbed his briefcase and rushed in – he shouldn't have stayed at Frank's bloody café, but she was so . . . so desirable.

He ran through the hallway of the station, past a copper carrying a dog. ('He got lost,' said the constable apologetically, feeling like a right pillock), and into the interview room which he had booked for his first meeting. The room had windows on both sides: one

49

onto the street, and one onto the hallway of the station. 'I'm sorry, I'm sorry,' he panted as he burst in. 'My last interview overran.'

Naylor, sitting at a table in the small, bare room, looked down at the ground with his arms folded. He had a good idea of whom that last 'interview' might have been, though he would have died rather than make a sarcastic remark about it, even if they had been alone in the room. On the opposite side of the table Sergeant Poynton and a representative from the Police Federation, both in uniform, stood up. Clark put his hand out, and Poynton took it first. 'Tony Clark.'

'Sergeant Poynton.' He was a tall man in his late forties with a mild face and a strong Liverpudlian accent.

'Alan Davies, Police Federation rep,' said the other man, older and white-haired, in a menacing tone of voice. I bet you haven't been drinking champagne this morning with a beautiful young woman, thought Clark as the rep sat there, looking dour and puritanical.

A large and sophisticated tape-recorder was already running, next to a jug of water.

'I understand you wish this interview to be taped, Sergeant Poynton, is that correct?' Clark asked briskly, and Poynton and the rep both nodded. They began the laborious process of recalling events surrounding Dicks' arrest two years previously. It was painstaking stuff. After almost an hour, Clark felt things warming up.

'He looked scared,' said Poynton, 'but drugs or drink, no.'

'Did you know him?' asked Clark.

'Knew of him.'

'What did you know of him?'

'When you've been in the force in one city for thirty years you get to know, or know of, most of the people who crop up. Teddy Dicks is one of them.' Poynton's tone was one of fairly relaxed but guarded co-operation.

'So you remember clearly what happened when Kendrick and McPherson brought him in?' asked Clark.

'Pretty clearly. I signed him in when they arrived, a couple of minutes after ten p.m. I asked him whether he required a solicitor. He made to sign the box indicating no solicitor. I checked with him that that was what he wanted and he said yes.'

'Would it surprise you' – now Clark took the bull by the horns – 'if he'd told us that he repeatedly asked for a solicitor all through that evening and was very disturbed that a solicitor only arrived at ten-thirty the following morning, eleven hours after he'd made his confession?'

'No sir. He's a liar.' Poynton remained calm. Clark looked mildly surprised. But he had to plough on. He could see that Poynton hated him and what he was doing. He was co-operating only because he absolutely had to.

'And would you be surprised to hear that the custody records for that day cannot be found?'

'No sir. The records are usually destroyed after eighteen months to two years. I'd be surprised if they still existed.' He was beginning to look unbearably smug.

'Do you resent me asking you these questions?'

Poynton looked at the surly rep for reassurance. 'As far as I'm concerned there are two or three officers under investigation by your mob that I'd be pleased to see put down for a decent stretch. But Kendrick . . . Kendrick's the best. He's the best. So yes, I do resent it.'

Clark stayed at the station all day, working through his material and checking out leads. He went down to the canteen with Naylor and Connell at lunchtime and ate chicken pie and chips. Naylor had liver and bacon, and Connell bought a sandwich, an apple and a can of diet Coke.

'No offence guys, but I think I'm going to get a breath of air,' she said, and left them at a small table in the corner where they were studiously ignored by everyone else. She took her lunch with her and strolled through the bollards at the end of the Huskisson Street and on to the stretch of greenery along one side of the cathedral. There was a bench next to a long stone buttress, and she sat on it to eat. She had got used to working in a male-dominated environment long ago, but sometimes she still felt the need to get away and snatch a break in the middle of a busy schedule. She wasn't a militant feminist, but she couldn't help feeling that she might have got further with her career than she had so far if she were male. She would certainly have been an inspector – Naylor's level. But her gut feeling was that life was too short to bother grinding that particular axe. Connell swallowed the last of her sandwich, screwed up the wrapper, stood up and tossed it in a rubbish bin as she walked past.

Something drew her inside the cathedral. She was wandering aimlessly, really, but the peace and tranquillity one always finds in cathedrals seemed to her the perfect antidote to the noisy, macho and slightly sweaty incident room. As soon as she went through the little wooden door next to the enormous main doors she was enveloped in the cool, almost cold air and smelled the sweet, musty smell of great churches.

Exhaling with pleasure, she strolled up the nave, looking up at the magnificent vaulted ceiling. Half a dozen people were dotted around the pews, kneeling or sitting and looking at the altar. One, in the back row, had a can of Special Brew in his hands. She liked that. It was his place as much as anyone else's, and there was

52

no reason why you couldn't talk to God after a few cans of beer.

Connell had worked with a specialist child protection unit for six years, but towards the end she had started to feel that she had effectively side-lined herself into a 'women's specialism'. Added to that, the burden of grief had become overwhelming – she was taking it too much on board. The choices were developing a rhinoceros-thick skin or burning out. After she had joined the CIB she was often asked how she could bear to investigate fellow officers. Everyone at the CIB was asked that with monotonous regularity: the culture that taught that it was a police officer's duty to stick by colleagues was so powerful that many within the force simply couldn't comprehend how anyone with a shred of sensibility could work for the CIB. Those who did were regarded much as collaborators were in occupied Europe during the Second World War. Maureen was inclined to say that compared to dealing with children who'd been sat on electric fires or buggered by their fathers at the age of five, investigating fellow officers wasn't so bad. Some people found her a bit prickly, but she wasn't really. Inside she was as soft as a marshmallow.

She stopped at a small chapel at the other end of the colossal building and rested her head on the cool, carved wooden screen. All women police officers were treading a tightrope, it wasn't just her. Try to be one of the lads and you could end up as the station bicycle; keep work and play strictly separate, and the view was that you just weren't behaving like a police officer. Find solidarity with other women, and you were a dike. Connell found it easier to function in a small unit like the CIB where the size of the team meant that myths, fantasies and speculations weren't given a breeding-ground. In police stations it was almost impossible to get the balance right, and she hoped she was never again going to have to run that gauntlet in her career.

She walked back down to the entrance, looking up at a seventeenth-century painting of the Virgin and child. Connell didn't have particularly acute religious sensibilities, but she felt there was something there – she wouldn't have put it in Christian terms, but she acknowledged that there was a spiritual dimension to life, and she found it surprising that it had been so effectively marginalised in the west. She thought probably it didn't matter too much if someone were a Muslim or a Jew or a Scottish Presbyterian: surely they were all methods of reaching out for the transcendental, and they all got to the same place in the end? She glanced over at a woman praying, and felt a very small stab that it wasn't an option open to her. She would have felt hypocritical, suddenly expecting God (or whoever it was) to listen to her after she had ignored him all these years. That was a shame, she reflected; it must be a great comfort.

Then she was horrified to hear the cathedral bells chiming three, and she turned her thoughts to pocketbooks and black eyes, and hurried back over to Huskisson Street, scrabbling for a pound coin to post in the collection slot as she rushed out of the door.

7

At three o'clock Clark and Naylor had an interview with McPherson in the same room where they had seen Poynton that morning. Sitting at one side of the table, they waited for a minute or two before they were joined by McPherson, the Kray lookalike, and his solicitor, a man in his late fifties dressed in a three-piece suit and a spotted tie. McPherson sat up close to the table and the lawyer sat behind him and started to speak. 'My client, Detective Constable McPherson, has prepared a written statement and has asked me to indicate that he doesn't wish to speak at this time.' With that the man handed Clark a sheet of paper from a sheaf on his knee.

The solicitor concealed his irritation. He had actually advised his client to speak, feeling strongly that this right-to-silence option made him look rather guilty. He had explained his reasoning very clearly to his client. But McPherson had got it into his head that he didn't have to speak unless he wanted to, and as he certainly didn't want to, he wasn't going to.

Clark was surprised. He was also pissed off. Just what were these boys up to? This was going to slow things up. McPherson sat there absolutely expressionless, his chalky face frozen. Hard as nails, thought Clark, and almost certainly guilty as hell. 'Fair enough,' he said, barely managing to conceal his irritation and looking steadily at McPherson, who returned his gaze without flinching, as ugly and unwieldy as a great bulldog.

Later that afternoon Clark and More talked the case over at More's desk at one end of the incident room. Naylor and Connell were sitting at their usual tables in the middle, poring over the pocketbooks of all the men involved in the case. As usual the room was bristling with people in uniform, looking at screens, filing and comparing notes. More liked to work in the incident room sometimes, as opposed to his office. It made him feel in touch with the team, and he liked to think that it made him more approachable, less of a distant authority figure.

Clark leaned over More's desk, positioned under a large framed map of the region. 'Poynton was superb,' he said. 'A dream defence witness: upright, indignant and believable.'

'And DC McPherson?'

'He exercised his option to remain silent.'

'Any idea why?'

'Probably because Poynton or Kendrick thought he *wouldn't* be a dream witness.'

'What about Dicks?'

'Two things really. Totally untrustworthy and totally believable.'

More laughed, with a touch of irony. 'Great. So is there a case against Kendrick and the others?'

'One unreliable witness and a claim of injuries that no one noticed at the Magistrates' Court,' said Clark despondently.

'No case?' asked More, raising his eyebrows.

'Well . . .'

'Clark, I'm a busy man.' He was losing patience. If you couldn't work fast in this business, you couldn't do the job.

'There is also a reporter with a more or less one hundred per cent hit rate who thinks she smells a rat,' continued Clark, now in full spate.

'You still haven't spoken to Kendrick?'

'No, I'm going to leave him till next week. He's at the centre of it and I want to know everything there is to know before I see him.'

Connell suddenly stood up and walked down the middle of the room to join them, concentrating on a police pocketbook she held open in her hand. 'Sir, look at this.' She stood in front of More's desk and held out the book to Clark. 'I got the pocketbooks of everyone on duty. PC Alfreds – Second June. "Twenty hundred hours: glass of water and bog paper to prisoners." From what we know without the custody sheets, there was no other prisoner apart from Dicks'– More looked on with interest at this – 'and he wasn't supposed to have arrived until ten.'

'Check it out with Alfreds asap,' said Clark.

The telephone on the middle table rang. Naylor picked it up, and after a moment he shouted, 'Call for you, Guv.'

So she had called him. She hadn't been able to stop herself, and she had almost convinced herself that she had telephoned him for professional reasons. She had told him to meet her for drinks at Wheeler's cocktail bar in town at eight-thirty because she had something to tell him, and of course he agreed.

She managed to get home first to change; it was quite an achievement, as she seldom left the newsroom before eight. She had been at the *Press* for five years, having joined straight from Liverpool polytechnic, where she had passed her BA in media studies with flying colours, and had risen up to chief reporter via the time-honoured secretarial route. She was good – everyone knew that. She was also becoming quite well-known in the community. She had grown up in Liverpool, which helped, though she had lost her accent. She had trained herself out of it at college. She thought it would help her career if she spoke in beautiful BBC English. Molly Cope could do things like that – just change her accent. She was formidably in control.

Clark was feeling pretty pleased with himself. He knew he had cracked this one and he was enjoying sitting there at the bar looking at her. She'd made a big effort. She was wearing a slinky dark blue velvet zip-up top edged with silver piping, and glass earrings like spinning tops. Her hair was swept back, and she had painted her lips an alluring shade of pink which suited her smooth milk chocolate skin. Carried away on a tide of euphoria, Clark was at his most charming. He turned it all on, full blast. They ordered Black Russians and sat facing each other, talking at first about uncontroversial topics such as how well he knew the north of England (not well) and her college course. It was inevitable that the conversation would turn to the police, and when it did she didn't have a good word to say about them. Despite the ostensible seduction scene she didn't hesitate to challenge him, spitting like a little tiger.

'If they were serious about getting to the truth in the West Midlands,' she said, 'why did they use West Yorkshire to do the investigation? They are the only one of forty-three forces with a worse record than West Midlands.'

'Record for what?' asked Clark.

'You name it – overall number of complaints, irregular arrests, irregular stop-and-search—'

He cut her off with a trace of contempt. 'Did you get that from the *Guardian*?'

'No, from the Police Complaints Authority Annual Report 1990, funded by the Home Office. And who do we get to clear up our little cesspit? The bloody Met. It makes me wild.'

'It makes me sad,' he jumped in while she paused. 'Most coppers, like me, join for the money, the excitement, the pension, all that sort of thing, but always, and even more so after training, with a sense of duty and responsibility to the community. Even in my job, where I see the absolute bottom of the barrel, I've only ever seen a handful of coppers who are bad, really bad. The rest are ordinary people who care. Somehow people don't believe that any more. I don't know what we have to do to persuade them.'

'Start with me. Persuade me.'

'I'd like to try,' he said meaningfully.

'I'll do a deal with you,' said Cope, suddenly remembering that she had asked him to meet her for professional purposes and snapping back into control mode, 'I'll give you what my informer gave me, if you'll use it.'

'Well, of course I will,' said Clark, mentally holding his breath.

'It makes all your three officers guilty of conspiracy to pervert the course of justice – amongst other things,' she said, her voice indicating that she wasn't at all convinced he would use it because it was so inflammatory.

'That's why I'm here – it's what I do for a living.' She looked exasperated, as if she were afraid of being taken for a fool. He pulled on his cigarette and she looked at him coolly. 'You really do think we've been brought here to cover up, don't you?' he said. Every ounce of his concentration was being channelled into making her trust him.

'Dicks was picked up at six p.m., not after nine,' she said quickly, as if she wanted to get it out, to get it over and done with. 'He was roughed up and taken to Egberth, a long way from being the nearest station.

59

The custody sergeant was an old pal of Kendrick's.'
Clark was riveted. 'Dicks was still high but not so out of
it that he didn't on repeated occasions ask for a
solicitor. When his solicitor finally arrived in the
morning Dicks told him he'd been beaten, intimidated
and kept cold and hungry. After several hours of this
treatment he had signed a—' she paused to place the
word between inverted commas '—"confession" which
had been dictated to him before the taped interview.'

'Strong stuff,' said Clark. 'Eyewitness or hearsay?'
She gave a little shrug. 'Is your informer reliable?' he
asked.

She looked away. She wasn't worried that he was
going to make her spill the beans. Once she had
decided something – end of story. They told her she
got her strong will from her father. He had died when
Molly was two, a year after the whole family had
moved from Mauritius. Her father had set up a
newsagent's and shop in Liverpool with his brother,
using money they had inherited when their own father
had died in 1962. It was just getting going when
Johnny Cope died of a heart-attack, quite suddenly.

Well, everyone was devastated, naturally. Molly's
mother still talked to her about how awful it was
during that period. There was talk of going back to
Mauritius, apparently; Molly often thought of that. It
made her realise how different her life could have
been, and it made her all the more determined to make
the most of the one she had. It wasn't just her at home
then. She had younger brothers – twins, eighteen
months younger than her. They both still lived in
Liverpool; one at home with her mum, the other
married but nearby. Molly's uncle Tom had struggled
on with the newsagent's after his brother died, and
after a few years the entire family was able to let out its
breath a little as the business stabilised. Molly couldn't
remember going without anything as she grew up.

What she could remember was getting up at five with her mum to unwrap the newspapers from their bundles.

She was the only one in the close-knit family who had gone to university; the only one who had stayed on at school beyond the statutory sixteen, come to that. Her mother had been so proud when she graduated. Molly smiled whenever she thought of it. She had a photo next to her bed of the two of them on that day, Molly in her academic gown and Mrs Cope in an absurd purple hat. They were very close. Molly's flat was a ten-minute drive away from the house she had grown up in, and she popped back at least twice a week. Everyone knew her there, and she felt at home walking around those streets. It had become an increasingly multi-cultural neighbourhood over the past ten years, but it was perfectly integrated – Molly had never heard a whisper of racial trouble, and she wondered why other places couldn't make it work too. But they couldn't, and that made her angry. She had lost count of the number of stories she had covered involving racial hatred in other districts of Liverpool or the surroundings towns and villages, usually per-petrated by a white majority on a black or Asian minority. It made her want to commit violence herself, but she didn't really think that was the way to get results. She used words instead.

Even at university she had developed a strong mistrust of the police, working on the student newspaper (which she edited, of course) and covering local stories of interest to the college community. She had come across a couple of cases of blatant incompetence within the force and two or three of obvious harassment of black men by white officers, and she had decided that they were all a bad lot.

It was nine o'clock that night before Naylor and

Connell found PC Alfreds at his station. He had been out on the beat when they arrived, and they had waited for an hour in the car outside the nick. They enjoyed each other's company. Of course, the well-oiled police force rumour machine had it that they had been at it once, but it wasn't true. Because Connell kept her personal life a closely guarded secret rumours about it were legion. They ranged from tales of voracious lesbianism to the story that she'd once given the commander of the Flying Squad one in a police station toilet, having lost a bet about how many fifty-pence pieces he could balance on his dick. Sensibly, Connell refused to confirm or deny any of this.

Naylor was devoted to Connell. Two months previously he had been given a few days off to deal with some problems at home, and Connell had been enormously supportive. Naylor found it very difficult to talk about personal matters at work, and Connell had helped him get it off his chest. He then relied on her to relay the information to the Guv'nor; Clark wasn't the most emotionally sensitive of people, though he did like to keep the troops happy.

It was a messy business. Mrs Naylor's brother had committed suicide out of the blue: hung himself from a tree in the garden. He was married, apparently happy, with two nice kids and a modestly successful butcher's shop in Waltham Forest.

It came out that he liked dressing up in women's clothes, and had been doing so for some time, on Wednesday evenings, when his wife thought he was at the skittles. It wasn't the kind of thing which integrated well into working-class east-end culture, but it probably wouldn't have come to anything if he hadn't been blackmailed by a young man with whom he had apparently been consorting for some time. The boy wanted money, and that was what he had been getting, funnelled out of the butcher's shop. But he got greedy, and started wanting more, threatening to blow the poor butcher's cover by sending photographs of him in a frock to the family.

The pressure killed him; it would probably have killed most people. Naylor felt sorry for him. He wouldn't have fancied dressing up in frocks himself, but he felt strongly that anything a bloke wanted to do which didn't harm anyone else was his own business. Being in the force, Naylor saw so much destructive behaviour and so many lives ruined by the actions of others that he thought people should concentrate on catching the real evildoers rather than exercising their judgement on those with unusual predilections who kept themselves to themselves. Leave them in peace to get on with whatever it was they liked doing, that was his view.

Anyway, it wasn't the brother-in-law who had worried him, it was his own wife. She had been terribly upset, and also seriously disturbed, and she had a kind of breakdown. The doctor had put her on tranquillisers, and one day – the worst – there had been talk of her going into the local psychiatric. That was when Naylor needed time off. He was devoted to her, and he had never seen her like that before. He found it very difficult to handle.

Mrs Naylor had started to improve after a few weeks, and she was well out of the woods by the time the Liverpool job came up. Naylor had never spoken of the problem since those first few chats with Connell, when it had all come out. He had found it all a very sobering experience. Although he had only talked to Connell about it two or three times, he had found her immensely helpful, and he was very grateful, in his way.

It was raining in Liverpool that evening. Alfreds agreed to talk, but didn't feel good about it, and he told

Naylor outright that he wanted their conversation to take place out of sight and earshot of the other guys.

Naylor found them a corridor beyond the bustle of the main thoroughfare of the station, and Connell stood with her back to them, looking into the station through a set of bars. A photographer was snapping away for a mugshot in the distance. Alfreds was twenty-five, and could have passed for younger; he looked scared but slightly defiant. He had a thin, quite hard face, though he was reasonably good-looking, and a wiry footballer's body.

'Probably don't remember this,' breathed Naylor, standing very close to the rigid constable as he pulled Alfreds' pocketbook from of his own pocket and pointed at it. 'On June the second 1990 you were on the night shift. You wrote "Twenty hundred hours: water and bog paper to prisoner." Do you recall which prisoner?' Naylor took a drag of his cigarette.

'Dicks.'

'You've got a good memory,' said Connell, turning and resting her head against the wall, half of her face lit up by the bright lights of the station and half shrouded in the darkness of the gloomy corridor.

'Not really,' said Alfreds. 'It's just been in all the papers.'

'Were you aware of anything unusual at the time?' asked Connell.

'Look, if this is going to become an interview, I'll have to have my solicitor . . .' protested Alfreds.

'Yeah,' said Naylor, hurriedly diffusing the tension. He was rather more aware of the sensitivity of respecting people's rights in these situations than Connell, and he was very anxious to get a story out of Alfreds without going through the whole bloody solicitor rigmarole. 'You wrote that you visited Dicks at eight. But he wasn't booked in until ten p.m.'

'I'd only been in the force a couple of months,' said

Alfreds without hesitation. 'I kept writing down ten p.m. as twenty hundred hours. I still do now, sometimes.'

'Yeah, it's a common mistake, isn't it?' said Naylor softly, looking into Alfreds' face. You, he was thinking, are hiding something from me, and you are very foolish, because I promise you, sonny, I'm going to find out what it is. I'll be back.

8

He had asked her back to his hotel for a nightcap. Molly didn't want to confront the reality of what a nightcap might mean just yet, so she didn't – she just agreed. How could she deny to herself that she really wanted this man? Clark paid the drinks bill at Wheeler's cocktail bar, and they took a taxi to the Shaftesbury, both feeling electrified.

The bar was heaving with punters. Clark looked around furtively: it was imperative that the other members of the team didn't see him, but he didn't want Cope to know he was behaving secretively. After all, there was nothing wrong with them having a drink in public. But Clark felt uncomfortable about the idea that everyone knew he was cheating on Sue, particularly as the news of his affair with WPC Dean had leaked out and seemed to be common knowledge. Cope didn't know he was married.

Clark caught sight of Naylor through a glass door. He was finishing a drink in another bar. Their eyes met. Naylor was with Deakin, their Chief Super and Clark's immediate boss, and they were coming through the door. Shit, Clark thought, I'm sailing close to the wind here. Cope was looking around the old-fashioned and slightly shabby hotel bar, an expression of surprised amusement on her face at the thought that Clark, Mr Smooth himself, should stay somewhere like this. She had been to all the cool hotels in Liverpool, but she had never heard of the Shaftesbury. Clark began to panic slightly and hustled her back through to reception. He thought he had got away with it – he was pretty certain Deakin hadn't seen them, anyway.

'Hi, er, two-one-two, please.' The night porter, a fat, balding individual wearing a bow tie who looked as though he'd seen off a few drunks in his time, handed over the key with an expression of disgust which clearly said 'I know what you're about to do and I wish you wouldn't do it in my bloody hotel – without paying for two people, at any road.' Clark looked nervously around: no sign of Deakin at least. It was essential that he got Cope into the room before they were seen.

Clark guided her up the stairs, along the corridor and into the room without turning the light on. She was extremely irritated that he hadn't bothered to explain himself. She hadn't a clue what this cloak-and-dagger behaviour was all about. Was she being set up, or what? How had she let this happen to her? Surely this wasn't his attempt at a seduction routine? Shit.

He shut the door and breathed a small sigh of relief.

'Look,' she started, 'I don't want to play pathetic and infantile little games. . .'

'I'm sorry,' he said, regaining his composure. 'It's stupid . . . stupid codes of conduct stuff – I'm sorry.' He gave her a peck on the lips, lit only by the light of a streetlamp through the window. He hadn't meant for that peck to begin things – not quite so quickly, anyway – but the electric current running between them pulled their lips together again, and then they were kissing each other deeply, and clawing at each other's clothes, and within two minutes of entering the room Clark's jacket, shirt and tie were on the floor, his keys and money falling on the carpet, and he had pulled down the zip on her blue velvet top and turned her round to

67

pull it off. Panting with desire, she leaned her head back to reach his lips: He was caressing her, he was overcome with passion for this strong, beautiful woman, and he turned her round to face him again and steered her towards the bed, pushing her down onto the red cover, not even pausing to take off her black bra, shaking off his trousers and kissing her, kissing her . . . she bit his shoulder and abandoned herself.

They made love for two hours, and when they finally fell asleep at two-thirty, it was into a deep sleep of physical exhaustion. The dim sound of carousing floated up from the bar, and a young woman in a red coat crossed the rainy street and entered the hotel.

The telephone rang. Clark picked it up drowsily. 'Hello,' he said muzzily. 'Where? *What!*' Suddenly he was wide awake. 'There's a young lady in reception,' a voice had said at the end of the phone. 'Shall we send her up?' 'No, *no*.' He meant it, there was no doubt about that. 'I'll come down.'

He slammed down the receiver. 'Something's come up, I'll be back in a tick.' He jumped out of bed, furious. He looked down at the woman who had been sleeping next to him, her long hair down and flowing over the sheets. God, he wanted her again. She stirred, and stretched a little, like a cat.

With an irritated sigh he struggled into his trousers, pulled on a shirt and headed for the door. 'Don't answer the phone,' he said to his sleeping beauty. Then, as an afterthought, 'And don't go away.'

He ran down two flights of stairs, buttoning up his shirt as he went, and saw Jenny Dean, sitting like a waif. She had taken off her red coat and was holding it over her arm, wearing a little black number she knew that he liked. Once he had told her that she looked so sexy in it he couldn't take his hands off her. But he didn't seem to be finding it very sexy now. He looked at her angrily. 'I just don't believe you.' In a desperate attempt to pretend everything was all right he walked past her to signal to the glaring porter at the end of the corridor that he was down, that he would take care of this late visitor, that the porter didn't need to call him in his room again. His mind was racing.

Then he turned back to Dean and faced her. 'You're bloody mad. I told you. . .'

'But I. . .'

'Bloody Deakin's here. You could have me thrown out of the force.' There was no doubt in his mind: it was that serious. His career was on the line here.

'Why didn't you answer my messages?' she said tearfully, wishing she hadn't come now, feeling desperate and wretched.

'I told you, it's over.'

'It may be for you, it's not that easy for me. I can't. . .'

She tried hard not to cry, but the corners of her mouth betrayed her, and she began to weep softly.

'Oh Christ,' said Clark, realising he was going to have to do the decent thing and see her all right. He had no choice, did he?

'I'm sorry, Tony. I couldn't stop myself. I thought you'd be pleased,' she said pitifully. A couple lurched past them in the hotel corridor, a blonde woman in a black mini-dress supporting a man in a rumpled white shirt who was singing 'We All Live in a Yellow Submarine.' They'd had a good night, at least. Clark drew close to Dean and moved her out of the couple's way.

'I'm sorry, but I'm not.' He was trying to be as kind as possible, but it was a difficult task. How the hell was he going to get rid of her? 'Got your car here?' he asked hopefully. She shook her head. 'Somewhere to stay?' She shook her head again. 'All right, we'll find you somewhere. Come on.' He was speaking gently now, and he took her arm and they walked out of the hotel into the drizzly night.

It took over an hour, but he found her a hotel in the end; it was small and pretty grim, but there wasn't exactly a lot of choice. As he walked hurriedly back to the Shaftesbury, hugging himself and rubbing his arms to keep warm, he thought that this had really got out of hand. It had been a very close shave there. By the time he reached the green wooden doors of the Shaftesbury he was frozen, as well as exasperated and guilty. He could see the night porter slumped over the desk and was too confused to notice the sign on the bell right in front of him which said 'Ring for Night Porter'. Eventually he did see it, after a lot of banging, and when he leaned on it the old man shuffled up and let him in.

He still had the strength to bound up the stairs, along the corridor, into the room and towards the double bed with the red cover – but she was gone. He sat on the edge of the bed and fell backwards onto it with a deep exhalation of breath, wondering if he was relieved or disappointed. But before he could work it out, he was asleep.

He had never really meant to have an affair with Dean – it had just sort of happened, in the way these things do to men like Clark. She had been a member of his team at Mulberry Street (he was rather embarrassed to recall that now). He had broken the rules to try to cover up the affair once or twice when it threatened to cause difficulties. A nasty sequence of events surrounding a surveillance operation had led to her being taken off the crime squad and put back into uniform, and there was a question-mark on her record that she believed was going to hang over her whole police career. Clark was never sure about that question-mark and how much it was merited.

Dean had learned something from her recent experiences in the force and her relationship with

Clark. She had become hardened to cutting corners and taking a manipulative approach to personal relationships. After the unfortunate business at Mulberry Street, in which Clark hadn't exactly done the decent thing and protected Dean, he had been flattered when she continued to take an interest in him: he thought it was a sign of her essential good nature that she was prepared to let bygones be bygones and not hold it all against him. He thought he had eased himself back into the highly convenient and undemanding casual leg-over situation at her flat in Mornington Crescent, north London, or in the back of his car.

He hadn't realised how much Jenny had learned about life, and wasn't aware of who was using whom. He had continued to believe that he was the one calling the shots, especially when she had made it just like old times by feeding him some useful information about a case he was investigating. What he hadn't seen – until it became abundantly clear – was that Dean had been anxious about a new case she was involved in.

It blew over, although it had left a nasty taste in Clark's mouth and he had decided to end the affair. But there was something else, now, something much more serious – even deadly. Jenny Dean had decided that she was in love with him.

Clark had the next day off; he had an important function to attend in London. It was a hard slog to make it from Liverpool to London and back in a day and perform well at a function to boot, even in the best of circumstances, and, well, these were hardly the best. He tried to work on the train, and drank a lot of coffee, but it was a hopeless task. He was knackered. At half-past eleven he was woken by someone knocking on the window. A British Rail guard was standing outside the carriage.

'Sir, sir!'

'Mmm?'

'It's London, sir.'

The function he had rushed down for was a lunch party at Deputy Chief Constable Dunning's house. Clark took a taxi home, kissed his wife Sue, had a shower, changed into a medium blue sports jacket, tie and navy slacks, and they were off. She drove. He tried hard to make conversation, asking her about her week at the hospital, but he kept dozing off – he couldn't help it. She looked at him sitting in the passenger seat, and wondered. She knew he had been at it, all right, and she now knew with whom. She suspected the affair was over, but she wasn't quite sure about that, either. She sighed deeply. She knew that she was going to have to be strong enough one day to leave him unless he stopped playing the field. She did love him; she loved him very much. But she wasn't going to let him cheat on her. She badly wanted to start trying for kids, but it was out of the question while their relationship was fundamentally unstable, as she thought it was (he didn't, but that was because he had different ideas about relationships). There was no doubt in her mind that she would rather live without him than live in misery as the wronged woman.

She turned off the M40 and drove through the pretty Oxfordshire countryside, following signs to Nannton. It was a beautiful sunny day.

'Tony! Tony, wake up. We're there! This is Nannton. What's the name of Dunning's house?'

'What? Shit . . . did I fall asleep? I'm sorry love . . . um, The Old Vicarage . . . ' They drove around the green and there it was, an Edwardian pile next to the old church. A line of cars were already parked in the drive, and they were all large, new and shiny. Sue parked, and they walked up to the house. The front door was open.

'Hello?' said Clark. Dunning swept through. 'Clark! Good to see you!'

'Hello, sir. Glad you managed to arrange the weather. This is my wife, Sue.'

'Pleased to meet you,' boomed the suave and be-suited Dunning, and they all shook hands. Their host took them through to the garden, where twenty or thirty people were standing around on the terrace at the back of the large and comfortable house – an interesting mix of people. As well as potentially high-flying coppers there were media folk, academic criminologists and bright sparks from the Home Office Research Unit. Clark wasn't used to mixing with high fliers – not socially, anyway – and he picked his way around the terrace and garden that afternoon as warily as he would have done around a council estate of crack dealers. He reckoned he could hold his own among them, and the prospects of prowling the corridors of power rather than the mean streets was looking increasingly attractive.

They moved among the hanging baskets, rose bushes and blooming plants, sipping drinks and eating canapés. The barbecue had been billed as a private celebration of Dunning's elevation from Assistant Commissioner to Deputy Chief Constable of a provincial force. It was widely perceived as the final stage of his grooming to become next Commissioner of the Met. The move had been announced the previous week, and Clark sniggered as he recounted later to Sue what Deakin's reaction had been.

'Ah! Nice to greet the old NTC syndrome again!' Deakin had said, and went on to elaborate his own more traditional philosophy of policing, contrasting it to the new and aggressive reform-orientated ideas expounded by the likes of Dunning. Policemen often reacted to new appointments with the cry 'NTC!' It stood for 'Not That Cunt!' Deakin also dropped some

73

broad hints that none of these 'thinking men's policemen' were really as squeaky clean as they liked to appear. He, Deakin, could tell some tales . . . but then he said that there was no point, some people were fireproof.

Clark kept his own counsel about the appointment. Privately he was quite chuffed that someone with whom he was on such good terms was tipped for the top. But he wasn't about to declare an ideological allegiance to Dunning and his henchmen yet. No point in getting up Deakin's nose, as he was such a good boss to have.

'I thought you were terribly good on telly last week,' said Sue to Dunning later when he appeared with an open bottle of champagne.

'Did you?' he replied politely.

'I thought you handled it very well, sir,' said Clark, ever the diplomat. If Tony Clark knew one thing, it was how to look after himself.

'Forget the sir here, Tony. It's Trevor.'

'Thank you, Trevor.' He hoped it didn't sound too awkward; but it did – it sounded like a prep school boy trying out his headmaster's first name. 'We have to do a good deal of work on our public image.'

An attractive woman of about forty-five with a suntan and a pink silk dress joined them with a tray of smoked salmon and cream cheese whirls and a bright smile.

'Ah,' said Dunning, every bit the lord of the manor now, 'this is my wife, Laura. Laura, Tony Clark, one of our rising stars at the CIB, and his wife Sue.'

'Pleased to meet you,' she beamed, proffering the tray. 'Trevor's told me a lot about you, Tony. We expect great things of you in the future.'

'Thank you, Laura. I hope I can deliver the goods. Can I help you with that tray?'

'No, that's quite all right, thank you. Someone

should be round in a moment with some more nibbles – Trevor, you're taking care of the drinks, I hope? We'll be gathering round the barbecue in about half an hour.'

Laura peeled off, and Commander Huxtable loomed. Dunning had been Huxtable's patron in the force from way back. Both had risen far and fast, and they weren't finished yet. 'Hello, Tony. Having a nice rest up in Liverpool?'

'Well . . . ' said Clark. Sarcastic bastard, he thought. You think we're having a rest up there, do you? ' . . . I'd hardly call it rest, sir. . .'

Sue continued confidently to Dunning. 'I also heard you on the radio talking about a non-adversarial system of trial.'

'Now that really was a debate,' said Dunning.

'Yes, but you got the point across,' said Huxtable.

'Do you think so?' said Dunning, genuinely interested now to know what people thought.

'Oh yes,' said Sue brightly. 'It's something one wouldn't normally think about – well, not as a layman, anyway. But it's so obvious.'

Clark was impressed – and totally lost. He hadn't picked up on this debate. He'd better catch up. 'Is it?' he said. 'I didn't hear the radio thing.'

'Well,' said Sue, 'how can the police be seen as impartial when the heart of their job, within our present judicial system, is to prove that members of the public are guilty?'

Clark looked at his wife in amazement. It ought to be him saying that. Now everyone was impressed by her succinct summing up of the situation.

'Do you want a job?' asked Dunning, putting his arm around her and smiling at the others.

Later in the afternoon, after they had eaten from the barbecue, Clark watched his wife moving among the other guests, chatting effortlessly. She was so bright, so

75

easy-going, so affable, so . . . giving. That was what had attracted him to her (besides the fact, of course, that he found her devastatingly physically attractive). Everyone liked her; he could see them gravitating towards her, engaging her in conversation and making her laugh. He suddenly realised how much he loved her. Her good looks were of the girl-next-door variety, not the smouldering sex-bomb style of Molly Cope, and they had a more lasting appeal. Sue looked especially beautiful that day, her sunny face fringed by her blonde hair and her terrific figure shown off by her simple apricot suit. She was a dark horse, he thought, and smiled to himself. Who would have thought she could rattle off all that stuff about adversarial systems of justice? He felt so proud of her, and he couldn't believe that he had ever risked losing her.

9

Clark arrived at Huskisson Street so early that the
cleaners were still there. He picked his way along the
corridor over patches of wet, freshly mopped floor. At
least he had been able to get back to Liverpool in time
for an early start. Sue had tried to persuade him to stay
the night in London after Dunning's party and take
the first train up to Liverpool the next morning, but he
had resisted and caught the last one back that evening
instead, returning sheepishly to the Shaftesbury, very
late, but at least alone.

'You're all the bloody same you lot with your big
bloody feet,' a disgruntled woman complained to the
duty sergeant at the station. 'Can't believe a word any
of you ever say. Look what happened to Jimmy in our
street last week ... you ought to be ashamed of
yourselves!'

'Will that be all, Mrs Campbell?' said the duty officer
wearily. 'There are three people waiting behind you.'

'No, it won't be all! I want to know when Kevin is
going to be out – or any road, when I can see him. I
don't want you lot leading us one of your monkey
dances again . . ..'

'I've told you Mrs Campbell, I don't know that yet.
Now step aside, please.'

Clark entered the by now very familiar incident
room. Deakin was in there. It took Clark aback, and he

paused for a moment before walking briskly towards the tables their team had commandeered. Deakin was sitting in front of the noticeboard with two photographs of Dicks pinned onto it. He was studying notes on the case. Otherwise the room was empty.

'Early bird,' said Deakin, without looking up.

'Two early birds,' replied Clark. 'Who's the worm?'

'I hope it's Dicks,' said the inscrutable Deakin.

'I'm afraid it might turn out to be Kendrick.'

Deakin fingered a file with one hand and a plastic cup of tea with the other. He was a pudgy man in his early fifties, built like a tank; if pressed he could still punch holes through most of his junior officers. He had spent most of his career in divisional posts, but he had done service with the SPG (before it was rebadged as the TSG), and he'd seen violent action on the streets. 'Hotting up, is it?' he asked Clark.

'Well, it's all a bit circumstantial, but it's building into a case. I was going to phone you to ask for a bit of advice about how to proceed.'

'Were you?' said Deakin without looking up from the piece of paper he was studying. 'What did Messrs Dunning and Huxtable have to say?'

'You don't miss much, do you?' said Clark, lighting up his first cigarette of the day.

'Almost nothing,' said Deakin, and Clark laughed. He felt comfortable. He had been socialising with his boss's superiors – Deakin hadn't been invited to the party – and Deakin had to let him know that he knew. But their relationship was solid enough to cope. 'I can even tell you what they said to you. Offer up the heads of all bent coppers on a silver salver, as a sacrifice to Mr bloody Dunning's media career. Gist of it?'

Clark nodded. 'So what do I do,' he said in response, 'stop the investigation and let them off?'

'That's not in your gift, Tony.' Deakin put down the piece of paper and looked Clark in the eye. 'This year's fashion is for coppers as clean as the driven snow so that's what we have to give them. Next year, when the crime figures go through the roof and the clear-up rates drop through the floor, they'll scream blue murder and we'll set up a couple of special squads and hey presto! – we're off again.'

Deakin would shrug his shoulders when he saw Dunning performing on television, delivering his piece about reforms of legal procedure. But he was strongly opposed to the way things were going.

'So I play it by the book?' said Tony, his hands on his hips, thinking privately that if the Huxtable-Dunning axis was the wave of the future, he was going to ride it. Deakin might be his immediate boss, but he wasn't going to be important to him in the long term.

'Whether you like it or not, you are the judge and the jury – we all are. Think how much they like it when they are stopped, say, for speeding and they get off with a verbal warning. You decide what to tell me, don't you? Naylor decides what to tell you, so does Dicks, so does Kendrick. The PCA, the press, Disgusted of Tunbridge Wells: all judge and jury. Now, the reason you're here is because we think you're smart enough, and somewhere inside strong enough, not to be a liability.'

'That sounds rather negative.'

'Yeah well, it's a sodding compliment. Oh, this bird rang for you,' he handed Clark a note.

'At this time of the morning?' What was Molly Cope doing up and about at that hour?

Clark began tackling a file, but his mind wasn't on the job. He was mulling over the implications of what his boss had said. Deakin could be very hard, and sometimes he was impenetrable, but Clark trusted him, liked him, and, most important of all in their line of country, he respected him very much indeed. In many ways Deakin was the best boss Clark had ever had.

They were completely different characters. Deakin had reached the end of the line as far as promotion was concerned. He was very happy with his rank. When he'd joined the force after five years in the army he hadn't thought in terms of anything more than maybe making sergeant and opening a nice steady business, like a menswear shop, at home in Enfield when shift work finally got him down. He turned out to be a good policeman, and one whose energy, zeal and physical courage recommended him to his superiors. With little in the way of formal education, Deakin had surprised himself with his capacity for responsibility, and though he'd make the odd obligatory cynical remark about 'the job', his real gut feeling was one of deep loyalty and gratitude to the organisation that had helped him realise his potential. He was genuinely concerned about the welfare of his officers, and it was this that had made him popular and respected when he was on divisional duties and had furnished him with a network of loyal contacts across the Met, which he could still call upon. He was a copper's copper, a copper of the old school. His equivalent of the barbecue at Dunning's would have been a round of golf, even a golfing holiday, or a lodge meeting or ladies' night.

Deakin looked forward to ending his career as divisional chief superintendent of a busy little area with, ideally, a Premier League football team within its boundaries. Sitting in the directors' box with the promise of a single malt or two in the bar afterwards, chewing over a good game – that was Deakin's idea of heaven. He had a rock-solid marriage of thirty years' standing, and, like many older men, surprised himself by finding that he got more out of his grandchildren than he ever had done out of his children. There were one or two things about him that no one closely connected with his life knew, and which he kept to himself.

In the meantime he put his head down and sniffed the ground for bent coppers. It wasn't exactly the area of the force he had aspired to – it wasn't the area of the force anyone aspired to – but he was there and so he was going to make the best of it. As he saw it, that meant binning the rotten apples but also – and this was never far from his mind – giving the benefit of the doubt to a decent officer who'd stumbled after years of good service, or to a young lad who'd shown excessive zeal. Essentially, he saw the CIB as an instrument for defending the good name of the police from the sabotage and carping of those who didn't – and couldn't – know the realities of the job.

He liked the team well enough. He tolerated the career policemen above him, and he found Clark sympathetic, although he hadn't known him long enough to come to a firm judgement. Loyalties took a long time to harden into reality in the force, which was one of the reasons why they were so meaningful once they were established. Clark had already noted that Deakin had a very benign, some might say indulgent, attitude towards Inspector Naylor, and he concluded that they were two of a kind – the old-school, dragged-themselves-up-by-the-bootlaces, no-poncing-around-with-academic-theory coppers.

'You bastard!' Cope burst into the café and hit Clark over the head with a copy of her own newspaper.

'What—' he spluttered. A couple of men looked up from their copies of the *Sun* and their bacon butties.

'Don't come the innocent with me. You nobbled my informer.'

'I did what?'

'You got to him. Shameless. The moment I'd spoken to you. Christ knows how you did it, but you got to him.' She ran her hands through her hair, absolutely furious.

'Did I?' Clark enjoyed seeing her angry. She was like a polecat. She stood there, eyes flashing at him, her hair down over her shoulders, looking every inch the career woman in her smart black double-breasted trouser suit. Clark folded up his *Independent* and took a swig of coffee. He genuinely didn't know what she was talking about.

'"Did I?"' she mocked. 'Your two gorillas were on him in a trice and now he's clammed up. He's wild with me, thinks I handed him over to you and now he . . .'

Clark was shaking his head and smiling, and she could see that she'd got something wrong. She had asked him to meet her there in order to say her piece and shame him, but now a doubt crept into her mind that it might be she who was shamed. She stopped. Clark was thinking fast. It came to him. 'Alfreds?'

She looked at him without any expression at all, but he knew he was right. He felt triumphant. By complete chance they had uncovered her informer. Connell had dug up the pocketbook that revealed the discrepancy in the booking-in time, and the young officer Naylor and Connell had talked to in the corridor of the nick was the one who had been feeding Cope the inflammatory information on the scandal surrounding the Dicks case. 'Coincidence. They found his pocket-book. It showed serious discrepancies concerning Dicks' treatment at the station.'

'I don't believe you,' she said quietly and defiantly.

'It's true,' he said.

'Oh shit,' she said honestly, feeling humiliated.

'My turn to deal,' said Clark, oozing victory and anxious to exploit the situation. 'I won't tell anyone who he is if he agrees to talk to me face to face.'

'Off the record?'

'Certainly, but I'd need my inspector present.'

'Why?'

'Without him it'd be useless.'

82

'That's exactly why he wouldn't agree to it,' said Cope, irritated. God, this guy was naive sometimes.

'Then I blow his cover,' said Clark.

'Then I stick to everything I said. You are a bastard.'

He chuckled and looked up at her, his face radiant with pleasure. 'Sit down,' he said amiably, pulling out a chair for her. She sighed and plonked herself onto the chair, swinging her large bag under the table. She had asked him to come to another greasy spoon not to annoy him but because she genuinely liked using them for meetings and often did so, especially when she wanted to pop out of the office mid-morning, like now. As she had been in the newsroom that morning she had asked him to meet her at Jack's Bar rather than Frank's. Jack's Bar was just about the only traditional establishment left among the welter of modern buildings around the *Press* offices.

'Hello, Molly love,' said a waitress who arrived at the table. 'Nice to see you.' She wiped her hands on her orange housecoat. 'Haven't you been doing us proud with all that stuff you've discovered on the Teddy Dicks business? Scandal!'

Molly smiled. 'How's Jack?'

'Not too good, love, thanks for asking.' She wrung her hands. 'Still, he's going back in next week for more tests, so we'll know summat then. Doctor says he can see some more shadows on the lungs, you know, in the X-rays, which is probably why the pain's come back, but he said that many shadows aren't harmful, you know, they're just summat there which irritates, like, and causes pain, and they can get rid of those easily enough. Want a coffee Moll?'

'Yes please, Jean. And a rock bun, please.'

'Pillar of the community, eh?' said Tony wryly, once the woman had gone.

'Salt of the earth, this lot,' said Molly, as softly as she ever said anything. 'I feel at home here – more at home than I do in that shark pit of a newsroom.'

'It seems you've managed to swim ahead of the other sharks without too much difficulty.'

'Well, yes, but I do wonder sometimes what personal cost is involved.' She checked herself. Why the hell had she said that? She hadn't meant to, it had just slipped out. She might be able to be relaxed and vulnerable occasionally with Jean and Jack, but not with anyone to do with work or with any man she was sleeping with! What was she thinking of? 'Any other interesting cases floating around at Huskisson Street?' She pulled herself up and tried to retrieve the situation. Jean arrived and put a mug of coffee and a plate with a buttered rock bun in front of her.

Tony looked away. If they had just hauled the crown jewels into Huskisson Street he couldn't have cared less about it. He had also been concentrating too hard on the task in hand, to get to her informer, to notice the chink in her armour she had just inadvertently revealed. But he cast around for some titbit to throw to her, as he still needed to soften her up. He was walking a tightrope, trying not to offend her sense of journalistic ethics while getting from her the information he needed to pursue the case to a successful conclusion.

'There was a rape last night in Berriman Park which they think they can link up with the two last month across the river.'

'Someone's onto that,' she said. Shit, he thought.

'Information's still coming in on that Securicor job last week.'

She raised her eyebrows. 'Where's this information coming from?'

'Straight up, Molly, it's not my case so I don't know. You know Chris Coles, the super on the case, don't you?'

'Oh yes,' she said, her eyes twinkling, 'I know Coles.'

84

Bloody hell, thought Clark. Is she doing him, too? A chill ran down his spine, though not through jealousy; through fear for his own exposure. Perhaps he wouldn't sleep with her again. 'Another coffee please, love,' he said as the waitress passed, holding out his mug.

After a short pause he decided to take the bull by the horns. 'Look, all you need to do is to get Alfreds to come down to Frank's or something, with you present if he feels safer, for a quick chat with Naylor and me. Let's say seven o'clock tonight.'

'Idiot,' she said with a toss of her head. 'First of all Frank's closes at six like all greasy spoons. Secondly, you call yourself a detective and you suggest that this sensitive meeting takes place in a public eatery in full view of the entire world?'

Clark didn't mind being humiliated. All he minded about at that moment was cajoling her into agreeing to deliver Alfreds up to him. 'OK, Molly, you call the shots. Whenever, wherever, as long as it's today, and I'm telling you that my inspector will be with me.'

She stirred her empty coffee mug and ate half a rock bun. She knew he was sweating, but she genuinely had to work out how she could arrange this meeting. Clark had actually moved quite smartly. If she didn't co-operate and he then blew Alfreds' cover, no policeman in Liverpool would ever trust Molly Cope again. Quite a few of them didn't already, of course, but she didn't need all of them, just the crucial few. She had spoken with Alfreds on the phone that morning and she knew he was off duty that night. She could simply drive him to a rendezvous and get Clark and Naylor to talk to him in the back of her car.

'Eight o'clock tonight, on the docks, at the end of Hart Street. You'll have half an hour, top whack.'

Clark mentally punched the air in victory.

85

'Constable Alfreds, please.' Molly was speaking quietly in the empty editorial conference room at the *Press*. You couldn't have this kind of phone call in the newsroom. It took Alfreds a few minutes to extricate himself from the duty desk.

'Hello?'

'Hi, Darren, it's me, Molly.'

'Not again,' he said, his voice hardening.

'Look, they found your pocketbook by chance. I promise you – it was a coincidence. Apparently the book reveals serious discrepancies concerning Dicks' treatment at the station.' Darren already knew that, of course; that was what his 'chat' with Naylor and Connell had been all about. 'I'll say it straight, Darren,' continued Cope. 'If you don't agree to meet the Met guys off the record and with me present for half an hour this evening they're going to blow your cover. They've put two and two together.'

'I still don't know how they made the connection between me and you,' said Darren. He was suspicious.

'Nor do I, but they're into this case up to their bloody eyes. As I see it, Darren, you've got no choice.' She decided on the spur of the moment to use steamroller tactics. 'Look, I'll pick you up at five to eight on the corner of Tanza Road and Randolph Avenue.' She put the phone down.

Darren listened to the dialling tone for a moment, then replaced the handset. His mouth was slightly dry. All he wanted to do was turn the clock back six months and start again. He shouldn't have started it. All right, he was appalled at the level of corruption and criminality he saw going on within his own nick, but he should have bloody well known that going to the press with it was going to be bad news for him. If it hadn't been for Cope, he probably never would have gone so far, but she had impressed him with her powerful ideas about right and wrong and how to clean up the force, and she made it all seem as easy as falling off a log: just pass the info over, she'd use it and the bad guys would get done in the end without he, Alfreds, getting a reputation as a grass. Molly seemed to think exactly the way he did. It was one of Cope's great skills, to make people believe that.

Alfreds had been in the force for only two years or so, but he had ingested enough of the culture to feel that coming clean and exposing fellow policemen through the correct channels was simply not an option. He could never live it down, either in the locker-room or in the street where he lived, where two other coppers who were neighbours would make sure everyone knew. Even his elder brother and his mates would despise him. And now he was going to have to do it secretly to some ponce from the Met. He swallowed hard, and returned to the duty desk.

Kendrick and his solicitor were seated on one side of the interview room table, Clark and Connell on the other. The solicitor and Connell had placed themselves behind their men, their backs against the walls, like seconds in a duel. Kendrick's face was always hard, but it was beginning to harden further as Clark pushed him to the limit. He had been in the force for twenty-five years, all of it at the sharp end. He didn't have much time for these designer-suited high fliers from the Met; he'd like to see how long they'd last on his beat.

'It seems from the taped interview,' said Clark, 'now referred to as the confession, that you'd spoken to Dicks before the interview began.'

'Yes, sir.'

'Yes?'

'Yes, sir.'

'Under caution?'

'Yes, sir.'

'Where's the tape?'

'The machine was faulty at the time, sir,' said Kendrick without flinching. 'I took contemporaneous notes.'

'Ah. And where are they?' It was clear that Clark didn't believe a word of it, and it rather looked as though he had decided not to believe it before Kendrick had even said it.

'They were sent along with all the other evidence to the Crown Prosecution Service.'

'Were they used in court?'

'I don't know, sir. It was the CPS's decision.'

'Were these notes signed by Dicks?'

'I think not, sir.'

'Where are they now?'

'Ask the CPS.'

'We have.' Seeing that he had at least succeeded in rattling Kendrick, Clark paused and then pressed on. 'Dicks' facial injuries. How did he come by them?'

'Self-inflicted.'

'Are you serious?' Clark couldn't go along with this charade any longer.

'You're facing a charge that could send you down for ten, fifteen, twenty years,' said Kendrick, his tone of voice suggesting that he was explaining the blindingly obvious to an imbecile. 'If you smack yourself in the eye or headbutt the bog there's an outside chance you might just walk in a week. Wouldn't you do it?'

'Did you write out the details of the robberies to jog Dicks' memory?'

'No, sir.'

'Were you aware that he was under the influence of drugs?'

'No, sir.'

'Did you interview him for several hours before

Poynton checked him in?'

'No.'

'Did you deny him access to a solicitor?'

'No.' Kendrick's voice was getting harsher. His solicitor fidgeted.

'Beat him?'

'No.' He felt outrage welling up inside him. Connell was riveted.

'Deny him food?'

If Clark thought he was going to wear his man down by that kind of method, he had badly misjudged the situation. Kendrick couldn't speak. He just smiled a small, cold smile.

'I think you did most or all of the above.'

'Prove it,' said Kendrick, twisting up his face.

10

At eight o'clock that night Clark pulled off the meeting with Alfreds. He had parked his pool car behind Cope's heavy and stylish old banger at the end of Hart Street on the docks, and he and Naylor had got into the back. Alfreds was in the passenger seat, and Cope was at the wheel. They had gone through the whole case, lit by a single streetlamp which cast a curious cadmium glow, like a Victorian gas lamp. The windows of the city buildings on the other side of the water twinkled. It was the dead zone, a no-through road where nobody ever had cause to go unless it was to buy drugs or execute some shady deal or screw anonymously in the back of a car. It was the province of the disaffected and the disenfranchised of Liverpool, and it was not a place to wander alone if you weren't one of their number.

Darren Alfreds was co-operating, but he wasn't happy. He looked straight ahead, into the rainy street. Cope was silent throughout.

'So why didn't the solicitor lodge a complaint for Dicks?' asked Clark.

'I'm not sure, but he knew Kendrick; they were certainly on first-name terms. I do know he advised the lad to keep schtumm. Don't make waves, plead guilty and serve your time. And the kid bought it.'

'Did you give Miss Cope all the stuff on the Serious

Crime Squad?'

'Some of it.' He hated this bit.

'Why?'

'Because the place is a mess.'

'Yeah, but why the press, why not tell a senior officer?'

'Because I didn't know how high I'd have to go to get out of this shit. And it doesn't matter how high you go, nobody likes a nark. Do they, Inspector?'

'No comment,' said Naylor, deadpan.

Clark looked at Naylor, registering the antipathy that had evolved between these two after just one meeting. As far as Naylor was concerned, grassing to the press was the lowest of the low. It wasn't right. If you have a genuine complaint against your own kind, fine – but have the guts to handle it straight and swim along the correct channels, don't go off up some sewer to protect yourself.

'But you won't speak?' said Clark to Alfreds.

'No,' he said firmly. 'You blow my cover and I leave the force and don't say a word.'

For many coppers, the stigma attached to betraying other members of the force was too much: they couldn't handle it. They couldn't live under that kind of peer-group pressure. Even if they knew they were doing the right thing, the just thing, by not condoning rank corruption, they weren't made of strong enough stuff to see it through. Alfreds was one of them, all right.

'This is much more like it,' she said. 'They even give you slippers.' He hadn't wasted any time. Clark never did. After the interview with Alfreds he had been obsessed with the need to arrange to see her again that night. First he had to get Naylor back into the pool car. He could only do that by getting in himself, which he did, and then as Naylor started the engine he opened his door again.

'I want to check on something,' he told Naylor. 'I'll be

right back.' Naylor looked out of the window and lit a cigarette. You must think I was born yesterday, guv, he thought. Clark ran back up to Molly's side of the car. She wound down the window, and he flicked his head back almost imperceptibly to indicate that he wanted to say something to her out of Alfreds' earshot. She got out, looking slightly cross. The meeting which had just taken place had been quite an ordeal for her; she would have much preferred it not to have happened.

'I want to see you later,' he said, his eyes blazing. 'Please, Ms Cope.'

She looked at him. 'Yes, but not in the same dump as before.' Without waiting to hear his suggestions, she said she'd see him at nine-fifteen in the bar of the Britannia Adelphi. It was Liverpool's most luxurious hotel.

She drove Alfreds back to his own car in Tanza Road. He was lost in his morose thoughts about integrity, humiliation and betrayal, she in hers about passion and desire. But her head was always in control of her heart, or at least, in partial control. If he wants me, she thought, he's going to have to pay. If he thinks he can palm me off with bloody cheapskate fleapits, he's mistaken; I have my pride.

There was something else, too. She had tried to get in touch with Clark on the day he had gone back to London. When she called the Shaftesbury they told her that he'd gone away for the day, so she asked if she could be put on to another member of the team. She got Naylor. She put on a Liverpool accent and said she was calling for Clark and did anyone know where he was.

'He's gone back to London for the day,' the unsuspecting Naylor had said over the phone.

'Would he be at his office there?'

'No, he's gone down for a social function, and to see his wife.'

'I see. Thanks.' She had put the phone down quickly, stunned. It had never occurred to her that he might be married. She couldn't explain why. She had never had an affair with a married man before – it was a bit of a principle with her (she certainly hadn't been short of offers). Damn! She felt a wave of panic rising up inside her. How dare he? But more importantly, how much of him could she lay claim to if there was another woman on the scene?

Perhaps his marriage is on the rocks, she thought hopefully as she dropped off the hapless Alfreds. Perhaps it's already over, and that's why he's made himself so available to me. Surely he can't be sleeping with his wife, otherwise he wouldn't have been so uncontrollably passionate. Or was she being taken for a fool? Damn, damn, damn!

She was going to punish him for it, in more ways than one. First of all he could spend his bloody money on somewhere decent for them. Second, she might play a few games herself, with the only weapon she had: material on the case.

When they met, he suggested that they didn't linger at the bar, indicating with a smouldering expression that he couldn't wait to make love to her. He assumed they'd go to her place. The reason he implied for this quick exit was only partly the truth: after the close shave of the other night, he simply didn't want to be seen in public with her in a social situation. No, she had said. Let's stay here. And she walked over to the reception desk, cool as a cucumber, and checked them in to a master suite. The receptionist was similarly cool. She was quite used to business people who weren't married to each other checking in without any luggage. It was a daily occurrence.

By the time they were in the room and had plundered the mini-bar for champagne and she had discovered the little velvet slippers, she was enjoying herself far too much to spoil the evening with a scene. It was a huge room with a plush deep-pile carpet, heavy velvet curtains with tassled tie-backs, several sumptuous armchairs, a television, a mini-bar, a jacuzzi in the large bathroom with a porcelain dish of bath pearls waiting on one corner: it was quite luxurious, and Molly loved to be pampered. She loved being with him, too, and she genuinely wanted him to have a good time with her. She could have her revenge quietly in the morning, after a wonderful night together. She undressed in the bathroom, down to a lacy navy all-in-one body and bra, brushed her hair and went through to the palatial bedroom, where Clark was lying on the bed in his boxers underneath a very grand sky-blue curtain, which was draped over the bedhead like half a wigwam. He was reading the *Police Gazette*.

She wanted to check one thing. 'You won't blow Alfreds' cover, will you?' she asked as she walked over to the dressing-table. Next to the empty bottle of champagne a huge bunch of lilies were arranged in a vase underneath a crystal wall lamp.

'You know I won't,' said Clark.

'Yes,' she said, smiling with relief as she picked up the room service card and scrutinised it. 'And Naylor? He did hate him, didn't he?'

'Yep, but he won't shop him.'

She ticked coffee for two, croissants and news-papers, scribbling the name of her own paper next to the box, and took it to the door. As she snuggled up to him in the king-size bed, Clark put the magazine on the bedside table and said, 'Why can't we spend the night at your place?' His tone of voice revealed that this had been exercising his mind.

'Because you can't get room service,' she said lightly. He looked at her face, indicating that he would actually appreciate a proper answer to that question. 'All right. I have a cat, and she thinks, and I agree with her, that men are dirty, disruptive creatures, you know, skiddies in the pan, drips on the seat, so we don't invite them home. OK?'

He did not believe this woman.

'And the bed's bigger here,' she finished off. Good, she thought. He suspects that I live with someone. Let him sweat. Actually she lived alone – as she had done ever since she left college – but she didn't see why he had to know that. She wanted power in this relationship.

'You've got enough to do them now, haven't you?' she said, nuzzling her nose into his neck like a cat asking for attention. He kissed her forehead.

'What?' He was still thinking about her domestic set-up. 'Oh, Kendrick. No, not at all. We may have enough to convince us, but the CPS would need a great deal more before they decided to bring a case to court.'

'What a shame,' she said calmly. 'What you need is another witness.' She turned round and switched off the chintzy lamp on her side of the bed.

Wait a minute, he thought. What's that supposed to mean? He leaned over to turn on his lamp. She looked a picture of innocence. 'You up to something?'

Of all the 'Who, me?' looks that have ever been cast between lovers, Cope executed that one most stylishly. She switched off the light, and he knew he was beaten.

'Sometimes,' he said, running his hand up over the blue lace and onto her breast, 'you make me nervous.'

'Why?' she said, plunging her hand down into his boxers as she spoke, and then licking his earlobe.

'I feel outnumbered,' he said, slipping one strap down over her shoulder.

'You are,' she said, helping him pull off her lacy undergarment and then pulling him over on top of her, her arms clasped firmly around his back. 'And surrounded.'

*

The alarm call came through at seven-thirty, and Clark struggled to think straight as he regained consciousness. I can't keep going on like this, he thought, wondering what time they had finally fallen asleep. Tonight, definitely, an early night, he promised himself, though he didn't believe it would happen for a minute. Hard living had become a way of life.

There was no question of a lie-in: he couldn't be late again. He struggled out of bed and drew the curtains. It was a beautiful morning. He blinked in the glare, and stumbled into the bathroom, where he splashed cold water on his face and looked into the mirror above the double sink. Rough, he thought, inspecting the fine lines around his eyes and the faint shadows underneath. He sighed, took a long white towelling robe from a brass hook on the wall and went to the bedroom door. As he stooped to pick up the breakfast tray on the floor outside, sunlight from the room spilling onto the hall carpet, his eye immediately fell on the headline on the front page of the *Liverpool Press*.

It saidNEW WITNESS IN DICKS' CASE, and it had Cope's byline. Next to it was the photograph of Dicks with the touched up black eye on the wrong side of his face. Clark was dumb-founded. Why hadn't she fucking told him? He left the tray and its little vase of tiny flowers where it was, shut the door again and walked over to the bed, spluttering. 'Hey,' he said, tapping her on the shoulder with the newspaper. She was pretending to be asleep. 'When did you find him?' he said, standing over her and looking mortified.

'Last week,' she said muzzily. Wow, was she enjoying this! Play it cool, she thought, stretching languorously. She had been bursting to tell him. Her excellent network of contacts on the ground in the seedier districts of Liverpool had come through with the news that a shopkeeper had seen Dicks and Kendrick together on the day Dicks was taken in. She had gone to see him at his junk shop immediately, and he had turned out to be a dream witness. Cope had kept it to herself to show Clark that he wasn't holding all the cards. He'd better play a straight bat with her in future.

'Why didn't you tell me?' said Clark plaintively. He was genuinely upset.

She played her ace. 'Why didn't you tell me you were married?'

Clark had found the new witness by nine-thirty, and was chatting to him outside his shop in Victoria Road, New Brighton. Cope had simply handed over the address of the junk shop before Clark left the room in the Adelphi. There was no harm in doing that, at this stage of the game; he could find the guy easily enough now that it was all over the papers. And it gave Cope no small pleasure to write Mike Attwood, 47 Victoria Road, New Brighton on a stiff sheet of cream paper encrusted with the words Britannia Adelphi in a heavy Gothic script.

Clark had returned to the Shaftesbury early that morning and had slunk in, trying to avoid the gaze of the bold old porter. The man slapped the key down on the counter, staring at Clark as if he were a small dog turd. Well fuck you, thought Clark, picking up the key and looking right into the ugly old face. Don't you take the moral high ground with me. You're getting your money for my room, and that's all you need worry about. Why should I come over all embarrassed in front of you, you scumbag? You're jealous. You probably haven't had it for twenty years. And he held his head up high as he strode upstairs.

As soon as he reached 212 he lay on the bed and called Connell's room. 'Maureen? Morning. Seen today's *Press*?'

'Give me a chance, Guv,' she said. 'It's only eight-fifteen.' She was sitting at her dressing-table eating breakfast. She had made a special request to have it delivered outside her room every day; the Shaftesbury management had agreed only on condition that she didn't want full English. They wouldn't normally even have agreed that much, but they didn't want to lose the lucrative Met contract. Connell had made it clear that it was an important request. She always made a point of having breakfast in her room whenever she travelled on business. It was bad enough almost always having lunch and dinner on the job and spending the whole day in male company pretending she was one of the gang. But breakfast too? Not likely. She needed those few minutes of calm to get to grips with the new day and prepare herself for the onslaught. Anyway, she didn't much enjoy watching a load of men tucking into greasy bacon, fried bread (yuk!) and acres of toast loaded with butter. She enjoyed tea, cereal (Shredded Wheat was all that was on offer at the Shaftesbury) and a piece of fruit (she had to provide that herself) in her bedroom.

'There's another witness. We should get down to New Brighton asap. Can you ring Naylor's room and tell him we're taking the pool car, and we'll meet him at Huskisson Street later? I'll see you downstairs in twenty minutes.'

'Right you are, Guv.' Good, she thought. A bit of a break before I have to confront that bloody incident room again.

The old-fashioned pram remained unsold and stood on the pavement outside the junk shop as stately as a galleon. Connell leaned on the car right in front of the shop as Clark went in. She looked around the dreary street at the out-of-date posters for fleabitten music venues which were peeling off the hoardings.

'Oh yes. I know Dicks,' said the chubby shopkeeper,

still wearing the cream peaked cap. 'He's been nicking stuff off me most of his life. When I saw Kendrick with him I was chuffed. I thought it was about bloody time the police did something about him.' He had watched Dicks grow up. Most of the kids around there stole almost as soon as they could breathe, but some were worse than others. Usually it was irregular, petty stuff. But Dicks – Dicks was a hard case. Mike Attwood had seen Dicks throw a few punches.

'So you must have known Kendrick too, if you recognised them both?'

'Yes. He's been trying to clean up this area for donkeys' years.' He chuckled. 'Bloody thankless task that is!' The pair of them walked back to the door of the small, dank shop, stepping over a mound of unsorted underwear the man had picked up from a smelly old house whose sole occupant had recently died. 'Need any new pants, guv?' asked the shop-keeper, scooping up a pair of saggy pre-war men's pants with holes in strategic places. 'Or how about something nice to keep you warm in the winter?' He had picked up a brown china cylinder about a foot long, with a stopper at the top. Clark looked at it. It was a hot-water bottle. He took it from the man and examined it. Sue collected things like that in the garden. 'How much?'

'To you, guv, two-fifty.' Clark got the change out of his pocket, thinking that it would keep the old man sweet, if nothing else.

'What time did you see them?' he asked, getting back to the task in hand as they emerged onto the pavement.

'Between five-thirty and six. I was shutting up shop, see. I remember it because there was a bit in the next day's evening paper and I realised that's what I'd seen the day before. It's not exactly a regular daily occurrence to see someone getting picked up for armed robbery. Not even in New Brighton.'

Clark smirked at Connell, who was still leaning on the car. 'What sort of state was Dicks in?'

'Well, he was always unhealthy, too much wacky baccy.'

'And that day?'

'Same, I think.'

'So you don't remember him being exceptionally stoned, or high?'

'No.'

'What was going on between him and Kendrick?'

'Like I said, I was pleased, 'cos it looked like Kendrick was giving him a good talking to.'

'Was he hitting him?'

'Oh no, I don't think so. Maybe holding him. I don't remember.'

'Did Kendrick take Dicks away or did he leave him there?' The man walked along the pavement a few yards to the place he had been standing that day two years previously when he witnessed the encounter between Kendrick and Dicks. He screwed up his eyes and looked at the exact spot where they had been positioned, and he tried hard to bring that moment back. But it was no good. It wouldn't come. 'I just don't remember.'

Clark and Connell looked at each other, frustration written on both their faces. But there was nothing they could do. It was natural enough that the man couldn't remember the details.

'Thanks very much for your help,' said Clark, placing his hand on the shopkeeper's shoulder. 'We'll be in touch.'

He walked slowly along Victoria Road for a few minutes before getting back into the car, one hand in his pocket, the other cradling the hot-water bottle, with Connell at his side. They were both deep in thought. Three kids ran out of a side street, shouting obscenities behind them. They had come from a house with boarded windows. Squatters had got in by burning away the lower half of the front door.

They drove to Huskisson Street in silence, the pair of them troubled, turning over this opaque case in their minds. It wasn't straightforward, that was for sure. They had both had a gut feeling for a period that Kendrick was as bent as hell and had nobbled Dicks. But now – well, they weren't convinced. Then Connell spoke up.

'He doesn't like him, does he?'

'Hmmm?'

'The shopkeeper, he doesn't like Dicks?'

'No.'

'Do you think he realises his evidence might get Dicks released?'

'No.' Clark was right. The shopkeeper hadn't thought it through. If he had, he wouldn't have spoken up – might even have told a few porkies. He didn't want that Dicks back on the streets of New Brighton, no thank you.

'I don't like this case,' said Connell.

'No,' said Clark, his face grim.

11

Clark dropped Connell at Huskisson Street and said he was going to look into one or two things alone. 'See you back here later,' he called as she slid out of the car and he walked round to the driver's side to take the wheel. He lit a cigarette as he pulled away, and almost failed to stop at a zebra crossing at the end of the road over which a little old woman was pushing a shopping trolley. Clark was feeling uncomfortable. He had to talk to Kendrick, see if he would crack, try to frighten him into some kind of admission, then offer him a deal. Kendrick wasn't an easy kind of man to frighten, but Clark badly wanted to put the case to bed. He was nervous about it – very nervous.

It was a Saturday, and he knew Kendrick wasn't working from a riffle through the duty rosters at the station the day before, so he drove along the pleasant, suburban street where Kendrick lived, the neat semis exuding complacency. Well-scrubbed children rode mountain bikes along the pavements and laughed, while their dads threw buckets of sudsy water over the cars parked in the driveways. Domestic bliss, thought Clark, looking at Kendrick's comfortable home as he drove past. He pulled up around the corner, next to a typical Liverpudlian Victorian pub, sat still in the driver's seat for a few moments, and then walked over to a red telephone box.

Kendrick was at that moment pinned down on the stairs in the hall of his house by his son, aged nine, and his eleven-year-old daughter. This kind of rugby scrum was quite usual for a Saturday morning in the lively Kendrick household.

'Pick on someone your own size!' shouted Kendrick as his son held him in a half-nelson and his daughter tickled him under both arms. 'Not unless you agree to take us to the pool!' squealed the young boy. 'It's a fair cop!' said Kendrick, peeling one of his daughter's arms away from his armpit. 'When?' she shrieked, immediately clamping the arm back in position. 'This afternoon. Aaargh!'

Kendrick's wife watched from the doorway of the living-room, smiling. It was a bright, airy house, decorated with care and pride. Kendrick had built an extension at the back, and there was a greenhouse at the bottom of the garden where he grew his own tomatoes and cucumbers. Behind the stairs where they were wrestling the windows still had their original stained glass.

The telephone rang, and Kendrick's wife picked it up on the mobile. She was an attractive woman, in an ordinary, homely kind of way, without make-up or pretension of any kind. It was a very happy marriage.

'Hello?' she said. 'Quiet, I can hardly hear the phone!' she said, her hand over the receiver, trying to restrain her laughter at the sight of her husband spreadeagled on the stairs.

'Hello? . . . Yes, he is. Who is it?' She took the phone over to Kendrick, who had extricated himself and was sitting at the foot of the stairs, panting. 'For you, Bill,' she said as she handed over the phone. 'Someone called Clark.'

Kendrick's face hardened as he took the phone from her, and he got up and moved to the far corner of the hall, stopping underneath an attractive reproduction mirror and speaking in a low voice right into the handset. 'You! . . . No, I won't speak to you without my solicitor.'

'I appreciate that, Bill,' Clark's voice came over with an echo. Kendrick registered the calculated use of his Christian name. 'I want to talk to you, without prejudice and completely off the record.'

'Fuck off.' Stella Kendrick heard this, and she opened her mouth to remonstrate with him. Then she realised it was serious, and left it.

'It's getting too hot now and I regret it,' continued Clark purposefully. 'I want to talk to you about damage limitation.'

'You are in no position to deal and you know it,' said Kendrick, his voice menacing as he moved back to the stairs, vacated now by the kids, and sat down on the third from the bottom. Going to come the chum, was he? Not bloody likely.

'Aren't I?' Clark was riled. 'Well, if you don't come to the pub round the corner from your house in the next twenty minutes you'll never know, will you?' The phone went dead. Kendrick stared at it. Arrogant bastard, he thought, well aware that he had no choice but to go.

'I have to pop out, love,' he said to his wife. She looked at him with a mixture of astonishment and worry. There were no secrets between them. 'That bastard from the Met sniffing around.' He picked up his black bomber jacket from a hook inside a small downstairs cloakroom. 'Won't be long.'

'Dad, what about the pool . . .?'

Clark had bought himself a drink in The Black Dog and was sitting at the bar next to the pumps trying to ignore the musak. A man in a singlet was finishing a pint at another corner of the bar and a couple of old regulars were ensconced at tables with *Daily Mirrors*;

apart from that, the pub was empty. It was only a quarter to twelve, which was early even for the hard drinkers.

Kendrick pushed open the swing door and sauntered over. The man in the singlet moved off, and Kendrick sat on a barstool next to Clark. He wasn't a regular in The Black Dog, although it was the nearest pub to his house. He wasn't a pub kind of guy; he preferred being at home with the family, if the truth were told. And unlike most detectives he didn't drink much, either – in fact he rarely drank anything at all.

'No drink,' he said, looking straight ahead. Clark had bought himself a pint. Kendrick had no intention of moving from the hostile position he had taken up with Clark and his team from the moment they stepped onto his territory. If they thought they could just pitch up there, playing the high and bloody mighty, with no conception whatsoever of what kind of a hardened criminal community coppers like Kendrick were working in, peopled with the likes of Dicks . . . Oh no. He wasn't getting into cosy drinks with this smart alec.

'I'll be straight with you,' said Clark coolly. 'I'm stuck between the devil and the deep blue sea. I can't just drop this case. I've got too close, too many people are waiting for a result. But I honestly don't want a full-scale, no-holds-barred scrap because I believe all three of you will go down, and Dicks will get out.'

'I don't agree,' said Kendrick, looking at Clark for the first time.

'That's because you don't know how close we are to you,' said Clark, quick as a flash. 'We have the original complaint. We then have a witness who will testify that Dicks was high. We now have a witness who will testify that he saw you behaving roughly towards Dicks three to four hours before you admit to speaking to him. We have the prison doctor. We have the solicitor advising

Dicks, who turns out to have been a friend of yours. We have a confession to one job that doesn't match the eyewitness details. We have McPherson, who I believe will crack under pressure.'

Kendrick turned to Clark ponderously. 'A lot of hot air,' he said. He was completely confident. 'Wouldn't frighten anyone, even if they were guilty.'

Clark played his best shot now.

'And we have an inside informer who is now willing to testify' – Kendrick raised his eyes sharply, without turning his head towards Clark – 'that he saw Dicks inside Egberth nick at least two hours before Poynton signed him in.'

It was a bluff, but it was a good one. Kendrick didn't believe Clark really did have this insider. Was Clark so low that he was going to set him up?

'Produce him,' growled Kendrick.

'I will,' said Clark. 'But first I wanted to offer you something.'

Kendrick would have liked to have said no there and then, but he couldn't stop himself hearing Clark out.

'If you admit to taking Dicks to the river, thumping him and being aware that he was high, I will not spring the informer and McPherson and Poynton will not be implicated.'

Kendrick turned away.

'There's every chance that they will not be touched, or they might just get "advice". There's every chance that you will just get a caution. I can't promise you won't be kicked out but frankly, in view of your record, I think you'd swing it.'

'And Dicks?' Kendrick simply could not countenance the thought of that young criminal being let out onto the streets. If Clark had seen the trauma, distress and pain Dicks had caused on a regular basis in that city ever since he had been old enough to run fast, he wouldn't have wanted to risk seeing him back on the streets either – even the streets of Liverpool.

'That's up to the Appeal Court,' said Clark. That wasn't his responsibility, at least.

'Funny old world, isn't it?' snarled Kendrick.

'Yes,' said Clark, his heart beating slightly faster. I think he's going to buy it! he thought triumphantly.

'No deal,' said Kendrick as he got up and walked out of the bar, disgusted, furious – but not scared.

Naylor and Connell had spent a reasonably quiet couple of hours before lunch sifting through material in the incident room after Clark had dropped Connell off and gone to find Kendrick. When Connell had arrived at their tables she found Naylor absorbed in the *Daily Mail*.

'Morning Harry. Anything of interest?'

He stubbed out a cigarette and folded up the paper. 'Another load of guff about these ideas for reforming the legal system. Dunning's really stirred it up, no doubt to get his name put about, and now the media are into bloody rent-a-quote – everyone and his dog gets wheeled out to say their piece. I ask you.'

Connell smiled to herself and picked up the *Mail*. 'What d'you reckon, then, Inspector Naylor? What would you say if they walked in here now and asked you for a quote?'

Naylor drew his chair up close to his desk as if he were about to start work in earnest. 'Well, they wouldn't, would they? Never ask someone at the bleedin' sharp end who actually knows what he's on about. Nah, policing's never going to be all that different, Maureen, you've seen enough to know that. Leave us alone, that's what I say, leave things be and let us get on with the job.'

Connell read through the articles and editorial. She went along with the idea of reform, but she was similarly sceptical. She had lived through programmes and initiatives before, and apart from making work for desk jockeys, she wasn't sure they did anything to alter the sad truths of human nature – whether police or criminal – whose perpetual interplay was the endless cynical drama of police work.

Later, just as they were putting on their jackets to go and grab some lunch, Clark came in.

'Morning, Guv,' said Naylor.

'I've just seen Kendrick,' said Clark. 'He wouldn't buy a deal. I'm worried.'

'Let's not go to the canteen,' said Connell as they walked out of the incident room. 'I don't know if my internal central heating can cope with the icy blasts we get from everyone down there.'

They went to the pub around the corner and ate a poor imitation of chilli con carne. All three of them were restless, and as soon as they had finished eating they were ineluctably drawn back to the incident room. Half an hour after they had sat down again to wade through more documents and toss ideas and theories on the case to each other like tennis balls, More stormed in. Connell was sitting on one of their tables in the middle, legs crossed, facing Clark. The room was full of officers.

'What's all this nonsense about suspending Poynton, Kendrick and McPherson?' barked More, imperious and tall in his immaculate uniform, a piece of paper dangling from his hand.

'Well, I—' began Clark defensively.

'I will not suspend officers on the basis of circumstantial bits and pieces,' said More in the voice of a threatening schoolmaster.

'Don't you think the Crown Prosecution Service has enough to build a case?' asked Clark, looking quizzical. Surely More agreed with him – the evidence against Kendrick was becoming irrefutable, wasn't it?

'No,' snapped the Deputy Assistant Commissioner, irritation gleaming in his eyes.

'This new witness may have tipped the scales in favour of the prosecution,' said Naylor.

'What about the *theory* that the newspaper reporter, Cope, has an informer inside the force?' said More. That story had been circulating for some time now, since before Clark and the team came across her, luckily for Clark.

'From some of the leads she's come up with,' said Connell, 'there's no doubt about it.'

More turned to Clark and said without irony, 'You've been trying to wheedle your way in there. Any progress?'

Clark cut into the uncomfortable pause. 'I've spoken to her.' Naylor looked at Clark, his face frozen into utter impassivity. Clark regained his composure. 'Naturally she won't reveal her sources, or whether she has any.'

'I don't mind saying that I'm not happy about the way this is going. I've got enough headaches without this little molehill turning into a ruddy mountain.'

'Are you saying you want me to stop the investigation?' said Clark, looking More in the eye. More looked back at him coldly, as if to say, If you don't bloody well know the answer to that, you're stupid. Clark didn't flinch, and More stomped out of the incident room. At that moment a constable came in, holding a large and weighty object at arm's length. 'Left in the back of pool car nine-one-four,' he shouted ostentatiously. 'Anybody know anything about it?'

It was the hot-water bottle.

It had been a tough day. Nerve-endings were fraying. At six, four hours after the unpleasant encounter with More, which had rattled them all, Clark and Naylor had found themselves outside the police club bar. Without actually verbalising the decision to have a drink together they were drawn in, like iron filings to a

109

magnet, and they were onto their second pints before they had exchanged more than a couple of sentences. Their minds began to loosen up. Clark took off his tie. They smoked a lot of cigarettes, like most of the other officers in the crowded bar. The atmosphere was thick.

'If they blow out the confession,' said Naylor, 'Dicks will be released. The helmet, gloves and jacket are bollocks as evidence. There was no money found, no positive identification.'

'Maybe he didn't do it,' said Clark, standing back from the bar a few drinks later. They were both regular and hard drinkers; had been for years.

'Well, well, well,' said Naylor, hunched over the bar. His face twisted. 'D'you know that's the first time since we've been on this case that anyone has bothered to ask did the little bastard rob those post offices? Well 'course he did, didn't he, we all know he did. It's just possible that he may not have done the New Brighton job, but how many others has he done? How many others that we don't know about, eh?'

'That's not really the point,' said Clark, not tuning in to Naylor's wavelength.

'Well, if putting villains behind bars isn't the point, I don't know what I'm doing the job for,' said Naylor huffily.

'It's how you do it. If we don't play it by the book, we just become vigilantes.'

Naylor's face turned vicious, and he spat at Clark, 'Jeez, you're beginning to sound like that bedfellow of yours.'

It was a savage moment. Naylor held his boss's eye, but he wondered if he'd gone too far. Anger flashed through Clark's mind, and if it had been another man he would have swung a punch at his inspector. But the rage settled; he couldn't be angry at Naylor for long, he trusted him too much. Anyway, Naylor had a hold over him now.

'Did you tell Deakin?' said Clark quietly, taking a slug of bitter and thinking of that moment, the first night he slept with Molly, when he had seen Deakin and Naylor having a drink together in the Shaftesbury.

'I should've,' said Naylor, facing him. 'I should've told him a lot of things, but I used my judgement. Does that make me a vigilante?'

'No,' said Clark, feeling defeated.

'Well, you'll excuse me, Guv'nor, but I think you're being a bit naive. If you choose to play it by the book there isn't one of us you couldn't haul in for something. Me, you, Deakin, Huxtable, Dunning. I bet you a hundred quid you couldn't drive across London without breaking the law. Have you ever tried to drive at thirty miles an hour for more than a couple of minutes? It can't be done.'

'We're not talking about breaking the speed limit, we're talking about conspiracy to pervert the course of justice.'

'Words. What the fuck would you think if he blew your wife away? That little shit's lethal.' He meant Dicks. 'All right, so they slapped him around a bit, but they got a confession.' He paused. 'So he was scared for an hour or so, and they bent the rules. How scared are the old ladies he waved guns in front of, hey? How scared are the little kids he's forced to lie on the floor?' Naylor's voice rose, and cracked slightly. 'How many nightmares? How many wet beds?' Clark never thought in those kind of small, concrete details. Naylor rarely thought in any other way. That was the big difference between them.

They drank for a minute in silence.

'No,' said Naylor into his glass. 'If Kendrick had played it by the book he would never have got him.' That had been his intuition from the start. He had learned to trust his feelings. 'And now,' he said quietly and bitterly, 'Dicks has got you, me, half the bloody

111

Met, the PCA, the CPS, the DPP, his lawyer, the papers, the officers under question, the courts, all running round like headless chickens, and for the first time, three minutes ago, someone, you, bothered to ask' – he turned to look at Clark meaningfully – 'did the little bastard to it?'

Clark left shortly after that, and Naylor stayed alone for a while. He didn't regret letting Clark know that he knew about his affair with Cope, and he wouldn't tomorrow when he was sober, either. He despised that kind of behaviour and wasn't going to condone it. He wasn't prepared to go along pretending to be one of the lads, supporting the 'any-bird-is-fair-game-and-the-more-extra-marital-bonking-the-better' mentality. He was a bit of a puritan at heart. He had never been unfaithful to his wife in nineteen years of marriage, and he never would. Yes, he despised his boss for that.

He met her at the Adelphi. He was drunk. They booked into a regular room – though it was still luxurious – and they made love and drank champagne, pretty much simultaneously; she was full of energy and vitality, and for a short while she lifted him above his troubles. But when he broke away from her, tired and sweaty, he came down to earth quickly. He got out of bed straight away and took a shower. She lay on the bed, feeling delicious, abandoning herself to the paradise of post-coital languor and thinking about what he had done to her just then . . .

Underneath the hot jets Clark's thoughts began to penetrate the fog of alcohol, and immediately the case filled his mind. He just didn't know how to proceed; he couldn't trust his instincts – in fact, he wondered if he had any instincts. He dried himself slowly, combed back his wet hair and wrapped a towel around his waist. Then he lay down on the sofa on one side of the bedroom and smoked, staring up at the ceiling.

112

She was lying naked on her front, her hair falling loose over the pillow and a glass of champagne on the ledge next to her. 'You're very quiet,' she said. She had propped herself up on her elbows and she was glowing: she felt wonderful after sex. She had expected him to join her back on the bed after he had showered. She wanted more. She always wanted more of him. She was totally transfixed by his body; the thought of it kept cutting into her mind as she hurried about her business in the newsroom. That day the editor had caught her out when she was staring out of the window during the daily editorial conference. He had said, 'What do you think, Molly?' and she had replied gauchely, 'What? Oh, sorry Jock, I was thinking about another story. Run it past me again.' The editor had been quite amused, actually; Cope was usually the keenest of the pack. She must be in love! What a hoot! He resolved to tease her about it.

Cope looked at Clark, lying there, oblivious to her presence, deep in his own internal world. She sighed, got up and walked to the sofa, grabbing a robe from the floor as she did so. She stood in front of him and put it on. He just about raised enough interest to admire her smooth, supple brown body.

'What's wrong?' she asked gently, sitting down on the edge of the sofa and sweeping her hair to one side. He took a drag of his cigarette, and massaged his stomach, wondering if he should have another drink.

'What's wrong?' she asked again, stroking his face as she did so.

'Big question,' he said, unhelpfully.

'Is it you and me?'

'What?' She realised from his blank expression and total lack of comprehension that 'you and me' hadn't crossed his mind. It wasn't a concept he had recognised. There was no such thing as 'you and me' for him, there were just interludes of enjoyable sex

113

when it suited him. That caused her a small, painful stab of anxiety, and she got up from the sofa. But she pressed down her pain and her fear, summoned up her strength and carried on. What choice did she have?

'You must be fairly close by now, aren't you?'

'I don't know,' he said. 'If I push on I might get closer, I might not.'

'But you must, you must push on, you promised me.'

'What?'

'At the beginning you said you'd convince me that there were honest coppers. You also promised that if I gave you the stuff from Alfreds, you'd use it.'

'Yes.'

'Are you getting cold feet?' It was an accusation.

'No. It's my job to collect evidence, and I think I've got all there is to get. It was so long ago. People's memories are unreliable. We've nibbled away, a bit here and a bit there, but when you add it all together it doesn't amount to much. What we're supposed to find is the truth, and really I wonder if there is such a thing.'

'There is,' she said coldly. He was silent. I think you are misguided, he was thinking. I think you're young and angry and that clouds your judgement. And I'm beginning to wonder if you're not capable of an awful lot of harm. But he kept his silence.

'You're worried,' she said, returning to the sofa, 'because you think Dicks did it.' He nodded. 'All those bastards who beat up the Birmingham Six . . . you've seen the pictures. They all thought those six men were guilty. Actually, no, that's wrong – they *knew* they were guilty. They were beaten by copper after copper, warder after warder, they even let other prisoners at the Birmingham prison in to beat them up.' The passion rose in her voice, and she drew her face close to his. 'They all *knew* they were guilty, and now we *know* they weren't. No one, *no one* has the right to do that to someone in a civilised society, least of all policemen.'

114

'It's completely different.' He dismissed her tour-de-force icily.

'No it isn't,' she snapped. 'They think they have the right to be judge and jury. Well you don't. You don't in South Africa, you don't in Ireland, you don't in Chile, you don't in Romania and surely *for Christ's sake* you don't here?' He lay there looking at her, his face expressionless. She really believed all that. It really mattered. There were few things that mattered more in Molly Cope's world.

'Come to bed, you're tired,' she said, standing up and holding out her hand to him. He took it, and struggled to his feet.

'Yes,' he said.

'And half pissed.'

'Yes,' he said again as he fell into bed.

12

Kendrick, Poynton and McPherson had settled down in Kendrick's sitting-room. The door onto the hallway was shut, but the sound of children's laughter came through it and irritated McPherson and Poynton, both of whom just wanted to be reassured by Kendrick. Poynton was in uniform. The three of them had been at Huskisson Street together the previous afternoon, and seeing McPherson's ever-increasing anxiety, and how quickly things were heating up, Kendrick had told them to drop over to his place at four-thirty the following afternoon. It would give them a chance to swap information, too, on what the team from the Met had been up to – they made sure they knew where they were almost all the time. It was McPherson's day off, and Poynton had easily managed to get over to Kendrick's for half an hour.

They had been kicking bits and pieces of news and gossip around for ten minutes, but it hadn't got them very far. They had known that Clark was screwing Cope almost before he did, but it didn't look like that was going to do them much good. They couldn't use it in any constructive way. Clark didn't realise how much more they despised him because of his affair. It confirmed all their suspicions about career detectives from the Met who turned up without the slightest knowledge of the turf and poked their noses and dicks into whatever took their fancy.

There was a gentle knock on the door, and Kendrick's wife pushed it open with her elbow and walked in carrying a tray which she placed on the coffee table in front of them.

'Thanks, Stella,' said Kendrick, looking up at her. She smiled at him, and went out, shutting the door behind her. Kendrick passed the tea and Hobnobs round. 'I've told you, don't worry. Keep your head,' he told McPherson, who was the tallest and the heaviest of the three of them by a long way, but the most scared, too. In his years in the force Kendrick had noticed that physical size was rarely commensurate with courage, guts and moral fibre.

'I think we'll be OK,' said Poynton, whose conscience was clear – more or less. He wasn't easily intimidated, and he had absolute trust in Kendrick. 'Though I'm afraid Dicks'll get out.'

'I'm afraid of that, too,' said Kendrick grimly.

'How can we get a fair trial?' blubbered the massive McPherson. 'The press are baying for our blood.' He gestured at a dog-eared copy of that day's *Liverpool Press* on the coffee table. The Dicks' case was the top story again, and there was no doubt where the finger of guilt was pointing: at the coppers who arrested him, who were at that moment gathered in a comfy semi drinking PG Tips.

McPherson smoothed his brylcreemed hair and looked wildly at Kendrick, then at Poynton. Kendrick looked down into his teacup.

'Relax, boy,' said Poynton. 'Inspector Kendrick will deal with Clark.' He swivelled his head to look at Kendrick, who returned his gaze and held it. He had made his decision.

After the other two had left Kendrick looked for Stella. He saw her at the bottom of the garden, moving the

117

clay chimneypots through which they grew a healthy crop of rhubarb. He walked through the kitchen and down the neat gravel path towards her, glancing over the fence to see if there were any neighbours about.

'Have they gone?' Stella asked, pushing her hair from her eyes.

'Yes, love,' he said, looking at her. She sensed that he wanted to say something, and so she stood there in silence, letting him compose his words. 'Stell, I'm going to be straight. I think I'm going to be nailed for a fit-up. The consequences could be very serious.'

'I know you didn't do it,' she said, holding his gaze, 'so I'm not going to ask you that. If you came down here to justify yourself to me you ought to be ashamed of yourself. No matter who else you ever have to justify yourself to, Bill, you never have to do that to me.' She paused. He looked at her, and for the first time for a number of weeks he felt something warm swelling up inside him. 'I know you, Bill. I know you'd never do more than twist the rules just a little bit to prove something you knew beyond any remote shadow of a doubt to be true. And that's what matters to me. So don't worry. We'll make it, whatever those bastards try to pin on you.'

At about the same time Clark and Cope were walking towards Huskisson Street station. He had called into the *Press* offices to ask her to help him find a few old cuttings on cases Kendrick had handled. She had found the material easily, but it wasn't any good to him. Clark had hoped to get some kind of handle on Kendrick which might shed some light on his character; he was clutching at straws, actually. He had reached the conclusion that there was nothing else he could do in Liverpool. If Kendrick didn't accept his deal and admit to bashing Dicks about, Clark wasn't prepared to go any further. He simply didn't think

Kendrick was guilty any more. Not guilty of a fit-up, anyway; he thought he had probably just gilded the lily – improved the case, rather than inventing it. He thought Dicks was in prison for a crime he did indeed commit. But Clark knew that if it went to appeal, the conviction was almost certain to be found unsafe because the evidence had been tampered with. Then Kendrick would get it – a court case, probably. He was gloomy. It was the kind of day on which he questioned the validity of his job, and felt there was no point in it. The detractors of the CIB were right: they should let things take their natural course. All they were doing in Liverpool was causing trouble. Clark's moments of self-doubt were rare, but when they assailed him he suffered as much as anybody else.

'Going back to Huskisson Street?' Cope asked him as he sat with his arms folded in a conference room, pursing his lips and looking out of the window over the city. He nodded.

'I've got to call in there myself, on that Securicor story. Coles is there, and I need to chat it over with him.' Clark looked at her. 'Don't worry!' she said, laughing and rumpling his hair. 'I'm not knocking off Superintendent Chris Coles too. One copper at a time's quite enough, thank you.' He had been thinking about Kendrick. It hadn't even registered that she had mentioned Coles. Frankly, he didn't much care who she was knocking off, as long as she wasn't talking to them about him.

'Let's go to Huskisson Street together,' she said, realising that she was going to get only a fraction of his attention that morning, even if she took off all her clothes and did the tango across the conference room table. So he had given her a lift. He didn't suppose that was out of order, seeing as it was office hours and they were both clearly working, but he didn't like it much. They talked the case through yet again as he parked the pool car in the car park behind the station.

Clark explained the deal he had offered Kendrick that morning. 'And if he doesn't accept I'll close the case anyway, send the stuff to the PCA and the Crown Prosecution Service and let them decide what to do with it.' He looked straight ahead as he walked, his hands in his pockets.

Molly Cope swung her large leather duffel bag over her shoulder. Her hair was piled up in a bun, and she was wearing a stern dark grey dress and a string of pearls. 'Either way the other two will get off scot-free,' she said irritably. He shrugged. 'Whitewash,' she hissed. She wanted to see all three of them – Kendrick, Poynton and McPherson – in the slammer. Her mind was closed on the subject.

'I thought that would be your reaction,' he said, turning to her, his eyes cold. 'Actually, I've gone as far as I can without Alfreds speaking,' he continued, 'and I've left him alone as a favour to you.' He was trying to make sure she understood that his mind was made up, and that if she pressed him, or started ferreting around again herself, his next move would be to expose Alfreds as an informer and make him go public. Not only would that ruin Alfreds' career, but it would land Cope in the shit too. 'We've talked to everyone . . . end of the road.'

As they turned the corner to the front of the station they saw a knot of people eddying around the swing doors, and quickly realised they were press photographers and a television crew. Cope immediately ran up and into the throng, talking to a young photographer she knew and grasping for her notebook in her bag at the same time.

Clark quickened his pace, but didn't run, and he crossed the station hallway, punching the code into the security door and then walking as fast as he could along the corridors and up the stairs towards the incident room. Connell came rushing out of the Ladies and collided with him. She was obviously in a hurry, and looked either panicked or excited – Clark wasn't sure which. 'What's all this?' said Clark, baffled.

'They've just released another prisoner whose case was thrown out on appeal,' said Connell. 'They want a statement from Deputy Assistant Commissioner More.' Shit, thought Clark. This is going to make More even more vituperative. He resolved that he really would do as he had told Cope a few minutes earlier: he'd close the case. 'Which prisoner?'

'Foreman – Tim Foreman.' Clark clocked the case. Then Connell gave him a piece of news. 'We've had a message from Kendrick, sir. He wants to talk.' She looked at Clark's face. She knew how important this was: if Kendrick came clean it would be a great victory for Clark and the team. Tony smiled broadly, and slapped Connell on the back.

Clark skipped along to the incident room, which was buzzing even more loudly than usual. Naylor looked up and raised his eyes to the ceiling as if to say, We could have done without this, eh, boss? Clark wasn't thinking about Tim Foreman. He sat down heavily in his usual seat and called Kendrick at home, drumming his fingers on the table. 'Bill?' he said quickly when he heard Kendrick's voice at the other end.

'I'll meet you at the docks, at the end of Hurlington Street, at four-fifteen,' said a surly Kendrick, and put the phone down.

They strolled along the towpath next to the river for a few minutes before Kendrick started talking. It was a pale, dreary afternoon; the sun was like a watermark on the matt sky, and the Mersey was a dull steely grey. Alone they loitered next to the corrugated iron fence, both with their hands in their pockets. Traffic was racing across the huge bridge behind them, and an emaciated cat mewled as it loped past, staring hopefully down into the murky water. A thin, metallic smell of petrol hung in the air. They struck an odd contrast, the handsome Clark in his well-cut navy suit, razor-creased shirt and Next tie, and the short, pug-faced Kendrick with his crinkly hair, jeans and buttoned up bomber jacket.

'I'm going to make a statement,' said Kendrick all of a sudden, as if he were announcing some great surprise event. 'I want you to understand one thing. I am making this not out of fear but out of anger. Because the longer this and all the other investigations carry on, the more mud gets thrown, and mud sticks, believe me, it sticks. You and your team, your journalist friend . . .' He walked in front of Clark, turned to face him and stopped. This was a confrontation. Clark couldn't conceal his surprise, and looked at Kendrick with wide, astonished eyes. A chill wind off the river whipped up his straight hair. How the hell did Kendrick know about his affair with Cope? Did everyone in South Lancs know.

'My God, you're naive,' said Kendrick, sounding disgusted. 'We're all detectives, you know. We don't just sit around playing with ourselves, we watch our tails. We know where any of you are at any time. Did you prefer the Adelphi hotel – the free slippers? I could use that. I could offer *you* a deal. But I won't.

'I *did* bring him down here,' he said, looking around. 'And I *was* aware that he was high. I could hardly fail to be. When I saw him in Victoria Road at around six o'clock he was so freaked out he just surrendered himself to me. He couldn't stop talking. I never had to ask him a question, it all came tumbling out. But I knew I couldn't take him in in that state. I didn't want to lose him, so I decided to walk him round a bit. I never hit him, not then, not later, and nor did anyone else.' Kendrick paused and looked at Clark. He was

122

confident that Clark would believe him. He didn't think Clark was stupid, just misguided, innocent, caught up in fancy ideas and theories and too concerned with personal success and promotion.

'I bought him a McDonald's and a coffee,' said Kendrick, snarling at the irony of what he had done for this man he was accused of beating up. 'When I thought he'd sobered up enough I rang McPherson. On our way in we picked up his helmet, gloves and jacket from where he'd told us they were hidden. We booked him in at Egberth when we said we did. We fed him, gave him some water, and asked him if he wanted a solicitor. Everything was as we said it was. And that is all there is to it.' He spoke the last sentence slowly and meaningfully, and Clark looked at him intently. Kendrick drew nearer to Clark as the wind began to blow harder, and he started to pronounce his words in a peculiarly exaggerated way, as people do when they are aware of some great import in what they are saying.

'Now, you can't touch the other two because they didn't do anything, and me, well, I walked a man who said he'd committed several armed robberies around a bit. I fed him hamburgers and coffee and presumed, to my lasting shame, that it was my duty not to lose him but to get him to confess so that he could be put somewhere where he wasn't going to kill an innocent person. *Mea culpa. Mea maxima culpa.*'

He stared at Clark, as if to say, are you satisfied now, you cocky bastard? *Look what you've done.* 'And do you know something else?' he ended quietly. 'We never did find the gun. Chilling, isn't it?' He turned and walked away, brushing past Clark, and sauntered back down the towpath with his swaggery, slightly bowlegged walk. Clark instinctively needed to lash out in self-defence. 'You fucked up,' he said to Kendrick's back. 'You broke the rules.' He was thinking, I believe

123

you. I got it all wrong at the beginning. I think Poynton might have been right when he said you were the best.

But Kendrick didn't bother to turn around.

Clark and Cope spent one last night at the Adelphi together. They had pretty much moved in, and a lot of his gear was there. He was slightly pissed off, as it was going to cost him a fortune. They didn't meet there until midnight that last time, as Clark had to work through outstanding business concerning the case at Huskisson Street in the evening: it was all over bar the shouting now, his work in Liverpool was at an end, and he was catching the train home with Connell and Naylor the following morning. By the time he got to the Adelphi he was exhausted, and she was already in bed. She had worked on the Foreman story herself until the last edition went down at nine; then, when she had called him and found out that he couldn't get away until much later, to kill time she had driven over to see her mum, where she had eaten supper. Spending an hour or two there had calmed her down a bit. It had been a hectic day, and she was very aware that this was her last night with her new lover.

At eleven she had parked her car underneath the Adelphi, trying to ignore her heavy heart.

They made love. It was the first time they had ever made love just once and then fallen asleep. It was pretty good, but not the best. He fell asleep immediately, but she didn't. She lay awake, thinking.

The next morning he woke at eight and realised he had to be away by eight-thirty. He called down to reception and asked them to make up his bill.

'Cash,' he said, when they asked how he'd be paying. He could hardly put it on any of his credit cards – they were all held jointly with Sue and she saw the bills. They wouldn't take a cheque for over seventy-five quid, as that was all his cheque card guaranteed him.

First of all Sue knew he'd officially been staying at the Shaftesbury because she'd called him there, and secondly she knew that as far as accommodation was concerned he didn't pay and then claim it back, it was all taken care of by the Met. Thirdly, since when did the Met put him in places costing a hundred quid a night? He had arranged to pick up a load of cash from a local branch of his own bank the previous day. For no particular reason he and Sue didn't have a joint current account, so at least she wouldn't see the stonking withdrawal he had been obliged to make. He was grateful for that, at least.

He talked the case over with a sleepy Cope as he packed. Although he was leaving Liverpool, not a word had passed between them about the possibilities of their affair continuing. It hadn't crossed his mind – one of the reasons it had all been so easy for him was that he knew the relationship would reach a neat conclusion when he had to go back to London and Sue. He had made a resolution, since the barbecue at Dunning's, to make a real effort with Sue from now on. He was going to straighten out the tensions of the past few months and show her how much he loved her, make her feel confident about him again, as she had done at the beginning. He had started making a few plans: a surprise holiday, try to get back home before eight when she wasn't working nights, flowers – the usual kind of thing, but it was all genuine stuff.

As for Cope, she knew better than to mention it – she knew she was the one who couldn't bear the thought of it ending. She knew his feelings for her amounted to no more than short-term lust. That hurt. But there was another reason why she didn't mention the implications of this parting. The editor of the *Guardian* had been in town two days previously, and he had called her and asked if they could meet for an informal chat. She had seen him at Wheeler's, the same cocktail bar that she had taken Clark to on the night they slept together for the first time. The editor had said that he was most impressed with her investigative work with the *Press*, especially on the Dicks case. He couldn't commit himself to anything, but if ever there happened to be an opening for a keen reporter on the *Guardian* home newsdesk down in Farringdon Road, would she . . . Molly Cope sensed the advent of her finest hour.

'Do you know what that means?' Clark asked Cope, when he had given his resumé of what had really happened on the night Dicks was arrested and how Dicks had subsequently massaged the story. He zipped up his holdall smartly. She was silent, and Clark noted that. She must have been feeling guilty. 'There wasn't a single accusation that Dicks made that we didn't believe,' said Clark, his hands on his hips. 'We just believed him, as if it were the most natural thing in the world to hear about a copper nailing an innocent man. Where have we come to?'

'To the point where we automatically believe the criminal not the copper,' she retorted. 'Whose fault is that?'

They looked at each other. 'Yours,' they said simultaneously, and started laughing.

He met the others back at the Shaftesbury. He had never checked out of his room there; he couldn't, could he? It was the team hotel, and the Met were picking up the bill. What was he going to say, that he'd moved into the most luxurious hotel in town because he was screwing the local star reporter, and that he'd pay the difference himself? No, he had to go through the charade, though Naylor and Connell knew perfectly well that he hadn't been sleeping in the Shaftesbury. For all he knew, bloody Deakin was *au fait* as well.

He waited outside in the watery morning sun in order to avoid making conversation with the bald porter, who was still looking at him suspiciously.

'Morning, Guv,' said Naylor, plonking a battered Samsonite on the pavement.

'Morning, Harry. Sleep well?'

'Yes, sir, thank you,' said Naylor, ostentatiously not asking the same question back. 'Morning, guys,' said Connell, a rich red carpetbag over her shoulder. Clark looked at his watch. 'I've ordered a taxi for ten,' he said.

They were all tired, and the train journey passed largely in silence. Connell and Naylor got their laptops out on the table and stabbed at their work half-heartedly, toying with data. Clark didn't even bother doing that. He slumped in his seat, staring out of the window. The only things really in use on the table were the three packets of Silk Cut. They were all thinking, really. They were all thinking sheepishly that maybe they had barged in up there and got things rather wrong. Naylor felt vindicated, as he knew Clark was now on Kendrick's side, and Naylor thought that was right. Connell was surprised at how much she had learned from this case, and she thought she'd always be more careful in future before making up her mind. And Clark – Clark was the most thoughtful of all. How many cases was he going to have to see off before he learned that very few of them were painted in black and white?

13

Two weeks later Clark was sitting in a white plastic chair in his garden in south Clapham on a beautiful Sunday afternoon, reading the papers. He had just mown the lawn, and Sue was at the garden table cutting up runner beans for a late lunch. He felt pretty good. Things had been going well between them. To his surprise as much as hers, he had actually managed to get home before nine every night she was at home. The previous evening he had taken her to Harvey's on Wandsworth Common, supposedly one of the best restaurants in London and certainly the one everyone was talking about. He knew she'd enjoy it – and she did, although it cost him an arm and a leg. But he had enjoyed it too, and half way down the second bottle of St Emilion he had said. 'Look, darling, I want you to know that I'm really sorry things haven't been too good between us over the past few months. I know I've been difficult. I know I haven't paid you enough attention. I know I've set too much store by the job. But I do love you, you know, and I'm really determined to make it work.'

He clasped her hand on the tabletop. 'I really missed you when I was in Liverpool.' That was a bit of a lie, actually, but it didn't matter, did it? The most important thing was that he meant what he was saying. If he invented one or two small details to add credibility to his case, it wasn't important, was it?

Sue, who had gone into the house, walked out again holding the mobile phone. He hadn't even heard it ringing. 'For you,' she said. '*Liverpool Press*.'

'Oh,' he said, trying to sound normal, glancing behind him to see how far away from him his wife was. 'Hello?'

'Hello, Tony,' said Cope bouncily. She was sitting at her desk, working on Monday's top story. There hadn't been any contact between them since he left Liverpool, and she thrilled to hear his voice.

'Hello, Miss Cope. What can I do for you?'

'Now there's a question. Are you overheard?'

'Yes.'

'Good. First you can take me to a nice sunny beach under some palm trees.'

'Oh yes?'

'Yes. Then you can undress me.'

'Yes, yes, that should be fine,' he said, half enjoying the game but half scared of her and the possible consequences. 'When?'

'Thursday, I'm coming down to London for the appeal hearing – meet you outside?'

'Fine,' said Clark. It was Dicks' appeal, and he'd have to be at the court anyway. 'What time?' Sue finished the beans, and moved a chair so that she could sit behind him, in the sun. 'Noon.' Cope paused for dramatic effect. 'By the way, Kendrick, Poynton and McPherson have all been suspended. Word is that the CPS is going to prosecute.' She enjoyed telling him that; she had been waiting until she had some card to play before she called about meeting him in London. As long as she kept control, she wasn't going to get upset, was she?

The news about the suspensions was true. They had received notification that morning. Clark switched off the phone, his mind in turmoil. First of all he felt a stirring in his loins. Secondly, he felt a heaviness behind his breastbone. He could have stopped this. It was down to him, basically, that Kendrick had been suspended. He found that very hard to live with.

By four o'clock Kendrick was clearing his desk at Huskisson Street. He felt numb, but he was trying to shock himself back to life with his usual pragmatism. What upset him most was the effect the news had had on Stella; that really cracked him up. And as he faced the real possibility that he might soon be unemployed on Merseyside with two kids to finish bringing up, he experienced a nauseous feeling in the pit of his stomach. He didn't think evil thoughts about Clark. What was the point of that? This kind of thing had happened many times within the force, and beyond any doubt it would happen again many more times. Rough justice, for some.

At the same time Poynton was clearing his locker at Egberth. He had never envisaged this – not suspension. He had had such great faith in Kendrick to see those guys from the Met straight. He could hardly believe this was happening. A self-preservation mechanism took over. Of course, the mistake would soon be found out and life would return to normal. The three of them would be heroes, actually: victims of the ponces from London. Might even be a promotion at the end of it. The lads had been supportive when they'd heard the news; they were all behind him. But he felt uncomfortable; he didn't enjoy running that particular gauntlet. He took a deep breath, and left the locker room to walk through the station.

As for McPherson, he was sitting in his solicitor's office. He was in such a blind panic that he couldn't sit still at home. The solicitor had told him over the telephone he was doing all he could, and that McPherson should keep calm and not worry, but it was like telling a sheep not to bleat. McPherson had gone to the office anyway, though he couldn't have told you why. He just felt safer there. His solicitor's secretary had told him that he'd have to wait, because Mr Smith was in a meeting, and would be some time, possibly as long as two hours. She and Smith had anticipated that this news would shift McPherson, but not a bit of it – he would happily have sat there all day. Lurking in his subconscious was some confused idea that nothing bad could happen to him while he was in a lawyer's office, as if it were some kind of untouchable sanctuary. He wondered if he'd ever sleep again, and felt sweat pricking at his big, shiny brow.

Meanwhile, in his prison cell, Dicks was doing his fortieth press-up and humming 'Eye of the Tiger'. He did press-ups every day, and he could keep going for a long time – he didn't know how many, but it was a lot. It helped control the rage which was constantly simmering within him, threatening to boil over. That morning he had been told that the three coppers who had arrested him were being suspended, so he was exercising with a new zest. It was great news, coming so shortly before his appeal hearing. His solicitor had told him there was a very real chance he would be out within the week. He savoured the vision of Kendrick disgraced in the dock, and for the thousandth time he imagined confronting him as he got out of his car late one night. He was going to get him, there wasn't the slightest doubt in Dicks' mind about that. His mouth began to water, the blue eyes shone, and he lay on the floor, his breathing shallow, cutting short the press-ups so he could concentrate on the vision of Kendrick underneath his boot. Or perhaps . . .

Clark was waiting outside the Appeal Court at noon on Thursday morning. It was a fine day, and the grand old building looked magnificent. Makes a change from stinking, piss-stained nicks, he thought. He felt perky;

131

he was looking forward to seeing Molly, actually. More than he had anticipated. His intellect had tried to persuade him to resist, to take her for a nice lunch, enjoy a flirtation and then say goodbye and go back to Sue as early as possible. But he was beaten before he started. He had told Sue he suspected that Deakin was going to corner him for a long briefing session that evening. It was a lie, but it was wise to arrange a late pass, even if when it came to it you didn't feel like using it.

Bewigged barristers hustled in and out of the massive court building, photographers and journalists loitered on the short flight of steps, and interested parties waited nervously, pacing around below the huge, vaulted stone doorway. A police siren wailed in the distance. And then he saw her. Her hair was loose, and she was wearing a simple cobalt-blue suit with a knee-length skirt. Underneath the jacket peeked the top of a scarlet camisole. She looked soft; she was like a vision, and the sight of her almost made him gasp. She could see the effect she was having on him, and it made her feel warm inside. She smiled, and kissed him on the cheek. He returned the kiss, tenderly. 'You look wonderful,' he breathed, turning the charm up to full power, and she smiled again, melting.

Cope had been feeling good even before she met him. She had caught the train down from Liverpool the previous afternoon and stayed the night in north London with an old university chum, another journalist. At nine o'clock that morning she had had a meeting at the *Guardian*'s offices. It had gone exceptionally well.

He touched her lightly on the back as they walked up the steps and into the building, a pair of lawyers hard on their heels. He wondered how he was going to make it through until the evening, or whatever time he could undress her again. He wondered if anyone had ever made it in the Appeal Court toilets. Now, that would be a coup.

The hearing only took about three hours. Clark and Cope were sitting next to each other in the public gallery when the decision was delivered. Deputy Assistant Commissioner More was in the row behind them, looking very grim. Dicks was standing in the dock, looking ridiculous in an ill-fitting jacket and ratty red tie, his hair greased back, and he gripped the rail in front of him. His friend Clive was sitting in the front of the public gallery; he had come down by coach specially. Their little group was like that; they stuck together. There wasn't much loyalty where they came from, but if you couldn't unite against public enemy number one – the law – well, it would be a poor show. Anyway, this one was shaping up for a right gala.

The judge was a beak-faced individual who looked as though he had been defrosted after twenty years in a medical school freezer. He was wearing half-glasses, and he was flanked by two other judges, a woman and a man. They remained silent and stony-faced while he spoke emphatically. He didn't make any bones about his decision. 'In the light of the new evidence I can do nothing except throw out this confession and the subsequent conviction as wholly unsafe. I will make no comment on what action should be taken against the officers concerned as this is now in the hands of the Department of Public Prosecutions. I will just say that it is a black day indeed when an innocent man is imprisoned in this manner.'

His words echoed through the lofty room and floated over the heads of the clerks, the stenographer, the court officials, the lawyers and their small mountains of paper, the police officer standing next to the ex-prisoner, a jubilant Dicks, the journalists, Clive, sitting in his plaid shirt next to the dour blackness that

133

envelops the entire legal profession, and they floated over Clark and Cope and More and over Kendrick, who was standing up at the back, his hands in his pockets. Clark turned to Cope, who was beaming. 'Innocent?' he whispered.

'Until proven guilty in a court of law,' she said piously.

Dicks had broken into a broad grin, and he turned to Clive, who punched the air.

As they walked through the crowded corridors afterwards Cope said to Clark, 'You can't believe that he might have been innocent, can you?'

'I suppose not,' he said. He thought about it. No, it just wasn't possible. Kendrick just couldn't have been lying. It didn't add up.

'Maybe Dicks was just showing off to his friends and taunting Kendrick, maybe Kendrick really did beat a confession out of him.'

'I believe Kendrick,' said Clark, mournfully.

'I don't. I'm not sure I believe Dicks either, but I'm glad he's been given the benefit of the doubt.' They continued through the ornate doors encrusted with worked gilt and across the echoing, flagged hallway with its enormously high ceiling. When they had got about twenty yards across it, Kendrick appeared in the doorway behind them. He was wearing his best suit, a smart and shiny double-breasted grey number.

'My trial next,' he called. Clark and Cope stopped, and turned to look at him. He began walking towards them. Cope didn't lose her nerve, though she was aware that Kendrick knew that it was she who had nailed him. She was the woman who had brought him down. 'I expect you'll be there,' he said to her. It was a statement rather than a question.

'Yes. You'll get off,' she said confidently, not to reassure him, but to show that she still didn't believe there was such a thing as justice within the police force.

'Will I?' said Kendrick, his tone of voice indicating that he thought it was unlikely. 'Both times?'

'What do you mean?' she said, genuinely confused.

'We're tried twice,' he explained. 'Once by the courts and once by the police.'

'You'll get off,' she said again, facing him square-on.

'I wish I shared your confidence,' he said. 'And you. What will you get?'

'Me?' she said, even more baffled.

'For tampering with the evidence. That photograph of Dicks that led to the public outrage that led to the appeal – you even blacked in the wrong eye.' His contempt for her knew no bounds. 'I have a photograph of the man he headbutted. Do you want to use it? It's quite shocking enough as it is, it doesn't need retouching.'

She looked absolutely crushed. Her heart was hammering against the red camisole, and her lips quivered at the edges. Her face – well, it almost *crumpled*. It hadn't crossed her mind for a second that anyone knew about that. What were the implications of Kendrick's announcement? Was it really a criminal offence? Oh my God . . . her mind was racing, and her mouth went dry . . . the new job . . . her reputation . . . what would Clark think, he would despise her . . .

'Funny old world,' said Kendrick, quoting Mrs Thatcher to Clark for the second time as he walked between them. As he passed Clark's pensive face Kendrick turned his head towards him and said softly, 'Isn't it?' before walking on, disappearing out of the main doors, down the steps and across the busy road outside the court.

Before the pair of them had time to react, Dicks and Clive were crossing the hallway. They walked purposefully, and they too approached Cope and Clark, but they did so in a more overtly provocative manner than Kendrick had. Clark and Cope froze.

135

When the two men had passed, Dicks turned, looked at Clark in a curiously flirtatious way, and gave him a little wink.

A minute later the last double door of the Appeal Court burst open and Dicks emerged into the sunlight, a grinning Clive at his side. 'Mr Dicks, Mr Dicks!' shouted numerous photographers simultaneously as they homed in on the innocent victim of a corrupt system, gnashing their collective teeth for a picture. Dicks raised his arms above his head in a gesture of victory as he savoured this moment of glory. His eyes clenched shut for a moment and his face twisted into the ugliest of ugly expressions as the photographers clicked away and the television cameras whirred, and his whole being exuded hatred, determination, aggression and revenge. Clive chirrupped away next to him, enjoying his mate's deliverance and wondering if his mum would see him on telly.

'Mr Dicks! Mr Dicks! What steps do you intend to take to seek redress for your two wasted years?'

'Mr Dicks! How do you feel about the men who distorted the evidence against you?'

'Mr Dicks! Would you like to say anything about the legal system which locked you up on the wrong information?'

'Bastards!' was all Dicks managed to say; he couldn't quite articulate anything else. Then he caught sight of Kendrick, walking away from the court in the street opposite. 'Hey!' screamed Dicks. Kendrick stopped, and slowly swivelled round.

The two men eyeballed each other. Dicks lifted his right arm, formed a mock gun with his hand, and, supporting his right elbow with his other hand, he pointed the imaginary gun at Kendrick's head. Fire shone in his blue eyes. Then he squeezed the trigger.

14

Molly's new job was sewn up. A week after their first
meeting in Liverpool, the editor of the *Guardian* had
called her. Could she come down? There were a few
people he'd like her to meet. She'd tied in the trip with
the Dicks appeal, which she was covering for the *Press*,
and had taken an Intercity down to London with a
tight feeling in her stomach and an effervescent smile
on her lips. At the *Guardian* offices in Farringdon Road
she'd met the home news editor and two reporters, and
she spent an hour and a half with the editor of the
paper. She had felt good about it all from the moment
she set foot in the building.

The editor had called offering her the job two days
later, and on the fourth day, after the envelope
containing formal confirmation had dropped onto the
mat, she handed in her notice at the *Press*. She typed
out a letter of resignation, but she took it in to Jock
herself. She thought it was the decent thing to do; she
owed him that much.

'Well, Moll,' he said, 'I knew it was coming, I saw it
from afar. Reporters like you never stay in the
provinces. We did well to hold you for so long, I
reckon. I'm going to struggle to fill your gap on the
paper, Molly. I'm very sorry to lose you. But I'm
pleased for you.'

He smiled affably and came round to her side of the

desk. 'Now,' he said. 'We'd better start planning the mother of all leaving parties.'

They agreed on a month's notice. That gave Cope a week to get herself down to London and settle in before turning up for duty in Farringdon Road. She was beside herself with excitement, anxiety – and fear. It turned out that Sabine, the college friend with whom she had stayed in Burleigh Road, Kentish Town when she had gone to London for the interview, was about to depart on a foreign assignment for six weeks, and she had asked Cope if she'd house-sit for her. It was an ideal arrangement for them both: Cope had a comfortable place to stay while she sifted the papers and agencies for a permanent flat, and Sabine had her place looked after, her plants watered and the cat fed. Molly thought it was a good start.

The only person who wasn't happy was Molly's mum. There had been much wailing when the news was broken. 'I know I've been lucky, the three of you always being in Liverpool near me,' said Mrs Cope querulously a few days after Molly had told her she was moving away. 'But Moll, I'll miss you so badly!'

'Look, Mum,' said Molly firmly. 'I'm not going to Siberia, am I? I'll be back – holidays, weekends; probably I'll get to come up here on a few stories. You'll see me. You can come down to stay. We can speak on the phone – every day, if you like.' She looked at her mother. They were both close to tears.

Cope seemed to get busier every day. Finishing off work at the *Press*, packing up at her flat in the wonderful art deco building (she was really going to miss that), organising the trip down to London, saying goodbyes – she hardly had time to think. She certainly didn't have time to think about Tony Clark – or not much, anyway. He was always there, lurking just at the top of her subconscious. All he'd said about the future when he left was that she should get in touch if ever she was in town, and they could do lunch. She called him once, when she'd got back home after the Appeal Court hearing, but he never returned her call. She didn't dwell on that – she was too busy. It was only when she lay awake in the small hours, staring into the darkness, that she could admit that part of the reason she was so thrilled at the prospect of moving down to London was that she would be near that man.

The leaving party was a wild success. The editor had booked the top floor of their local wine bar, a business kept going almost exclusively by thirsty *Press* hacks. He had called the woman who catered for their office lunches and organised a finger buffet, and he had put a few hundred quid of *Press* money down for the first couple of hours of drinks. He knew he could get that past the proprietors by disguising it as something else on his expenses; when it ran out, guests could bloody well buy their own drinks.

He was determined to do a good job, to give her a big send-off. She had done wonders at the paper; she had started stories rolling which had captured the punters' imagination because they seemed to revolve around all the big issues of the beleaguered city. It hadn't gone unnoticed, and advertising was up. This had put the editor in good odour with the proprietors, who were, naturally enough, always baying for advertising revenue. Yes, Molly Cope had been a good thing. He watched her hustling around the newsroom on the day of the party. She was a looker, too, and he contemplated another wasted opportunity with genuine regret. Molly's personal life had always been the subject of keen speculation in the office. A rumour had circulated that she was involved with a prominent local businessman, but nobody really believed it: they simply wanted something to talk about, something to chew over as they lingered in the wine bar, gossiping and speculating about the sexual peccadillos of the absentees. Cope had cocooned herself in the highly seductive mystique of the single, unavailable woman, and her colleagues and associates simply refused to believe that there wasn't a scandal to be uncovered, if only they were to search hard enough. But she had always been very, very careful. She was a professional, after all.

Molly had invited a few of her regular contacts along to the party, and a number of other people had found out about it and were coming anyway, to pay their last respects, as it were. By seven the large room was packed full of people, all chucking wine down their throats as if it were going out of fashion. A healthy contingent of humble types had turned up, like Jean from Jack's Bar, for example. Molly was extremely popular among ordinary folk like Jean. She could be as prickly as a gorse bush with important people whom she perceived as a threat, or with bolshy individuals, but she was as mild as a saucer of warm milk with the harmless, unassuming Liverpudlians she saw every day as they struggled to rise above their troubles.

Jock, the editor of the *Press*, had hired a trio of ukelele players who were favourites among the staff at the newspaper, and they had written a song about Molly to the tune of 'My Old Man's a Dustman'. Jock made a speech later. They had already given her a gift, privately, in the newsroom that afternoon. It was a beautiful Gladstone carpetbag, and inside it was her leaving card: a mock-up of a *Vogue* cover, featuring Cope's face surrounded by spiced-up headlines from some of her most stinging stories.

She even had a few glasses of wine herself, although she was high enough without them. She felt she was poised on the threshold of a brave new world, and it was gratifying to know that the one she was leaving behind would remember her so warmly.

'Don't forget us, Moll!' said Jock much later, in his cups. 'I won't,' she said, putting her hand on his shoulder and her feet on a stool.

'We'll all be looking forward to seeing what you turn up down there in the big smoke! Flush out more of those bent coppers, knowing you!'

The week that Cope moved down to London, Tony and Sue Clark were invited to dinner at the Huxtables. Clark was chuffed. From his conversation with Commander Huxtable at Deputy Chief Constable Dunning's barbecue in Nannton he knew he was well positioned on the outer circle of the 'culture club', as the commander's informal network was known, but now, to have moved straight to the exclusive dinner party – well, that was something. He had always thought he was well in with the Commander, and this seemed to prove it. Ever since he had joined the CIB Clark had been moving closer to Huxtable as partial role model and patron. Huxtable was impressed by the way Clark had handled himself within the CIB so far: he was always on the look-out for ambitious and forward-thinking officers to take with him on his way up to the stratosphere. As far as Clark knew it was going to be just the four of them at dinner – a real chance to cement a personal relationship with Huxtable which could do Clark a lot of good in the future. He was bristling with confidence when he and Sue locked up the house. 'I suppose I'm driving?' she said, smiling knowingly and getting into the driver's seat of the Sierra without waiting for a reply. She never drank more than two glasses of wine.

'By the way,' said Clark after he had lowered himself into the passenger seat. 'Did I tell you that you look absolutely magnificent tonight?' She was wearing a short, sleeveless black dress embroidered with tiny gold filaments, and it hugged her slim figure. Clark leaned over and kissed her on the cheek as she turned the key in the ignition. He felt that they were going places as a partnership.

The dinner went swimmingly. The Huxtables lived in a huge Regency pile in Pimlico with high ceilings and large rooms, all tastefully decorated in pastel shades and hung with interesting modern art as well as nineteenth-century etchings. After drinks in the stunning morning-room they moved through to the dining-room, where the Huxtables had created sculpted alcoves to display their antique porcelain. A large weeping fig filled one corner of the spacious room, which was lit by white lamps on discreet walnut Regency tables. Tina Huxtable, younger than her husband and very laid-back, produced a cordon bleu meal of curried parsnip and apple soup followed by duck breast in ginger with wild rice and a julienne of spring vegetables. They even managed to keep the conversation off police-related issues for most of the evening.

After the brandied oranges had been dispatched, however, and the four of them were lingering at the table over liqueurs and coffee, they slid effortlessly into the debate over the public image of the police. The table was lit by eight candles in silver candelabra on either side of an elaborate floral decoration.

'I'd say it's much more about image than information,' said the urbane Huxtable, pulling on a panatella while Clark puffed away at his usual Silk Cut. 'The public judge you on what you look like, they're not really interested in what you say.'

'But it's your manner as well, isn't it?' added Clark. 'You know the sort of Heseltine smile, however tricky the question.'

'True,' said Huxtable as he and his wife chuckled at Clark's turn of phrase.

Tina stood up and started gathering up the dessert plates. 'More coffee, anyone?' she asked.

142

'No thanks, Tina,' said Clark. Huxtable and Sue shook their heads, and Sue stood up. 'I'll give you a hand clearing up, then I really think we should be going,' she said. 'It's after midnight.' The women disappeared into the kitchen, carrying some of the debris of a good evening's entertainment.

'Well, we're all politicians now,' said Huxtable ponderously. 'There are cameras everywhere, just waiting to catch us out. But,' and here he pointed meaningfully at Clark, 'if the camera likes us – up we go.'

'It still helps to be a good copper,' said Clark, thinking that he was understating the obvious.

'It helps, but it's not essential,' said his host. Clark was surprised, and showed it. 'You're on the way up, you know.'

'Thanks, Brian.'

'It was a good show in Liverpool. You managed it well,' Huxtable paused, but only slightly, 'especially the press.' Clark was looking straight at him when that came out, and he tried not to flinch. Shit! he thought. Just when things seemed to be going so well. Was it a barbed remark, or was it innocent? Clark just didn't know. Seemed a funny thing for Huxtable to mention if he didn't know, and yet, and yet . . .

Sue returned from the kitchen. If Huxtable was trying to show him that he knew, and warn him off that kind of behaviour, he could at least have had the grace to do it when Sue wasn't around.

'Tony,' she said, putting her hand on his shoulder. 'We really should be going. You need your sleep.'

'Yes,' he said, getting up from the table.

In the car on the way home through London to south Clapham Sue was pensive. Suddenly she said, 'He likes you, doesn't he?'

'Yeah,' said Clark, looking out of the window.

'That can't do you any harm,' she continued.

'No. "Chief Superintendent Clark", thirty-five grand a year, I think we could handle that, couldn't we?'

'Yes,' she said with a smile, and they drove on in silence for a mile or so. She bit her lip; she was obviously preparing to say something, but he was too absorbed in the night landscape passing outside the window to notice. And he was slightly pissed.

'Tony?' she said as they headed through Stockwell.

'Yeah?'

'Will you give me an honest answer to a straight question?'

He thought for a moment, then, with a mischievous grin, he said 'Possibly.'

Sue smiled. His sense of humour had always appealed to her. Then she hit him with it. 'Is your affair over?'

He froze, then relaxed a little and mentally limbered up to deny it, to mollify her, to make it all right. His instinct – to laugh it all off with some flippant joke – had to be suppressed. He was about to speak. But he hadn't heard anything yet.

'With Jenny Dean. I know about it. Is it over, Tony?'

He was poleaxed. How the fuck did she know? He contemplated bluffing it out for a couple of seconds and then realised, sensibly, that she had found out, it was a fair cop, and that if he started denying what she knew to be correct he'd be insulting her further and making it all worse – if that were possible. He stared at her. He was terrified, and looked it. He felt about as accomplished and secure as a ten-year-old caught shoplifting. He nodded, almost imperceptibly.

'I thought it was,' she said.

She had found out who he was screwing easily enough. One morning two months previously, after he had got home late the night before, shown no interest (yet again) in making love to her despite her best efforts,

144

and they had squabbled pointlessly in bed, she heard him making a telephone call before he left the house.

'Yes,' he had said. 'I'll see you down at the river at six-thirty, at one of the tables outside The Dog and Duck.' Then he had giggled. 'You bet!'

A chill ran through her like a stream of ice. It was her day off, and at six o'clock, after the most miserable day of her life, she steeled herself to drive over to the towpath along the Thames which meandered past the beer garden of The Dog and Duck. It was typical of him to have chosen that pub for his dirty little assignment. The Cabinet Maker's Arms fifty yards downstream was much more popular and much, much nicer: there was far less chance of being seen at The Dog, which was never crowded.

Sue knew there was a bench partially obscured by willow trees where she could sit and observe her husband without any chance of being seen. It was a very mild day, but she felt chilly nonetheless. Jenny Dean arrived at the pub at twenty-five past six. As soon as Sue saw her, she knew she was the one. She recognised her from social functions at Mulberry Street, of course, and she knew the saga of how Dean had been taken off the crime squad and put back into uniform. Sue wasn't surprised. But when Tony arrived and she saw the concrete evidence in front of her, how he kissed her, flirted outrageously with her, how they laughed all the time, as people do sometimes when they are gripped by passion, she couldn't stand it — after ten minutes she fled back to her car, sobbing uncontrollably, and when she got home she put her head under the duvet and wept for three hours. When Clark slid in to join her, much, much later, she pretended to be asleep, and when he woke the next morning she had left for her early shift.

Later, after dinner at the Huxtables', Tony and Sue

made love. So much for him needing his sleep. They both felt like it, because they both sensed that things were going to be all right now. His affair was out in the open, it was over, and Tony still loved Sue. Not only that, but Sue still loved Tony. He felt great. He didn't seem to recall that after the Jenny Dean affair there had been a certain Molly Cope. Clark could do that. He could just push things out of his sight if he didn't want to look at them. Anyway, as far as he was concerned Molly represented an emotionally cost-free leg-over out of town. Sue was lying on top of him, and they were kissing eagerly, even voraciously, building up to a second round of sex, when he said to her, 'I love you.' And then she said a funny thing. She said, 'I know.' She felt very much in control of their relationship then, after so many months of helplessness. She hardly dared believe it had come together. But what she had experienced had developed her self-protection mechanisms, and she automatically activated them at that moment.

'One thing you must understand, Tony. Ever again and I leave you. And no discussions. I couldn't go through all that pain again.'

He nodded, and leaned up to her. They kissed, and they melted into one another again, losing themselves absolutely in their love and ardour.

The idea was that Molly Cope should be eased into the hard-hitting life of a reporter on a national newspaper. There were a whole raft of soft stories which needed to be covered and which had her name pencilled next to them on the day she turned up at Farringdon Road, looking spruce in a new dark pink jacket and navy pleated skirt. She had barely learned the coffee ropes, however, when the home news editor beckoned her over to his overflowing desk. 'Look, Molly, I'm sorry, but everything's going haywire. Somehow or other I haven't got the top story covered. You'll have to do it.'

He looked her in the eye. He wasn't trying her out — he really was in a fix. He would have preferred to have sent a more senior member of the team, but they were all God knows where. 'The industrial dispute at the meat pie factory has turned nasty. Our industrial relations correspondent is up in Nottingham with the miners. I need you to go to the meat place right away and stay there until you've got the story. You can file over the phone as it hunkers down. Gerard's around somewhere — he'll be with you all the time, taking pictures. He's going on his motorbike so he can get the films back quickly to the picture desk. Tracey's arranging a car to take you now.' She stood there in front of him, mesmerised. 'Good luck.' She turned to walk away.

'Molly — get the car to take you home first. You need to change. Warm, waterproof and casual.' His telephone rang. 'Philip Kolvin. Sam! Where the fuck are you? Yes, I need about six hundred words . . .'

Molly felt as if she were limping back to her desk. She hurriedly shoved the few possessions she had taken out of her dark pink leather bag back in to it, and made her way to the lift, desperately trying to recall what she had read about the meat pie factory case. A dispute over redundancies had escalated to the point where communications had broken down between the union and management. Production was continuing, and the union had organised pickets. It was somewhere on the outskirts of London. And that was all she knew.

She blinked in the sunlight and acknowledged the driver of a black Honda Accord who was waiting outside the front door. 'Hi,' she said breathlessly. 'We need to go to Burleigh Road in Kentish Town first, and then on to the meat pie factory . . . er, I'm afraid I'm not sure where that is. I suppose we need to get there as quickly as possible.'

'Factory's in Bishopston, love. Don't worry – I know. You'll have your work cut out there.'

At home she quickly changed into her jeans and two sweaters, and realised she didn't have anything rainproof. She rifled Sabine's cupboards and found a bright orange cagoule. That was fine. She looked at herself briefly in the mirror. It wasn't quite the glamorous national reporter image she had envisaged, but never mind.

Half an hour later she was there, drinking coffee out of a plastic cup with Gerard and leaning against a barricade. Nothing much was happening.

'I reckon it'll be quiet until tonight,' said Gerard, an old workhorse of a photographer who had been at the *Guardian* for ten years. 'That's when the lorries go out. They make all the gear during the day, after the meat comes in at about nine, and then take it out at night, so they can distribute it when the streets are clear.'

Molly looked around. A dozen pickets loitered about on the gravel tracks, eyeing the entrance to the factory a few hundred yards away on the other side of a perimeter fence with newly positioned rolls of barbed wire on top. About twenty-five policemen stood in small groups, obviously relaxed and not anticipating any immediate trouble. Molly relaxed too. At least she had a few hours to catch her breath.

15

At a quarter to midnight that evening a lonely figure in an orange boilersuit wandered across the large and brightly lit factory yard. The yard was deserted, except for a couple of very new-looking Leyland lorries which were backed up to loading bays. The side hatches were down, but the lorries were still empty. The man moved across the yard towards the perimeter fence. A policeman and a dog were inconspicuously patrolling the shadows, and a windowless police van was parked next to a yellow portakabin in the yard. Beyond the first fence one or two figures were just distinguishable, and the man in the yard could hear the sound of distant shouting.

As the man walked towards the gates the one or two figures developed into tens and then hundreds, and the distant shouting became the roar of a considerable crowd. Outside the gates the crowds were brightly lit by the street and factory lighting, as well as a few large halogen lamps installed by the police. Several photographers and two television news crews were on the edge of the seething mass of men, the whole lot contained by a minimal cordon of police in yellow rainjackets with some mounted policemen behind them. The atmosphere was high-spirited without being particularly menacing, but there was a sense, among police ranks at least, that something, sometime, had to break. Men didn't hang around in anger and despair at cold barricades for days on end without releasing their feelings somehow. Chanting just wasn't enough.

The lone factory worker reached the fence, and through a small door a few yards along from the main gates he spoke to Inspector Offer on the other side. Offer was wearing full riot gear, and his visor was down. Between the lines of police and the crowd behind Offer stood Commander Paddy Neame, top dog at the Territorial Support Group. He was addressing the crowd through a small but powerful electronic loud-hailer, and cut a fine figure with his tall, slim body, erect bearing and good-natured, confident manner, as well as with the total lack of fear he showed when confronted by this potentially dangerous crowd.

'It's been the same thing every night on this picket,' his firm voice boomed out to the milling crowd. 'There's nothing to see, and there's no reason to stay here. You all have homes to go to. Surely the innocent residents of these houses have the right to their sleep. So please, just peacefully—'

At that point the crowd caught sight of the factory worker walking back across the yard, and they began a forceful chant of 'Scab! Scab! Scab!' jabbing the air with their fingers and waving their placards which said 'Jobs not Cuts' or 'Join the Strike – Fight the Cuts' or 'Official Picket'. The man in the boilersuit ambled back up to the factory without looking back. He just chewed his gum and raised one finger nonchalantly in the air: stuff you.

Neame, his loud-hailer at his side, thought about resuming his appeal, but realised that it would be pointless. In a dark back street behind him more mounted police and a hundred or so of his TSG men were waiting in full riot gear. 'Look after that, would you?' he said to one of his officers who was standing near him, and he handed over his electronic loud-hailer.

Molly Cope was still leaning on a barricade, pen poised, and she was talking to one of the coppers in yellow. Gerard, positioned next to her, had three films in the bag already, and was raring to go. Their partnership was shaping up nicely, and they were both fired up to get a really good story.

'We know what you're doing, we know what you're doing!' taunted the pickets to the unseen factory workers on the other side of the perimeter fence. They too were fired up, and most of them had nothing whatever to lose. They had already lost the most important thing. Anger was a potent motivator.

Neame hurried through the crowd, into the temporary police encampment, past a mobile snack van and into the TSG control vehicle. Three officers in shirt-sleeves were sitting at a desk in front of two monitors surrounded by white wipe-clean notice-boards, and the atmosphere was extremely tense. The noticeboards indicated where the TSG units were deployed, and Neame scrutinised them as he walked past: though he knew it all by heart, he couldn't resist a final check. He was a very thorough police officer, which was one of the reasons why he had risen so high. His men had absolute confidence in his capabilities, and he inspired great trust.

One monitor showed TSG reserves almost pawing the ground, like eager horses, and the other the street outside. 'Well?' said Neame, running his hands through his dark grey and silver hair and putting his hat down on the desk. He was addressing a sergeant who had also entered the van. He was not in office gear: he had been out at the sharp end and was buttoned up in a navy-blue riot police windcheater. He was sitting at another desk with his hands clasped in front of him, looking grim.

151

'A few of the pub chuck-outs have wandered off but if you want my honest opinion the crowd's bigger than ever,' said Sergeant Richardson. Neame looked at the monitors.

'Damn,' he said, leaning his arms on the main desk. Inspector Offer came in. He spoke with an upper-crust accent. 'They want to load the lorries, sir. If they're going to get them on the road for three a.m. they have to start now.'

'Can they be seen by the pickets?' asked Neame.

'They reckon not,' said Offer.

Neame looked anxiously at his watch and pursed his lips. 'Tell them to wait till midnight then to go ahead. But carefully.'

'Sir,' said Offer, and turned to go.

'Oh, Jim,' said Neame, leaning on the table. 'Break the men for hot food as and when. It's going to be a long night.'

Outside, Colin Page was standing at a barricade with his two sons, Billy and Dan, amid a forest of placards. All three of them had been made redundant shortly before the mass lockout at the factory, and they were angry. Colin had been loading meat pies at Bishopston for twenty years. He had been a rock solid member of the union for all of that time, of course, but he wasn't confrontational, certainly not violent. He felt that management had tricked, lied and deceived, and that once again it was the workers who were suffering. Besides that, he wanted to work.

He was a mild-mannered, reasonable man who knew what he thought. He wanted a quiet life: plenty of time with his wife Brenda, the footie of a Saturday, a few pints occasionally, a flutter – and the bloody boys to stay in line. They were a very close family, but Dan, at twenty-three the eldest son by two years, was a hothead, and there always seemed to be trouble of

152

some kind lingering around him. Touch wood it had never been very serious, and Colin and Brenda just hoped he'd grow out of it.

The three of them were a bit cold, but there was something about the carnival atmosphere which the two lads were enjoying. Billy went off to search for something to eat and drink, and arrived back at the barricade with three cups of soup and three packets of crisps just as his dad and brother were joining in the taunts at the man in the orange boilersuit.

'Nice one, Billy,' said Dan. 'Where d'you get it?'

'Pakis 'bout a mile away,' said Billy. 'Filth told them to close just after I got there.'

'Bastards,' said Dan, taking a sip of soup. As far as he was concerned, the police – all of them – were the lowest of the low. 'What is this?' he barked suspiciously.

'Mango and coriander,' said Billy cheerfully, raising his cup as if to say 'cheers!'

'Eh?' said Colin.

'You come out of the closet or something?' said Dan. When the two lads were together barely a moment passed without banter of one kind or another, whether it was abusive, mocking, humorous or obscene.

'It's all they 'ad,' said Billy with a broad grin.

Just across the barricade from the Pages, three TSG men, PCs Dunn, Hartwell and Cameron, one of the two West Indians on the team, were about to take their dinner break. The three of them were close buddies, and they were in good spirits, despite having been standing for a couple of weeks outside this factory waiting for the shit to hit the fan. They had been working in the same team within the Territorials for a couple of years, and spent a lot of time together socially as well as on duty. Dunn was going out with Hartwell's younger sister, and the three lads were often at each other's houses if they weren't working at weekends, driving their mothers mad. Cameron's dad

153

called them 'The three musketeers'. The only real bone of contention between them was that Cameron was Arsenal, but Dunn and Hartwell were Spurs.

As another batch of men returned from their meal break the three friends stood with their visors up, looking across at Inspector Offer, their boss, with hangdog expressions.

'All right,' said Offer. 'You three next. But don't hang about.' Dunn looked at him with mock innocence, as if to say, Would *we* ever hang about, sir?

'Sir?' he said, feigning amazement.

'Well, go on then,' said Offer with a smile, and they raced off, taking off their helmets and leather gloves as they ran. At least they've still got plenty of energy, thought Offer. A constable opened a gate into the police encampment zone and they turned up at the mobile snack van where they stood in a queue while various other TSG men eddied around, eating and drinking quickly. Sergeant Richardson was waiting for his oxtail soup to be ladled from an urn when the lads rolled up. He took the cup from the counter and stood in front of the van, his helmet tucked under his arm.

'Anything good on, Sarge?' asked Ian Hartwell.

'Soup and burgers,' said the unsuspecting Richardson.

'No, I meant is there anything good on the box?'

Richardson looked at him po-faced, and Cameron and Dunn squirmed theatrically, quite accustomed to their mate's bold cheek. Hartwell wasn't afraid of anybody. He was as tough as they came.

'It was – like – a joke,' said Hartwell, leaning his arm on Cameron's shoulder.

'It was like a joke, only jokes usually have a funny bit at the end, d'you know what I mean,' said Cameron.

'Oh, I see,' said Hartwell. He hadn't finished yet. 'So, Sarge, how is it in the executive suite? Drinks cabinet running low?'

'You're a cheeky bastard, Hartwell,' said Richardson, not quite smiling.

'Yeah, well, right now I'm a cheeky, cold, tired bastard, Sarge.' That was the point.

Suddenly a milk bottle crashed into the side of the food van. The woman dispensing the soup screamed. Richardson put down his styrofoam cup, spilling oxtail soup all over the counter, and ran back to forward control, shouting, 'Here we go!' The three lads also charged off.

In a way, it was a relief to them all that it was starting at last.

Back at the Pages' barricade, objects were flying and the noise level had risen considerably. The two brothers and their dad were being jostled and pushed against the metal barricade. 'What idiot did that?' shouted Colin as something large and sharp flew over his head. He turned round and shouted into the crowd, 'Pack it in, you idiots!' He was worried. This was simply not the way to go about things. Violence would considerably, if not fatally, weaken public sympathy for the pickets and give management the upper hand. It would be like handing them victory on a plate. Why couldn't these stupid, aggressive bastards see that? He hoped they'd be bloody well careful. It made him mad. People were going to get hurt if they didn't simmer down – and for what? Colin remembered the last industrial dispute, during the winter of discontent. There had been ugly scenes then, and Colin didn't want to see them again in Bishopston.

The boys, however, were enjoying it. 'I reckon we should rip up the pavement and stone the bastards,' shouted Dan cheerfully. They had to shout at each other now to be heard. 'Shut up and finish your soup,' yelled his dad, who felt as if he had been saying that or the equivalent to his eldest son since the day he was born.

'Can't I chuck this at them?' mouthed Dan, really getting into the spirit of the fight.

Billy shook his head and grinned. He was far more easy-going than his brother. 'Germ warfare!'

Colin looked nervously into the crowd again. He could see that things were beginning to get out of control. Large white horses were being led down the ramps of police lorries, tossing their heads in expectation. Richardson got out of a van and walked through assembled ranks of TSG men to speak to Offer. Dunn and the other two lads were now back in their positions, this time with batons at the ready and riot shields held in front of them, already deployed to fend off flying bottles.

Offer, standing next to them, took a few steps back and continued a conversation into the mouthpiece of his walkie-talkie. He was annoyed, agitated and strung-out. 'It's not just the crowd,' he said, 'it's the idiots in the factory. They said they'd be discreet.'

'And aren't they being?' replied Neame from the TSG forward control vehicle.

'Well,' continued Offer, 'I'm standing right next to the crowd and I can see people coming and going from the backs of the lorries clear as day.'

'Why haven't the crowd seen them?' asked Neame.

'Too busy chucking things at us,' said Offer grimly as another missile skidded on the ground next to him. 'I tell you, sir, they'll go crazy when they realise. And as for trying to get the lorries out . . .'

Neame made a quick decision. 'I'm going to disperse the crowd.'

'Couldn't we just stop the lorries?' suggested Offer hopefully.

'We'd have the same problem tomorrow night,' said Neame. He was right. Anyway, the lorries had been loaded, their side hatches were bolted shut, and the petrified drivers were revving the engines. They switched on their headlights.

Neame studied the monitors for a few moments in silence, marshalling his thoughts and confirming his decision to himself. 'Right,' he said to Richardson and the two officers in the van. 'We're going to drive a wedge through the middle of them . . .'

'Disperse!' Offer had begun to yell through his loud-hailer. 'Horses will be used . . . please disperse . . .'

The Pages and many other pickets saw that the lorries were being loaded. The news spread through the crowd like a fire in a dry wheatfield, and pent-up rage and hatred exploded like a firework. It was the ultimate insult for a group of men who had already been insulted to the limit. Molly Cope walked past, right in the heart of what was about to become the action.

Behind the crowd a small group of photographers had collected five masked rioters by a garage wall that had the slogan 'Scabs Out' daubed on it. They were encouraging the rioters to pose with bricks and wooden staves in their hands as if in the act of throwing them at police lines. A photographer went forward and adjusted the pose of one of the rioters. But it wasn't Gerard. He was with Molly. He loaded his tenth film of the day into the Nikon, zipping the cartridge containing the last one into a security pouch strapped firmly around his waist underneath his Berghaus Gore-tex jacket.

'Horses first,' instructed Neame, channelling every ounce of his concentration into the planning of this critical operation. He raised his voice to ensure that the jeering outside the vehicle didn't drown him out. 'Followed by sections one, three, four and five. We'll keep two in reserve here and four at control. I just want it fast and physical. Tell the men to keep the momentum up until we've secured the area within a hundred yards of the gates in all directions. Right, ready to go in five minutes.'

'Scab! Scab! Scab! Scab! Scab! Scab!' pounded the chant outside relentlessly.

Meanwhile, behind the crowds, a knot of young men had gathered behind a high concrete wall. They were sitting around in a circle, and two of them were shining torches down on the ground in front of them. A lad with glasses, only eighteen years old, was pouring petrol from a can through a small funnel.

· 'Hurry up Stu, for fuck's sake. The party'll be over before· we get this thing going.' The young man making the incendiary device was silent, and kept working. The man who had spoken, a skinhead with a swastika tattooed on his arm, got up and paced the scrubby wasteland.

'Got any blow left, Simon?' he asked one of the others, who came up to join him and handed him a grimy plastic bag. Carefully taking apart a Marlboro in the palm of his hand, the skinhead mixed some of the very low-grade dope in the grimy bag with the tobacco from the cigarette. The dope had already been cut at least six times, so there wasn't much chance of it doing great things to his head. But he smoked his joint, anyway.

He was going to get them good and proper tonight, the fuzz. He didn't even work at the meat pie factory, and never had, but wherever there was trouble in London or the surrounding area, he gravitated towards it. Here was a man who had been born at the bottom of the heap and had been burrowing further down ever since. Abandoned by his mother, a prostitute, he had been brought up in a notoriously scandal-prone children's home in the roughest part of the capital, and he had learned how to steal well at a very tender age. He had gone to school fairly regularly until he was eleven, but after that it failed to hold his attention, and he had put in only intermittent appearances at Crow Street Secondary. He had usually gone only when he couldn't think of anything else to do, or sometimes when he was so hungry that even a school dinner was appealing.

He had never had a job. He collected his dole each week, and there had been a few half-hearted attempts at getting him on a Government training scheme. But he was suspicious of all that; he thought it was all a load of cobblers, a trick to get him either to work for nothing or to screw him out of some of his money. He lived in a squat on a council estate in Battersea with his dog, a terrier he called Sutcliffe after the Yorkshire Ripper, and whoever else turned up – as long as he liked them, of course. If he didn't like them he set fire to their sleeping bags, and they usually left pretty sharpish.

The police knew him, of course. They had known him since he was a little boy. They had had him in the cells for the night on numerous occasions, but they had never managed to put him away. He was quite proud of that. He had been beaten up several times, but not really badly. His hatred of the police was predicated less on personal experience and more on the fact that they represented authority, the establishment and even the other side of life in general – the side which worked, which went about its business, which had opportunities and which motivated itself to get on.

It would have been difficult to over-estimate his hatred of the police. It was a profound, white-hot rage, and there was nothing he wouldn't do to indulge it – nothing at all. He sucked the joint dry. 'Finished, Stu?' he said to the kid, whom he knew from the estate and who was a dab hand at making petrol bombs. The skinhead had promised to get hold of a bit of E for the kid if he came along to Bishopston that night to do the business. All the kids on the estate were desperate to get hold of E. It was a great weapon for the skinhead, and he used it indiscriminately.

The TSG lines were preparing to charge. They were tense, determined and disciplined. Eight horses cantered into view, ridden by policemen in yellow rainproofs. The crowd were incensed. Dunn and the two others were in the front line of the TSG men who nosed in front of the horses, crouching slightly. They drew down their visors and edged towards the crowd. Cope was bunched up nearby, next to the Page family, struggling to keep tabs on what was shaking down and pointing out potential shots to Gerard, who stuck with her, his Nikon glued to his face and his flashgun hot with over-use. Suddenly the weight of the crowd pushed down the barricade in front of the Pages, and everyone rushed forward. The two sides met, and man-to-man skirmishes erupted everywhere around, the confrontation swiftly degenerating into a lawless mêlée which was further confused by the arrival of more white horses. Everyone was shouting and screaming. A flare was thrown, a horse reared and its rider was dragged to the ground while three other TSG men were punched and several of the rioters lay groaning on the gravel. A lad of about Billy's age ran past the Pages, the wild and vicious skinhead whose anger was uncontrollable. He lobbed a petrol bomb at the police line. The whole scene was horribly lit for a second. Billy was knocked into a barrier. 'Fucking hell!' shouted Dunn to Cameron as he put his helmet back on. 'What a shambles, all for some bloody—' Then he disappeared in a ball of flame. The petrol bomb had hit him in the ribs, and his whole body was on fire. He ran forward, screaming hideously, and fell to the ground, throwing his body around while Cameron looked at him in pure horror. He had never heard a human being make that kind of noise before. Hartwell began pumping away frantically at the flailing limbs with his small green extinguisher, shooting the jets at his flaming mate. 'Medics!' screamed Dunn, almost ripping his vocal chords. The fire subsided and Cameron and Hartwell began dragging Dunn back. A medical team came running up, knelt down next to him and began gently levering the burned man onto a stretcher. The two friends stood looking at them as they trotted off, one of Dunn's legs dangling over the side of the stretcher, and then they remembered the riot. They resumed their places in the line. Cameron glanced across at Hartwell. He was staring ahead, and under his visor Cameron could see that his thin mouth was set hard with determination.

Hartwell rushed forward, taut with concentration, and Cameron followed. The three Pages had been separated, and Colin was looking around wildly for his youngest son. 'Billy!' he screamed, and then cupped his hands around his mouth in a vain attempt to make his voice carry. 'Billy!' There wasn't a hope of being heard. Hartwell reached the crowd. 'You!' he screamed, and headed for Billy, thinking of nothing except revenge for his burned mate. Billy didn't see Hartwell until he was almost upon him, and he realised immediately that the copper was going to clobber him, so he scarpered. In his fluster to get away he ran straight for the perimeter fence in front of the yard, and then he had no option but to start climbing it, the red hood of his sweatshirt top dangling out onto his cream bomber jacket. He never stood a chance. Hartwell slammed him across the back with his baton, and Billy crumpled to the gravel at the foot of the fence. Then Hartwell hit him on the back of the neck. He hit him hard. Everything around this ugly little scene was in chaos, and although Colin Page dimly saw someone being struck through the pullulating crowd, he was powerless to intervene. Cameron finally caught

161

up with Hartwell and tried to restrain him, but it was too late. After just two blows Hartwell saw that his victim – the bastard who had thrown the petrol bomb, as far as he was concerned – had lost consciousness, and he ran off and lost himself in the crowd, swinging his baton.

Cameron crouched down by Billy and a medic ran past a few feet away, carrying a small orange suitcase and wearing a white crash helmet. Cameron shouted, 'Over here!' and then he, too, was off.

16

Clark ran along the corridor at New Scotland Yard and
knocked on the door before entering Deakin's office,
running his fingers through his hair. It was ten to nine,
and Deakin, watching the TV AM news reports of the
riots, had his back to the door. On the screen an
ambulance was trying to get through the crowd and a
lorry was nosing along behind it. 'Pickets were
throwing stones and petrol bombs and obstructing
ambulances trying to ferry the injured to hospital,' said
the grave voice-over.

Deakin hit the off button on the remote control unit
and swung round abruptly in his swivel chair to face
Clark. Clark's hair was still slightly wet from his
morning shower. Deakin looked at his watch, and cast
a frosty glance at Clark. He was angry. 'Sorry sir,' said
Clark. He knew it was much too late. He hadn't got
much sleep; it was the morning after the dinner party
at the Huxtables.

'Have you seen this?' asked Deakin, clicking his head
back angrily at the screen.

'Yes, sir,' said Clark. He had watched ten minutes of
it in the bedroom as he was getting dressed.

Deakin never wore what might be described as a
benevolent expression, but that morning he was
looking daggers. 'One of the crowd is in a coma at St
Mary's,' he snapped. 'They give him fifty-fifty.

Commander Huxtable wants you leading the inquiry, starting' – he looked at his watch for the second time in two minutes – 'nearly an hour ago.'

All very well for bloody Huxtable, thought Clark. He probably went straight off to the land of nod when we left. I had to go through the third degree on the way home and then keep my lovely young wife satisfied for half the night after that.

He swung into his office down the corridor. Naylor and Connell were already sitting in it. 'Morning all,' he said breezily.

'Morning,' they chorused.

'Right, let's get started,' he said, taking off his jacket.

He stood up next to the window and told them what Deakin had told him, and they began piecing together the available material and how they could get hold of more of it. 'And of course we have one huge advantage,' said Clark, drumming a pen against the palm of one hand, 'which is that there were more cameras there than at the Coronation.'

'How would you know?' asked Connell, sitting on a table swinging her legs.

'Harry told me,' said Clark. Naylor smiled weakly. 'So for starters I want a video running on all four channels . . .'

'Been on since seven-thirty, Guv'nor,' said Naylor, who never sounded smug. He was sitting down with his back to an internal window overlooking the typing pool; leafing through a pile of papers on his knee, His jacket was hanging over the back of the chair.

'Brownie badge, Harry. Newspapers?'

Connell placed a huge pile on his desk, the *Guardian* on top. Clark was clearly very impressed at their efficiency. Connell played it up. 'Your coffee,' she positioned a plastic cup next to the newspapers, 'and your cheese roll.'

'What is this, *Little House on the Prairie*?' said Clark.

'Let's do some work. First we'll collate the media stuff, then we'll go over to the TSG area headquarters and seize the documents. Mo, ring Commander Neame at his office. Let him know we're coming and get him to send over the film they shot of the riot.'

The team slid into action, all keen to get their teeth into this one.

At St Mary's, Dan and Colin Page had been pacing the corridors all night. It had taken them hours to find Billy – he'd been carted off in an ambulance before they got to him. Eventually they'd made their separate ways back to Pemberton Road, where they lived. Dan hadn't been too worried; he reckoned they could all look after themselves. But Colin was beside himself. He had seen someone copping it. Who had it been?

Dan arrived at the terraced house first. He put the kettle on and rubbed his hands, deciding to stay up and wait for the others. His father came in before he had time to drink the tea. 'Where's Billy?' he said to his eldest son.

'Dunno, thought he was with you.'

And then the telephone rang.

Everything smelled of sickness in that hospital. They found a couple of smoking-rooms, and drifted out of one or the other. When the call had come through to Pemberton Road Colin had woken Brenda and they had leaped into Dan's ten-year-old Capri as fast as possible, faces blenched in the darkness, each thinking that this couldn't really be happening to them, and that they were going to wake up soon.

They weren't allowed to see him until three o'clock in the morning. He was on a ventilator. The funny thing was that he looked totally undamaged – he looked peaceful and healthy, his smooth pink skin utterly unblemished. Just this tube coming out of the

side of his mouth attached to a green nozzle, and a
white band half an inch thick strapped around his face.
Nurses in thin rubber gloves came and went, tinkering
with the bottles suspended from poles next to the bed
and twiddling dials in the wall. And always the terrible
bleeping and the rasp of the ventilator at his side. They
had taken it in turns to sit with him, or sometimes they
all sat together. Mrs Page rarely left the room. The
doctor hadn't said much, except that people sometimes
came out of comas and sometimes didn't. Well, what
was that supposed to mean? Mrs Page sat there, her
face expressionless, willing her child to open his eyes.

Meanwhile, along the corridor in another ward,
Dunn was lying in bed in a Michelin Man set of
bandages, sedated but awake. Cameron was sitting at
the bedside, now wearing regular police uniform.
Hartwell arrived, his jacket in his hand.

'Hi, Col,' he whispered to Cameron, looking down at
Dunn with a grim, frightened face. 'How's he doing?'

'He's going to be all right, ain't you, Tiger?'

Dunn made a big effort, and spoke in a muffled
voice without moving his facial muscles, like someone
trying not to crack a facepack. His nose was blistered a
horrible yellow colour, and weeping, and his chin and
neck were mottled with an angry red and brown
swelling. He was peeping out of slit eyes. The bandages
were striped with brown elastoplast. 'I'm going to have
a bit of a tan though,' he said.

Hartwell was genuinely surprised. 'Shit, are you
awake?'

'Course I am,' said Dunn heroically, his Geordie
accent more pronounced than usual.

'There's no way of shutting you up, is there?' said
Hartwell.

'No.'

Hartwell lowered his voice and leaned forward. 'We
got the bastard for you.' Cameron looked really

166

shocked, and recoiled slightly.

'Thanks mate,' murmured Dunn, and closed his eyes.

Half an hour later the two friends left Dunn and walked through the swing doors of the ward. Cameron, who led the way, was furious. He couldn't contain himself. As soon as he had put on his jacket he rounded on Hartwell and pushed him up against the wall. 'Are you serious?' he said, almost tearfully, scrutinising his mate's face.

'What, about squaring it for Dunny? Yeah,' said Hartwell, surprised and indignant.

'But you just laid into the first poor bastard you came across,' said Cameron, becoming more agitated by the minute.

'No I didn't,' said Hartwell, quickly reverting to cool and weary mode. 'I clocked him, and I went for him.'

'Why didn't you nick him?' said Cameron, almost wailing in despair.

'What's up with you?' asked Hartwell, genuinely surprised now. He looked down the corridor. 'Look, I sticked him, he had it coming. I'd have done the same for you. Come on, let's get some coffee,' he said benignly, his tone indicating that it had been a long, hard day's night for everyone, and a traumatic one for the pair of them, seeing their mate go up in smoke. Cameron was tired and distressed. Hartwell was confident that he would calm down and return to his senses once he had time to stand back and take a cool look at the situation.

Hartwell exemplified a certain stereotype within the force. There were a lot like him. Putting villains behind bars was one thing. But when it came to villains doing in your mates or your fellow PCs – well, you went above the law, then, didn't you? Simply took the matter into your own hands. That was the first rule in the book, as far as Hartwell was concerned, and never,

ever, did he feel a moment's compunction. Loyalty to mates was one of the very few fixed points in his life, and he was the kind of bloke who liked to demonstrate his loyalty in overt, practical ways. It was the tribal morality of the force that had attracted Hartwell to it when he left school three years previously, aged sixteen. He wanted to belong somewhere, to identify, and the force offered him the opportunity to do that in a very meaningful way.

Cameron, on the other hand, had a clearly defined moral sense, and it happened to coincide with the law. He wouldn't have dreamed of taking the law into his own hands, under any circumstances. There was always a way of doing things properly. Even if the bastard who Hartwell thought had got Dunny was as guilty as hell, there was a right way of going about things, and that was to arrest the cunt. Cameron wasn't a saint: rough him up a bit once you've nicked him, of course, if you're sure you've got your man. But not this.

Clark was sitting in his office, smoking and concentrating on video footage of the riot. 'Guv,' Naylor shouted from the next-door office, separated by a glass wall. He appeared through the sliding door. 'Got Commander Neame live on BBC 1.'

Clark stopped the video and switched to the BBC, where he saw Neame standing on a platform outside St Mary's, a small group of hacks and photographers clustered in front of him. '. . . and naturally,' he was saying, 'I'm concerned, as we all are, about all the injured – the police, the protesters and the innocent members of the public. Concerned as I am about Mr Page I must remind you that there were twelve people seriously injured last night and nine of those were police.'

'Commander Neame,' butted in an interviewer, 'do —'

'Sorry,' Neame continued forcefully, determined to set his own agenda, 'but I must also point out that it's by no means certain, with all the lethal missiles being hurled about by the rioters, that Mr Page was not injured by them.'

Neame was a skilful manipulator of the media – he was a skilful manipulator of most people, come to that. He was the consummate smooth-talking copper. He had excelled himself during a spell with the Special Branch, and his record was unblemished. 'Straight as a die' was an expression often used of Neame within the force. It wasn't that he couldn't fight dirty, because he certainly could, but he was forgiven for that because he was always fighting for the right team.

He was an ordinary kind of chap, really: solid middle-class background, good grammar school education, joined the force at eighteen. He had married a girl-next-door type when he was twenty-two and they had lived happily ever after, spawning three sons along the way. One of the sons had followed his dad and become a policeman, but they had never worked together – Neame senior wouldn't have countenanced that. Neame enjoyed a round of golf, was quite a DIY man, and, like many coppers, he was a freemason.

Five years previously he had been Worshipful Master for a year. He had quite enjoyed it, but he wasn't sorry when it ended – there had been too many social functions for his liking. Small talk was all right, but only in measured doses; besides, he never liked the food they served up at those dos. Lately Neame had lost a lot of his enthusiasm for lodge meetings, and for the lodge in general, after an extremely unpleasant incident involving a member who was also a policeman.

Neame had never learned the gory details, and he had never worked with the officer concerned. Things had gone badly wrong inside a nick and the officer had ended up grassing. The usual systematic hounding ensued, as it always did when the golden rule was broken ('Don't Rat on Your Mates'): the culprit was ostracised at the station: a can of paint was chucked over his car; obscene mail dropped onto his doormat; the entire bar at the police social club fell silent when he appeared – that kind of thing. Well, the bloke was a kind of man-and-boy copper, and he couldn't hack it, so he killed himself with carbon monoxide, locked in his garage wearing full uniform. Bad business.

Clark's little CIB team had worked on that case, too. It didn't endear them to Commander Neame. He suspected that they had coerced the officer into grassing.

Connell came into Clark's office as he was thinking about Neame. She had a couple of videotapes in her hand. Clark turned the television off. 'The tape's arrived from the TSG, sir,' she said.

'Good,' said Clark. The hard evidence of a videotape was worth a lot more than rhetoric, no matter how plausible and how smoothly delivered. 'Let's go through that now.'

'Before you do I've got a surprise for you on this one,' said Connell, and she perched on a corner of Clark's desk, put a tape in the machine in front of Clark and pressed play. Naylor had installed himself on the opposite corner of the desk.

In the middle of a crowd close-up from the television news footage shot at Bishopston was Molly Cope, darting about in the orange cagoule, prodding Gerard alongside her. Her hair was tied back and she looked every bit the beautiful and intrepid young reporter schoolgirls dream of becoming, risking life and limb for the story which would launch a glittering career. Naylor and Clark exchanged a very guarded look. 'It's that Cope woman from Liverpool,' said Connell lightly.

170

'Oh, right,' said Clark woodenly in reply.

'I thought she looked familiar,' chipped in Naylor. Clark darted a look at him.

'Could be useful to talk to her, sir,' said Connell, all wide-eyed innocence.

'Yes,' said Clark casually, glancing again at Naylor, who was leafing through newspapers with a hint of a smile on his face. 'Yes, I suppose I might as well.'

'She might be able to help getting the press to release their photos,' said Connell helpfully.

'Yeah. Look, Mo, have you got anywhere with the TV news?' Clark thought he was steering them smartly off the topic.

'Well, naturally they said they aren't prepared to release the film, but they are willing to see you tomorrow morning.'

'Good, good,' said Clark. Things were shaping up nicely. 'Well done. OK, that's enough of this one,' he said as Cope danced across the screen again. 'Let's have a look at the TSG tape.'

Connell swapped the tape. The TSG film began just before the men charged the crowd, and there was bloody Molly Cope again, notebook in hand. Naylor chuckled, and Clark shook his head. 'Well, she is very photogenic,' said Connell, looking at Naylor as the corners of her mouth curled up. What the hell, thought Clark, smiling too. So they know. No point in me giving any Oscar-winning performances about my innocence, is there? Naylor handed him a copy of the *Guardian*, and when he turned to the double-page spread on Bishopston, there was Molly's byline, underneath the screaming headline, 'VISION OF HELL' IN LONDON PIE FACTORY RIOT.

'No prizes for guessing which reporter,' said Clark. He was quite shocked to learn that Cope was in London, although he wasn't at all surprised to see that she'd been poached from the *Liverpool Press* by a

171

national. The shock came because her permanent presence in the capital presented him with a choice. Was he, or wasn't he, going to reactivate? Things were going so well with Sue, he mustn't think about it. Things were going well in all departments of Clark's life, in fact, an observation which hadn't escaped him. Before he could pursue this line of thought further the TSG men on the screen started running forward, and all three detectives in the office turned their attention to what went on in the crucial few seconds before Billy Page fell unconscious at the perimeter fence.

They watched the videos, and they watched them again, and then they watched them frame by frame. It was painstaking work because the picture was continually obscured by people rushing in front of the camera, or at least by a riot shield or two being brandished. The soundtrack was hopeless.

'No, there,' said Connell, pointing at the screen. 'Look, that's someone using a truncheon.' Several black silhouettes appeared to be dancing behind a thick net curtain.

'But Page went down at the foot of the perimeter fence, not there,' said Naylor.

'This is all very entertaining,' said Clark, his head propped up on his hand, 'but basically useless. We need to speak to Page's father and brother to find out exactly where they were and what they saw. I want you to set that up, Mo. And we need to install you,' he said to Naylor, 'at TSG HQ for a while.'

'Oh, that'll be nice,' said Naylor, sounding as if he thought it almost certainly wouldn't be. He got up, drawing on a fag.

'But first,' Clark continued to Naylor as he got up and grabbed his jacket, 'I'm taking you to lunch.' Naylor looked astonished. When he had recovered he smiled cheerily at Connell and followed Clark out of the office.

What this lunch involved was Naylor driving Clark around London and then sitting in the car outside a posh tapas bar eating a ham sandwich while Clark sweet-talked Molly Cope over Rioja and sundry delicacies inside the bar. The two men had simply turned up at the *Guardian*'s offices, and Clark had asked the commissionaire downstairs to call Cope. 'Who shall I say is waiting?' the man had asked.

'Tony Clark.'

'Miss Cope, a Mr Clark in reception for you.' The man paused, and put the phone down. 'She'll be with you in a moment.' Naylor was standing back, looking out of the window. 'I'll wait in the car, Guv,' he said, less to show tact to the loving couple than to spare himself a gooey scene. Naylor wasn't a great one for the public expression of sentiment. His wife would have said that he wasn't a great one for the private expression of sentiment, either.

Molly had emerged through a door, looking radiant. Seeing him had shocked her more than she would have admitted to anyone, least of all herself. He kissed her on both cheeks, and asked her if she could have lunch – he'd only just found out she was in town, and he had been passing, and wanted to see her as soon as possible, to congratulate her on the new job. It was lucky that Naylor did not witness this virtuoso performance. It would have made him puke.

She had actually brought food in from home that morning as she was planning on spending the whole day in the office writing up a couple of postscripts on Bishopston. But of course she agreed to have lunch with him.

Naylor had driven them to the tapas bar. It was a regular haunt of Clark's. He ordered a bottle of good Rioja and then drank it all himself; she drank mineral water. She never indulged in alcohol at lunchtime. Cope liked wine, but she never drank much, because she hated the idea of being out of control. They toyed around with their food, pushing the bits and pieces from the little earthenware dishes around their plates. The waitress thought they didn't like it. But really they were mesmerised by each other all over again.

They talked about developments in the Dicks case, and about Cope's move to London, and how the flat-hunting was going, and how she found the *Guardian* team. He chatted a bit about the small cases he had been working on since he left Liverpool six weeks or so previously. Eventually Clark worked his way round to the question of access to the *Guardian's* photos, and explained why he needed them: he thought it would appeal to her finely honed sense of justice.

'I'll see what I can do,' she said.

'Thanks,' he said, gazing seductively into her eyes. She was wearing a mustard suit, and her hair was loose. They sat there for a few moments, just looking.

'It hasn't changed, has it?' she said softly and meaningfully.

He shook his head.

This was how she wanted it to happen. But she had to challenge him first. 'So why didn't you return my call?'

'Doorstep syndrome,' he said, only half joking. As she looked at him she thought, surely, surely, when you feel this electricity between us like I do, you cannot perceive our relationship as predicated solely on the casual leg-over?

'I'm a married man,' he said, trying to brush the subject of the unreturned call away and normalize the atmosphere. He was not intending to sleep with Cope again.

'Isn't that supposed to be "happily married man?"' she asked sardonically. He looked at her, and a doubt about the harmless nature of this liaison flitted through his mind.

174

Naylor, meanwhile, was pissed off. Apart from anything else, they were going to be late for their next appointment. He got out of the car, slammed the door and walked into the tapas bar.

'We're going to be late, Guv,' he said to Clark. 'Sorry, Miss Cope.' Cope was looking very slightly crushed. Clark got up. He found it difficult to leave. Things seemed unresolved.

'I'll phone you,' she said as he smoothed down the sides of his jacket.

'Thanks,' he said. He turned and walked away towards the door, and then he stopped, swivelled round to her and said, 'In the office.'

Naylor had the engine running. Clark brazened it out. 'Thank you, Harry. Well, that was a very useful business lunch. Next appointment?'

This next appointment really was important: it was with Neame at the Territorial Support Group headquarters in South London. They drew up at the barrier, and Clark pressed his ID up to the window as the duty sergeant came out of his little box. He scrutinised it, then lifted the barrier. It wasn't until that moment that Clark realised he had left Cope to pay the bill at the tapas bar.

Inside the sinister and enormous red brick TSG building Cameron, who was a chunky young man, was hunched over a small desk filling out his Bishopston report. The office, lined with black leather chairs and with one row of desks positioned at the front, was empty. Hartwell was standing behind him, drinking coffee and looking over Cameron's shoulder, his hand in his pocket. 'Then I'll say that I went down Drake Street with you,' said Hartwell confidently.

'Ian, I can't put that, it doesn't make sense . . .'

'Davies made an arrest down there. If we're down as assisting him we can't have been anywhere near the perimeter fence.' They paused as a constable entered the room, walked through and went out of a door on the other side.

'You'd have to get him to agree,' said a miserable Cameron, and lit a cigarette.

Hartwell pulled a photocopied piece of paper out of his pocket and read from it. 'Zero thirteen hours, arrested Ralph Herberts with the assistance of Constables Hartwell and Cameron.' He had already fixed it all up with Davies. Davies was one of the boys. Hartwell leaned over and pointed to the place where Cameron should start writing, slightly irritated. 'Zero thirteen hours ...' he began again. Cameron reluctantly picked up his pen and started writing.

Just outside the room in which Hartwell and Cameron were cooking up their story Clark and Naylor were on their way to see Paddy Neame. Naylor straightened his tie as Clark knocked. Neame sprang up when they appeared at his office door, arm extended; he was affability itself. 'Tony Clark, isn't it?' he said with a warm smile on his face.

'Yes sir, and this is —'

'And you need no introducing, hello Harry, you old rogue, how are you?'

'Hello sir,' said Naylor, shaking hands. Clark was taken aback. Typical Harry. They'd probably watched two hours of Neame footage together that morning, and he hadn't even revealed that he knew him. Clark looked at Naylor, but failed to get a reaction. Naylor's middle name was inscrutable.

Richardson was standing up at the back of the office, reading a lever arch file, and Neame signalled for him to leave the room. 'Oh, Flossie,' Neame called to an officer in an adjoining office before he shut the door, 'could you do us three coffees, please? Now gentlemen,' he said as he settled back behind his desk. 'What can I do you for?'

'Well sir,' Clark began, 'to sort out what went down

176

last night we need to seize all relevant documents and I want to base Inspector—' he corrected himself '—I want to base Harry here for a while to collate all the relevant info.'

'Seizing the documents is a little melodramatic, don't you think?' said Neame, his hands clasped in front of him. A poster on his wall said LEADERSHIP in various shades of blue. 'No, everything you'll need to know will be in our report, which the Commissioner has asked for and will be with him, the Home Office, the PCA and you, hopefully by the early part of next week.' He smiled, as if this were a small matter which was going to be easily settled.

'Well, all the same sir—' said Clark, standing his ground.

'I hope, Superintendent Clark, that you are not judging the TSG to be guilty before proven innocent?'

'No sir, of course not.'

'Good. And I imagine you're not basing anyone at the union headquarters to discover whether the injuries to Mr Page were inflicted by one of the rioters?'

'No sir, but —'

'Then I'd rather you didn't base someone here. If you had clearly identified one of my men as being responsible I might feel differently, but you haven't, have you?' Neame bore into Clark with his gimlet eyes. He was like a weasel.

'No, sir.'

'Good.'

There was a heavy pause as Clark marshalled himself. 'However, I would like Inspector Naylor to take some preliminary statements from some of your men.'

'They are all filing their reports,' said Neame, as if that were the end of the matter.

'All the same sir—' continued Clark patiently.

'Clark! Don't rush in here like a bull in a china shop.' Neame tried the persuasive angle now.

'Sir, we have the press reports, and the videotape from your own camera which you very kindly sent us, and we are quite hopeful that we may even get the BBC news footage by tomorrow' – at this, Neame blinked and looked disconcerted – 'but without a clear idea of who was where we are unlikely to be able to make head or tail of what we are looking at.'

'As I told you, Mr Clark,' said Neame, his voice now plunging to sub-zero temperatures, 'you will have my report, and those of the TSG officers, by next week.'

'I'm afraid I must repeat that I want all documents now and I want to speak to those men. As the investigating officer confirmed by the PCA I have that authority and will use it with or without your co-operation.'

Flossie knew how to choose her moment, and in she marched, bearing the coffee tray in front of her like the crown jewels. She placed it on Neame's desk, and exited smartly.

Neame looked at Naylor, then back to Clark, and paused. 'Sugar?' he said, bright as a button.

17

So Clark got what he wanted. He left Naylor at the TSG that afternoon; he was anxious to get this thing speeded up. He was used to antipathetic officers trying to stop him doing his job. It didn't bother him. He wouldn't have got very far in the CIB if it had.

Naylor was ploughing through events at Bishopston with Richardson. They had spread a map of the riot scene on a large table and were poring over it. 'The medic found him here,' said Richardson. 'He reckoned he'd fallen over the crowd barrier, and maybe bashed his head against the gate.'

'Twice?' asked Naylor.

'Oh.' Richardson looked straight ahead guiltily as if to say yeah, that's a fair cop. He was doing his best.

'You see, the medical report indicates two blows, possibly with a baton, one on the back and one on the neck,' said Naylor slowly, making sure Richardson got the message. Hartwell busied himself behind them, picking up a file from a hook on the wall. He was trying to overhear; he knew where Naylor was from, and he knew what he was trying to find out. Was it going to get hot? Luckily he, Hartwell, was thick with Richardson, and would get the lowdown later. Cameron paused in a doorway, his palms sweating. 'Right,' mouthed Richardson, at a loss.

*

Clark was going great guns with Sue. He felt that he
had put the past behind them – he actually felt that he
didn't want any other woman except her, and he
enjoyed that feeling very much. She sensed his
commitment and determination to make the marriage
work, and it made her glow with pleasure. She also
appreciated his newly reawakened interest in sex – or
rather, in sex with her. She hated going without sex,
and didn't know how single women of her own age
who didn't have partners stood it. Mind you, his job still
tended to encroach rather too much on their marriage.
That evening he had got back from the office at the
reasonably civilised hour of eight o'clock, and they had
ended up in bed before supper. It was all great, until
the phone rang.

Clark was on top of his wife at the time. He stretched
across to pick up the receiver. 'Hello?'

It was Mo. She was sitting in front of a television at
the office, smoking, and the by-now familiar Bishopston scenes were playing across the screen. 'Sorry to
disturb you at home, Guv'nor. Just a quick message.
Billy Page's father lodged an official complaint against
the TSG this afternoon at his local station. He and
Billy's brother Dan also made a statement. Unfor-
tunately the family are refusing to speak to *us*. The
father has said that he saw Billy being hit by a
constable. Possibly black. I've got copies here.'

'Thanks, Maureen,' said Clark. 'I'm seeing the news
editor at nine and I'll be in after that. Bye.' He put the
phone down, and turned eagerly back to his wife, who
embraced him.

A very strange thing happened as Clark was going into
the BBC Television Centre at five to nine the next
morning. He was sitting in a taxi slowly going through

180

the entrance lane barrier when a car passed him travelling equally slowly out of the exit lane. It was Neame. The Commander acknowledged his new adversary with a regal wave of his hand.

Clark pondered this as he took the lift up to the third floor and entered the throbbing newsroom. Had Neame bloody well nobbled those tapes? He must know that he had someone to cover up for. Whom?

The news editor was a spiky blonde woman in her early forties wearing a funky blue cardigan with gold stars on it. She was in a bad mood, and she refused point blank to release the film. Clark followed her round the office, trying not to display his irritation at her lack of co-operation. Screens were flickering all over the place and glamorous young women scuttled around carrying videotapes and sheaves of fax paper.

'My brief is to investigate policemen,' he said. 'The tapes would only be used by me and my team to identify —'

'That's all very well,' she snapped, 'but Commander Neame wants to identify rioters. If I gave you the film I don't believe that other departments wouldn't get access ot it.'

Clark shrugged helplessly. 'They wouldn't. But I'm not surprised you don't believe it.' He tried to disarm her.

'What about the police cameras and the factory security cameras?' she asked, not really concentrating and trying to freeze him out of her office. 'I'm surprised there isn't enough footage there to sort things out.'

He thought for a moment. 'Did Commander Neame accept your decision?'

'No.' She straightened up from what she was doing and looked at Clark. 'He was bloody rude and threatened me with a production order. If he wants press co-operation he's going the wrong way about it.'

She was cross, and Clark was furious. He made to go. Neame had prepared the ground to ensure that the BBC film was not released to Clark; he had inserted a doubt in this woman's mind, so she believed that any film she released to anyone within the police force would be used against 'the enemy'. It was a sharp move.

'I think he's got exactly what he wants. Thanks for your time,' he said, as he shook her hand and swept out.

Meanwhile Naylor was fighting his own battles at the TSG headquarters. He was sitting in Neame's office, looking at him over his neat desk and drinking coffee. He had just reflected to himself that the Commander bore quite a strong resemblance to an old Rowan Atkinson. He drew on a cigarette and plunged in. 'Apart from Sergeant Richardson no one will speak to me,' said Naylor. 'Is that a result of official orders?'

'No, Harry,' said Neame, playing the avuncular role. 'They're just exercising their right to remain silent. I'm sure if your young boss was a little less impetuous and gave the dust some time to settle we'd all be keen to help. But barely twenty-four hours have elapsed. A lot of my men had close mates seriously hurt in that riot, and now is not the time to come looking for scapegoats. Do I make myself clear?'

'Could I have a list of those rioters you've identified and intend to charge?' It was like getting blood out of a stone.

'Can't do it, Harry. Not yet.' Neame began riffling through papers on his desk as if the matter were closed.

At that moment Naylor's young boss breezed in, barely pausing to knock and closing the door on Neame's secretary who had trotted after him down the corridor. 'Excuse me!' she was saying, exasperated at this handsome man's haste. Clark was carrying a bundle of papers, and he strode over to Harry and gave him one of them, remarking airily, 'Nice job.'

'I beg your pardon?' said Neame, looking mightily affronted.

'Nice job, with the BBC,' Clark looked down at the papers.

Neame stood up. 'You're way out of line, young man. What are you suggesting?'

'I'm just saying that it's a nice job, working for the BBC,' said Clark disingenuously, looking over the desk now. Neame glared at him. He turned to go. 'Oh, sir,' Clark continued as if everything were perfectly harmonious and he had simply omitted a small detail. Now he knew, from his experience at the BBC, that Neame was fighting dirty, he had rolled up his own sleeves. 'How many police cameras were operating on the night of the riot?'

'One,' said Neame sourly.

'Which was videotaped?'

'Yes.'

'And you also taped footage from the factory's own security cameras?'

'Yes, I think so. Why?' said Neame rapidly.

'Because we were only sent one tape.'

'Really?'

'I'll arrange for you to have the other tape. Obviously an oversight.'

'Really?'

Even Naylor was squirming now at the open hostility that had developed between his two superiors. 'Would you please get out of my office?' said Neame quietly to Clark, and turned to the business before him on his desk.

Clark duly left, feeling as if he had at least gained a point by exposing the security camera scam. The woman at the BBC had inadvertently put him on to that. Clark might well be used to hostility, but the extent of Neame's machinations to obstruct him had come as a shock. It made his blood boil, in fact, and it also made him absolutely determined to get to the bottom of this case, whatever it cost.

Meanwhile Naylor was left sitting in Neame's office like a silly little pig in the middle. The atmosphere had clearly degenerated to the point where he wasn't going to get anything more out of Neame that morning, so he decided to clear off. Furthermore, seeing as the Commander was hopping mad, Naylor decided to clear off there and then without saying anything. So he did. This leaves me in a fine position, he was thinking as he strolled back down the corridor and into the office where they had given him a mangy little desk in a corner next to the photocopier. It's all right for the Guv'nor to swan in here and put a bomb under them. Then he shoots back to the Yard, and where does that leave me? I have to sit here stewing in it all day, don't I?

Secretly, however, Naylor was pleased that Clark had got one over on the slippery Neame that morning. He, Naylor, had had one hell of a time getting nowhere at the TSG. It was very frustrating, and Harry wasn't eaily frustrated. It had convinced him that some kind of orchestrated cover-up was going down, and that Neame was at the head of it. Naylor could understand the impulse to protect your own men; Neame would have been a lousy officer if he hadn't tried to do that. But it didn't mean you had to make other coppers' lives a misery when you knew they were only doing their job. That made Harry cross. Everyone was cross now. And they were all going to get crosser before the case was put to bed.

At St Mary's that morning Dunn was taking his first steps, eased awkwardly off the bed by a nurse. At first he could barely tolerate the pain which shot through his body when he was doing no more than remaining in an upright position. But he forced himself to endure it, and after a minute or so it calmed down a little. 'Just try one small step, Graham,' said the nurse gently. 'Just one little one. I'm sure you can. Imagine how pleased your mates will be.'

He leaned heavily on her, his hands bandaged up like boxing gloves, and, looking straight ahead and breathing heavily, he did manage two tiny steps forward. It took the nurse a long time to get him back into bed, and when he was finally tucked up again, his eyes closed and his lungs working overtime, his heart was heavy as he realised what a long way he had to go.

Down the corridor, Billy Page had a lot further to travel. He had made no progress whatsoever. He lay there, and the ventilator rasped. His mother was at his bedside, looking tired and drawn. She had barely slept since her husband had woken her that fateful night. It seemed to her that the whole world had receded into soft focus, and that the volume had been turned down. There was nothing in the foreground now, nothing at all, except Billy, and the hope that one day, as she was sitting there listening to that artificial puffing, he was going to open his eyes and say, 'Hello, Mum.' She barely even registered a body leaving the ward on a trolley, entirely covered by a blanket.

She decided to get herself a cup of tea. Colin and Dan weren't due for two hours: they were carrying on with some part-time, cash-in-hand work laying concrete in a school playground for a local building contractor. It was only a very short-term job – three weeks at half-time, the man had said – but it would help pay the bills, even if it wouldn't pay them all. Mrs Page got up wearily, looked at her youngest son, picked up her bag and coat and left the ward, feeling numb.

Connell was sitting patiently and alone in the

corridor outside, reading the *Guardian* for the second time; she had already read an out-of-date copy of *Cosmopolitan* which she had found languishing among the dying parlour palms. She was lying in wait for Billy's mum: the plan was to have a woman-to-woman chat and to try to persuade her to work on her husband and eldest son to get them to co-operate with the CIB team. At eleven twenty-five, when Mrs Page came through the swing doors, looking like a corpse herself, Connell stood up. 'Mrs Page, may I have a word?'

Brenda turned and looked at her.

'I'm so sorry to bother you at this time, but it really is quite important. My name's Maureen Connell, and I work with the Complaints Investigation Bureau within the police force – our job is to find out what happened to Billy.' She paused to assess the impact of what she was saying. There didn't appear to be any. Well, no reaction was better than a hostile reaction. 'I wonder if you've got ten minutes for a coffee?'

Brenda had none of the fire of Dan Page, and she could see that Connell was a polite and friendly young woman. It wouldn't have crossed her mind to refuse to talk to her. Once they were settled into the bleak canteen, which seemed to be infused with the anguish of grief and endless waiting, Maureen explained how important it was for her team to speak to Colin and Dan, both crucial eyewitnesses, intimating that they might never find out who had done such a terrible thing to Billy if his father and brother didn't tell them what they had seen.

When Maureen had finished, and they had drunk their tea and each eaten one custard cream out of the little packets of three Maureen had picked up at the counter, Brenda pushed her dyed ash-blonde hair from her eyes and spoke softly. 'It's very nice of you to take such an interest in our Billy,' she said, as if Connell was

186

doing it out of the kindness of her heart. 'I think Colin should speak to you, and I'm sure he will, once I've had a word with him. You could come round to the house, whenever you like. We live in Pemberton Road, near the football ground. But Dan – I don't think so. Dan's a very wild boy. He's never been keen on the police, and he was very close to his brother. He's taken this very badly. I think it would end in tears if we made him talk to a policeman – or a policewoman.'

'I understand. When do you think you might get a chance to talk to your husband, to ask him if we can see him?'

'He'll be here at one-thirty. Can you pop back at two? Then we can make an arrangement for you to come to the house. I'm sure it'll be all right.'

'Thank you, Mrs Page.'

Naylor was pressing on although he had moved back to the Yard immediately after the dogfight between Clark and Neame that morning. He was glad, though, that it wasn't permanent; Clark had suggested that Naylor just leave the TSG mob to cool off for a day and consider their positions. Harry had stopped off at his favourite greasy spoon for liver and bacon on his way back to the Yard, then he had popped in to put some money on the dogs. That had cheered him up.

When he finally made it back he went to collect the next videotape from the secretary outside Huxtable's office. As she handed it to him Huxtable appeared at the open door and closed it in Naylor's face. Naylor registered surprise, and returned to Clark's office, where he put the tape into the machine and his feet on the desk and started watching. He could hear raised voices down the corridor.

The voices were raised at Clark. He was being given a sharp rap on the knuckles by Deakin about his conduct towards Neame, who had been on the phone to Deakin almost as soon as he had ordered Clark out of his office that morning, all guns blazing. Deakin obviously took Neame's word as gospel and was incensed that Clark had upset him. Huxtable was sitting at his desk quietly looking on, his hands forming a church steeple in front of his face. 'Commander Neame is a respected member of this force and you do not swagger in and out of his domain like some little Gestapo gauleitier,' snarled Deakin.

'He quite cynically prevented me from getting access to the TV film,' said Clark, genuinely aggrieved. He was standing in front of the two men with his back to the bookshelf like a schoolboy about to be caned in the headmaster's study.

'Doesn't he have the right to pursue his own attempts at prosecuting criminals?' said Deakin, standing at Huxtable's side.

'He has obstructed me every step of the way. He didn't give me the film from the second camera.'

'You have it now, don't you?'

'Yes sir, but —'

Huxtable jumped in. 'Tony, we can't function without the co-operation of other departments and their senior officers.'

'If everyone went barging in. . .' Deakin was furious. He and Huxtable made a perfect duo for a grilling: one irascible and verbally stomping over the victim, the other cool and unruffled, stroking him into submission.

'He was rude and obstructive from the start,' insisted Clark.

'He is a senior officer and he will be treated with respect. Do you understand me?' Deakin glared at his superintendent.

'Tony,' said Huxtable gently, 'I think we may have to take you off the case.' Clark was dumbstruck. They were simply putting Neame's point of view above his!

Was this their idea of loyalty? How was he supposed to go about his job if he didn't wield a bit of authority over tinpot dictators within the force doing their damnedest to pervert the course of justice? And if he were taken off the case, it would be in disgrace. It would spell failure – not officially, but the taint would linger. A thousand questions raced through Clark's mind, and there was a knock on the door.

'Come in,' said Huxtable. Naylor appeared, and exchanged a glance with Clark. He had guessed exactly what was going on in the office down the corridor, and as he watched the new tape he had made the decision to intervene. He had come to his boss's rescue, effectively.

'What is it, Inspector?' said Huxtable amiably.

'Something rather interesting has come up on the second TSG tape, sir.'

'Can't it wait?' Huxtable asked him.

'It's sort of relevant to your discussion, sir.' The three other men in the room all reflected that Naylor had worked out what was up pretty sharply. Clark looked hopeful.

'Well,' said Huxtable, getting up from his desk. 'I suppose we'd better go along to your office and see what the Inspector's turned up, Clark – if that's all right with you.'

'Of course, sir. Lead the way, sir,' said Clark, his mind still spinning. Deakin glared at him as he passed.

The four of them installed themselves in Clark's office, Naylor crouching next to the television with the remote control unit in his hand. He took them through the tape, Deakin at his side. '. . . that was the petrol bomb, the one that hit Dunn. Right, now here we go.' A white horse crossed the blurry screen. 'This is a really useful angle because the camera is following the middle group that headed towards the factory gates and the perimeter fence where Page was found.'

189

Billy Page was clearly seen leaping up onto the fence. At that moment the film of the riot was replaced with cartoons. Ed the Duck was quacking away instead of the TSG men. 'What are you doing, Harry?' said Clark from behind his desk, anxious to get to the point and irritated that Naylor could choose this critical moment to play silly buggers.

'I'm afraid I'm not doing anything, sir,' said Naylor triumphantly. 'That's what's on the tape.' Clark looked at Deakin. Perfect! Neame had walked right into it! He had spiked the critical bit of footage. Harry, thought Clark gratefully, you are a star.

The telephone on Clark's desk rang, and he picked it up. 'Superintendent Clark. Oh, hello.'

It was Cope. She was purring. 'I've got something for you . . . Yes, in fact I've got quite a lot for you.' She was sitting next to her VDU at the *Guardian*, holding a pile of black and white ten-by-eights which Gerard had printed up for her. He always collected his negatives from the picture desk after they had used them, and made copies for his files in his own darkroom before returning the originals. Cope had called on him at home and asked him to do her a favour. He had been pleased; he liked her, and as they would probably be working together a lot in the future he was pleased to cement the relationship by helping her out. Besides which, well, she was an attractive woman, and Gerard wouldn't have minded an extra bit of spice in his life. He was married, of course, but that hadn't seemed to matter to all the other female journalists he had bedded over the years.

Cope had already picked out one or two photographs which were likely to be useful to Clark, and she was fingering them. 'When can I collect them?' he asked her. In the background Naylor, Huxtable and Deakin were fast-forwarding the tape.

'About seven-thirty tonight?' Clark said, scribbling

on a piece of paper in front of him. 'Yes, that sounds fine.'

At that moment Connell arrived at the sliding door between the two offices, and registered surprise to see such a crowd.

'Sir?' she said to Clark as she stood in the doorway. He still had Cope on the line.

'Just a minute,' he said to Molly, and covered the receiver with his palm. 'What is it?' he asked Connell.

'I've arranged a meeting with Mr Page for six-thirty tonight, sir.'

'Excellent,' he said, beginning to feel perky again after Huxtable's bombshell. Three pieces of good news in a row which could clinch his victory over Neame: incriminating TSG film revealed by Naylor, press photos from Cope and an eyewitness account lined up by Connell. He turned back to the phone and Cope.

'Look,' he said to her. 'I've got a meeting at six-thirty. How about nine?'

'Even better,' she said. 'At my office?'

'Right. See you then. Bye bye.' Clark hung up, and pulled his desk diary across.

'Was that the TSG?' said the unsuspecting Connell.

'No, it was that journalist woman.' Clark was always uncomfortable when Cope came into the conversation (or onto the television screen), and he was relieved to find the other three men too busy watching the video to hear him.

'Cope?' continued Connell. 'Has she got the photos?'

'Yep,' said Clark smugly. He changed the subject smartish. 'And you've managed to get us a meet with Billy Page's dad?'

'Yes. I spoke to his wife, she had a quiet word with him and he agreed.'

'And the brother?'

'The parents reckon he's still too angry to co-operate. Best left out of it for now. Mother said she

191

couldn't guarantee he'd be able to restrain himself in front of a copper.'

'OK.'

'It's been quite a good day, huh?' she observed cheerfully. He made a face at her and turned to the other three.

'Well?' he said.

'It's a children's programme, right at the end,' said Naylor conclusively.

'Is he being bloody-minded, or is he trying to hide something?' said Clark, coming swiftly to the point.

'Or was it a mistake?' said Deakin. Clark looked at him in amazement. Why was he so thick with that fucker Neame? It was blindingly obvious to everyone by this stage of the game that Neame was up to something. How could Deakin even think of using the word 'mistake'? Naylor clocked the vibes between Deakin and Clark and didn't like the way things were going – though he understood the hidden agenda, which Clark didn't. Huxtable looked at Clark, trying to fathom him out. Was he out of order, or was he an efficient, sparky officer simply doing his job well? They were all going to be illuminated, sooner or later.

18

Dan Page sat next to his brother's bed with their mate Keith. They hadn't spoken since they entered the ward. Dan hadn't spoken much since the night it happened. He hadn't let any of it out, the grief, the anxiety, the pain or the rage. He was pale, and his fists were clenched. He looked at his brother's face, the closed eyes, the white band, the green nozzle and the tube. Wake up, he thought. Please, please, please, Bill, wake the fuck up. He even thought about God, in the way people do when they're on the ropes: dear God, if you make him better, I'll never steal anything again, I'll go to church every Sunday for the rest of my life and I'll give all my money to charity. But Dan didn't proceed very far down that route; it wasn't the kind of language he felt comfortable with. Tears pricked the back of his eyes, and his white-hot rage against the people who had done this to his brother blazed through his brain.

Meanwhile, Dunn's girlfriend had arrived to visit him. They had been going out together for three months; she was Hartwell's sister, and she was called Tracey. She was only seventeen. Nothing had prepared her for what he looked like. Luckily he was dozing when she appeared next to his bed, so he couldn't see the horror and revulsion on her face. She was speechless; she had never seen anyone so badly disfigured.

She had brought him a six-pack, nicely concealed in two Kwiksave carrier bags. Her dad often went into hospital for his skin, and that was what her mother always took him. He drank it secretly in the TV room when the nurses weren't snooping around. Tracey had thought that Graham might like the same. Couldn't give a bloke flowers, could you? Now she felt like a bit of a git, as he didn't look as though he'd be in the mood to motor through six cans of Special Brew; didn't look as though he'd be able to open his lips wide enough to drink one, even.

She sat on the chair next to his bed and looked at him. She was a pretty girl, with a red bob, blue eyes and pale, freckled skin; her paternal grandfather was Irish. There were three other Hartwell kids, besides her and Ian. Their father was a carpenter, but had been off work for a good portion of the past ten years with a serious skin condition related to psoriasis. They hadn't exactly gone without, but life hadn't been that easy, either. Their mother worked as a dinner-lady at the local school. Ian was generous with his police money. He was a rough diamond, Ian; often in trouble as a kid, and a bit of a bully, but when the chips were down he had done the decent thing. He was particularly close to his mum, though he found it hard to show it.

Dunn opened his eyes. At least, he opened them as far as he could. 'Hello, Trace,' he said weakly.

'Hello Graham,' she said, making to take his hand, her own hovering above one of the boxing gloves as she decided that perhaps it was better not to touch. She didn't know what to say, so she didn't say anything. It was one of those experiences that she would recall later in life and realise that it had made her grow up a little.

Huxtable had driven over to the TSG building himself to deliver the incriminating video with Ed the Duck on the end back to the culprit. After a chat in Neame's office, during which he didn't mention the video, he took the tape from his pocket and placed it on the desk, next to the commander's china coffeecup.

'Silly little joke,' said Huxtable, and got up to leave. Neame looked embarrassed, smiled lamely and took the video, which he placed in a drawer of his desk, and locked it.

'And Clark?' asked Neame after a pause. He had put a convincing case to Huxtable for Clark to be summarily removed from the inquiry. He had recounted in graphic detail how Clark had been rude and unreasonable, and how his heavy-handed approach was seriously jeopardising the likelihood of a sensible and balanced inquiry ever emerging on Bishopston. Clark was destablising the entire team at a time when they were shaken, sensitive and in need of reassurance. He, Neame, couldn't tolerate any more of it. He hadn't lost everything because of the Ed the Duck caper, surely?

'Clark? Clark stays on,' said Huxtable, as if there had never been any doubt about the matter.

'We'll see,' threatened Neame ominously.

'Yes, I think we will,' said Huxtable as he left the office, shutting the door behind him.

Huxtable was thinking about Clark as he left the red brick building and walked to his car. He thought Deakin had been a bit hasty. It was looking as though Neame was flaky, and Clark had got on to that quickly and followed his nose. That was good. Huxtable reckoned he had been right to trust his initial instincts about Clark.

Huxtable was the man at the top of the CIB, and he

knew where he was going: sooner or later he was going to be commissioner of the Metropolitan Police. He was in his late forties, younger than Deakin as well as further up the ladder, and he held a degree in sociology from Leicester University and an M.Phil in criminology from Cambridge, both taken while in service. He joined the police in the early sixties, in a provincial force, and saw with his own eyes the changes in social and political attitudes that put a brick through *The Blue Lamp*. Being an intelligent and adaptable man, he decided at an early stage in his career to go with the trends rather than rail against them. Having transferred to the Met in the seventies, he made no secret of his admiration and support for Robert Mark's clean-up of the Metropolitan CID. At the same time he tempered his enthusiasm for Mark as a professional with rather more liberal social and political views, making real efforts to enter into dialogue with the black community in a west London posting, and speaking up in no uncertain terms for Stanley Aldersons's ideas of community policing at a time when paramilitary postures were more in vogue.

He preferred to be seen out of uniform these days: in his grey suit he could mix comfortably and find common ground with senior managers, and in his sweater and corduroys he could hold his own at academic seminars. In a previous job as a staff officer at the Yard he popped up looking quite at home in a television studio, frankly decrying the 'dinosaurs of police canteen culture' to an audience of wary punks and rastafarians, expressing other liberal (but mostly circumspect) views about community, society and the possible reform of legal institutions, including the police, and skilfully fielding questions about police accountability. Huxtable was a political animal of a newer breed than Deakin, all right, and the television appearance had been greeted by Deakin at the time with an indulgent smile and the words, 'good career move'.

Huxtable's qualifications and virtues were undeniable, and his career development looked unstoppable, short of assassination. A large number of police officers, however, hated his guts. He knew it, which was partly why he didn't feel he was in danger of losing much popularity by taking over the CIB: he didn't have much to lose. He wanted a rigorous, efficient, honest job done in his department. But at the end of the day it was a stepping-stone to higher things, and he might confess over a brandy that he expected to do more to drag the police into the twenty-first century by becoming commissioner than by pursuing every politically sensitive complaint to its furthest possible point in the CIB.

Can anybody have survived thirty years as a policeman and stayed as squeaky clean as Huxtable? This was a question which Clark had often asked himself, without coming to any particular conclusion. A lot of interested observers doubted it, however. And if mud from the past ever did stick, there was going to be uncontrolled glee in a good number of police stations.

Connell was driving Clark to the Pages for the six-thirty interview, and he had taken the opportunity of a moment's pause in the busy day to call Sue from Connell's carphone and tell her he was going to be late. '. . .if it's going to be after midnight, I'll call . . . I know, darling, I'm sorry. Put it in the microwave . . . ' He laughed. 'Don't put that in the microwave, whatever you do! Bye bye.'

He switched the phone off and put it down, and they drove in silence for a while through the tree-lined streets of suburbia.

'Sir,' began Connell, sounding serious, 'I know this is

none of my business, and if you tell me to piss off I will understand, but, um . . .'

'Well, get on with it,' he said, looking straight at her. The triangular relationship between Naylor, Clark and Connell was predicated on the 'call a spade a spade and don't piss about' model.

'Jenny Dean, sir.'

His heart sank, and he turned to look out of the window. 'Well, what about her?'

'I saw her a couple of days ago. I know it's over and so does she. But, well, I think it would make it easier for her if you saw her. To let her down gently.'

Clark continued looking out of the window for a while. 'Has it hit her very hard?'

'Very,' said Connell, glancing across at him.

'I'll think about it,' said Clark quietly as they pulled up outside the Pages' terraced house in Pemberton Road.

Connell was being straight with him. It was typical that Dean's predicament had made an appeal to the compassionate side of Connell's nature. She had a great gift for stepping into other people's shoes. Nevertheless he was surprised. Connell had made no secret of the fact that she disliked and distrusted Jenny, as did Naylor. Perhaps she felt that she could afford to be a little more sympathetic now that the affair was over.

That's awkward, thought Clark. He was enjoying the experience of being faithful to Sue, and felt like a child with a good school report. Bit of bad luck that Jenny was taking it so rough; he felt guilty about that, and his inclination was indeed to see her, to soothe her and make it all fine. Perhaps he would. He was afraid of her, actually. There was something fundamentally unstable about her, and it made him nervous of what she might be capable of.

They got out of the unmarked car outside number

forty-one just as Dan Page and Keith were walking down the street on their way back from the hospital, their hands in their pockets and their faces glum. Clark put his jacket on and Connell went up to the front door, which opened directly onto the street, and rang the bell. As Dan reached the house he asked politely, 'Can I help you?'

'We've come to see Mr and Mrs Page,' said Clark, pulling his ID out of his pocket. 'I'm Superintendent Clark . . .'

Dan felt his head erupt. Everything that had been building up steam inside of him since that night at Bishopston burst into his consciousness, and he swung his arm back and hit Clark on the lip with a socking right hook. Clark fell over the bonnet of the car, and then rolled onto the street as Dan put the boot in. He was taking aim for another go when Clark snapped himself upright and went in to defend himself, twisting Dan down over the bonnet. As he had Dan pinioned there Keith, accustomed to a good scrap of a Saturday night, jumped onto Clark and began pummelling his back. Clark tried to kick Keith backwards, and they both fell to the ground. Connell came at the freed Dan from behind, preventing him from going in on Clark.

When Brenda Page heard the doorbell she said to Colin, slumped morosely in front of the telly in their small sitting-room, a framed photograph of Billy at his side, 'That'll be that nice policewoman,' and she took off her pinny and hurried to the front door. When she opened it, Superintendent Clark and Keith were panting on the pavement and Connell had her eldest son in a half-nelson.

'Any more of that,' Connell was spitting as she too fell to the ground, pinning Dan beneath her, 'and I'll break your bloody arm off.'

'Stop it!' said an affronted Mrs Page, glancing around to see if any neighbours were peeping through their curtains. 'Stop it, all of you!' If anyone had overheard, they would have thought she was speaking to a gang of naughty ten-year-olds. 'How dare you behave like this in the street! In front of everybody!' They all struggled up in silence, brushing themselves down and tending their wounds, feeling angry and humiliated.

'I'm sorry, Mrs Page but –' started Connell, desperately trying to retrieve the situation.

'I know exactly what happened,' said an angry Brenda. 'He's a hot-headed idiot. Daniel, this is Miss Connell and Mr . . .'

'Superintendent Clark,' said a shaken Tony, dabbing at his lip with a hanky.

'Sorry, Superintendent.' She turned to Dan. 'They've come to find out who it was that hurt our Billy.' Then she looked at Clark anxiously. 'Are you going to charge him, or are you going to accept an apology?'

Clark looked at Dan. He was still very angry, and his lip hurt like hell; he thought about what he'd like to do to the little bastard. But the kid had gone through a lot that week, after all, and Clark wasn't exactly going to endear himself to the family by nicking him. Besides, Clark had enough on his plate, and the last thing he wanted to do was piss about with the administration involved in petty charges. It wasn't bloody worth it. 'No, I won't charge him,' he said magnanimously. 'Buzz off,' he said to Dan and Keith. Dan thought for a moment about saying thank you, but it stuck in his throat, and he turned on his heels and sloped off, followed by an unrepentant Keith.

The first ten minutes in the Page household passed with a general examination and discussion of Clark's wounds. Mrs Page fussed around with TCP and tissues, and eventually they settled down in front of the electric fire with tea and digestives. It wasn't the first time Clark had been roughed up, and it certainly wouldn't be the last. It did hurt – his lip and back, at least – though it wasn't what anyone would call serious, and he didn't mind too much. He was a bit subdued, but his thoughts were back on the job already, and after all, he had to get on with it. 'I can't honestly tell you I saw anything clearly,' said Colin Page, trying hard to recall that night, wanting to co-operate. Besides being desperate to nail the man who got Billy, he felt rather embarrassed that the one policeman showing a genuine interest in their personal tragedy had just been beaten up by his eldest son. 'It was too frantic. The only thing I know is that I saw a black copper.'

'You're quite sure about that?' asked Clark, still dabbing at his lip.

'Well . . . yeah. Yeah, I'm sure,' he said, sounding as if he had just decided that he might as well be sure.

'And was he hitting Billy?'

'Yeah, I think so.' Connell and Clark were sitting on the low sofa, hunched over the coffee table without enough room for their legs. They weren't convinced.

At that moment, Colin Cameron was sitting at The Goose and Partridge along from the Yard, looking at the *Evening Standard*. He was a regular; they all were, and usually, if they went for a couple of pints after knocking off at six-thirty, he'd be over there at the pool table with the others, or laughing and smoking at one of the round wooden tables. But that night he was at the bar, reading quietly. He felt permanently sick at the bottom of his stomach. His overriding feeling was fear – fear of losing his job, losing face at home, being publicly humiliated for conniving in the permanent disablement of a man who was almost certainly innocent. But he also felt in a moral turmoil about

201

what his mate had done. It just wasn't right, was it? He was sure Hartwell had clocked any old bastard – how could he have known who threw that petrol bomb? None of them had even seen it coming. Loyalty was one thing. But suddenly the tight-knit group which had given Cameron the feeling of belonging and identity he had always sought didn't seem quite so great after all.

Along the bar Hartwell and Richardson were roaring with laughter at some anecdote another colleague had recounted about a woman in a house they had forcibly entered earlier that day. Apparently, the woman had been naked, and had refused to put her clothes on. Richardson took a swig of bitter and looked across at Cameron, registering that the lad had withdrawn into himself since the Bishopston debacle. He kept a close eye on his team, and Cameron had always been such a solid player, up until then. Richardson was worried. He suspected that Cameron couldn't hack it. Well, whether he could or couldn't, nobody was going to break ranks on Richardson's beat.

After they had left the Pages' Connell dropped Clark off at the *Guardian* offices. 'Thanks, Maureen,' he said as he got out. 'I'll make my own way home.' It was dead on nine.

'Goodnight, sir,' she said as she drove off. She hadn't expected to finish so early that night, and she decided to get an hour in at the gym. Although she smoked, Maureen was a keen trainer, and she was really quite fit. She drove off to her flat in Maclise Road in west London, situated directly behind the Olympia exhibition centre (estate agents liked to call it Olympia village, but there was nothing very villagey about it) and collected her kit.

The gym was in Kensington, off the high street. She had a good workout, and beat her personal best score on one of the cardiovascular machines. It filled her with energy. In the shower she saw her friend Caroline North, a chum from Edinburgh University days whom she liked very much, not least because she didn't have anything whatsoever to do with the police force.

'Mo! Haven't seen you much about here recently. How's it going?'

'Fine! Except I've been working too hard.'

'So what's new? I don't know why you put up with it, for the money you get.'

'Not exactly brilliantly qualified to do anything else, am I?'

'Fancy a drink?'

They settled into a wine bar across the street and had a heavy-duty talk about what was going on in their lives. The first bottle of Australian Chardonnay slipped down, and they agreed on another straight away. Mo could hold her booze, like most coppers, and certainly got plenty of training at it on the job, but it was rare for her to get slammed. She just felt like it that night – and she enjoyed doing it alone with a girlfriend, rather than surrounded by lecherous males at the police club bar.

When Connell dropped him off at the *Guardian* Clark crossed the busy road and walked through the revolving doors. The commissionaire looked up.

'Molly Cope, please.'

'She'll be right down,' said the man, after he had called Molly upstairs. As Clark waited, flicking through a copy of that day's paper on the reception desk, he couldn't help smiling to himself as he remembered asking for Molly in another newspaper office only – what was it now – two months earlier? He had been sent up to the third floor on that occasion, and she had barely found the time or enthusiasm to speak to him. A lot had happened since then, that was for sure. He was just thinking that it hurt to smile when she emerged from a pair of swing doors.

'Tony.' She looked wonderful. She was wearing that amazing blue suit she had had on at the appeal hearing, and her hair was back in a loose ponytail. The spark between them was still there; it had never gone away. The receptionist pressed a button to allow him through the barrier (they hadn't had those at the *Liverpool Press*) and as soon as the doors closed on the two of them in the lift they were close together, their lips touching. Clark hadn't intended this at all, but he couldn't help it – the old story. He couldn't help it. They kissed properly, but he drew away. It wasn't a prick of conscience. It was the cut on his lip. 'Ow!' he said, smiling, which made it worse, and putting his hand to his mouth.

'So who did that?' asked Cope, half laughing as she saw the split lip and swelling for the first time.

'I'm afraid there's another man.'

'Ooooh!' she said, and they kissed again.

They were laughing as they walked out of the lift. Quite a few people were still hanging around in the open-plan office space, some working at screens and some chatting, but the newsroom was quiet by its own standards, as it usually was by nine when the last edition had gone down and nobody was yet very worked up about the day after next's paper.

Clark walked straight ahead, assuming that they were going to be looking at the photos at her desk. But she stopped in front of the door of a large, windowless stationery cupboard next to the lift. 'Tony,' she said seductively, and she went in. He glanced around to see if anyone was looking (which was more than she had done), and then followed her. They were drawn together again by that irresistible current, and without turning the light on they clawed at each other's clothes, and as he winced in pain she pushed his jacket off, and he unbuttoned hers, and she fell back onto a mound of box files, and wrapped her legs around him as he put his hand up the blue silk skirt and over the suspenders, and she put her hand down and unzipped his flies, and within three minutes they were making love in the stationery cupboard.

When they were going through the ten-by-eights later he reflected that it was probably the first time anyone had bonked in that cupboard. But then he revised his opinion. This was a newspaper office! He knew what hacks were like. At it like rabbits. They were probably queuing up outside the cupboard each day in pairs to get in there.

She was sitting down behind her desk at a swivel chair, and he was perched on the corner of the desk. They looked through the pictures. They were very good. They were going to help Clark a lot. Cope registered her displeasure at the sight of so many baton-wielding coppers as she handed the shots, picture by picture, to Clark. He stopped, and looked at her. She suddenly became aware of his gaze, clicked out of professional mode and smiled, feeling that electric current all over again. She held his look. He didn't look away. She knew he wanted her, and it was she who swivelled away, beaming and positively glowing with pleasure. This was just how she had wanted it to be. She felt a swelling inside of her: she had made it work. She forgot the humiliation of the tapas bar. She was sure, now, that he was going to come running back for more.

It was one-thirty by the time he got out of a taxi and walked up his garden path in Clapham. Damn! He had forgotten to call Sue to tell her he'd be late. He felt euphoric – it had been wonderful sex, and he was fired up about the pictures, too. But he did feel a teeny bit guilty. And he was worried about what Cope might do; she wouldn't really cause trouble, would she? She might. She was a strong woman, and she had a great hold on him both professionally and personally. He thought that he'd better not dwell on that.

He tiptoed upstairs, hoping Sue wouldn't wake up. He didn't want her to know what time it was. It was most unusual for him to be at the office until that time in the morning. He opened the bedroom door. Good, looked like she was sleeping soundly. But as Clark stole into the bathroom his wife opened her eyes and looked at the digital alarm clock. She hadn't been asleep. She had been lying awake, constructing scenes in her imagination.

19

The next morning Connell and Clark were like two bears with sore heads when they got to the office. Connell struggled in for eight-thirty and Clark arrived ten minutes late with a bacon sandwich in his hand. After bickering over who had left the answering machine off, and snapping at each other over the papers, Naylor intervened.

'I don't know what you two were up to last night, or if you did it together, but it must have been good fun at the time.' They both looked at him.

Connell laughed. 'Sorry, guys. You got me, Harry, I admit it – I've got a terrible hangover. In fact, I could handle an aspirin or three; d'you know if we have any?'

'There's some in the Guv'nor's top drawer,' said Harry. 'I bought them for him last week.'

'Anyone we know?' asked Clark as he got out the aspirins and chucked the box at Connell, yawning as soon as he had finished speaking. His problem that morning wasn't the after-effects of booze (no more than usual, anyway) so much as lack of sleep: he felt as if he hadn't slept more than about four hours a night for months.

'You're too clean-living, Harry, that's your trouble,' said Connell, throwing her head back to swallow three aspirins with a gulp of coffee.

Later that morning Clark and Naylor interviewed

the medic who had attended to Billy Page on the night of the riot. He came to Clark's office, casually dressed, a visitor's badge clipped to the zip of his green jacket. He told them that the man who was with Page when he, the medic, got to him, was black; he couldn't really tell you anything else about him.

'But he was definitely black?' said Naylor.

'Oh yes,' said the medic confidently.

'West Indian or Asian?'

'West Indian, I'd say.'

Clark, who had been looking again at the photographs Cope had given him, didn't want to waste any more time with this man: they weren't going to get any more out of him. He got up, walked round to the other side of the large desk where the medic was sitting, and stretched out his hand. 'Thanks for coming in, David.'

'My pleasure.'

'Will it be all right if we call you in again?'

'No problem,' said Dave amiably.

'Thanks,' said Clark, and shut the door behind the man as he exited.

'So the medic thinks he's black as well. What have we got?' he asked Naylor, who picked a sheet detailing the TSG men on duty at Bishopston off a desk in front of him.

'Five officers. Two West Indian and three Asian.'

The telephone rang. 'Superintendent Clark. Ah, hello.' It was Dean. Clark covered the mouthpiece and looked at Naylor. 'Do you mind, Harry?'

'Course not, sir,' said Naylor as he left the room and shut the door.

'Hello, Jenny,' said Clark conspiratorially, settling back in his chair and concentrating.

'You rang,' said Dean. She was sitting on her bed in her flat in Mornington Crescent, smoking. It was a sparsely furnished, lonely kind of room. Dean had just got home from the station after a night shift, and had found a message from Clark on her answering machine. Her heart did not leap when she heard his voice. She was so sunk in misery and depression that she assumed he was going to berate her again about going up to Liverpool and all the trouble it had got him into. Anyway, on the message he had asked her to call him at the office, so she had. She didn't expect anything.

'Yes,' he said. I'd like to see you. To set things straight and to ... apologise. I'm afraid I behaved badly.'

'Yes,' she said, without bitterness. It was too late to get bitter, and it had hurt too acutely. 'You did.'

'You understand that it's over, don't you?'

There was a pause, then she said in a dull kind of voice, 'Yes.'

'Good, then let's meet ... Tomorrow lunchtime, possibly. I'll ring you first thing and confirm . . . Great. Bye bye.' He put the phone down. That was a good job done; that initial conversation was what he'd been dreading most.

She did feel a bit better after she'd spoken to him. As she was showering she thought, well, at least he thinks about me from time to time. At least he cares how I feel. Maybe it wasn't all one long lie. Maybe that's just what life is – a series of passionate affairs in which either you get crushed or you crush someone else. Her sister had told her that time was the great healer and that time was the only thing that would help her recover. It was little comfort, of course, seeing as time was the only thing Jenny couldn't buy or hasten along. But it was probably true. It was good that she was seeing Tony one last time. It would allow them to sign off properly. After that, life was going to get better for her. She was actually going to be able to contemplate a future without that bloody man. When she fell asleep that night, for the first time in weeks she was looking forward to waking up again.

'Harry!' yelled Clark, and the hapless Naylor trooped back in.

'Thanks,' said Clark. 'Now, do we have enough eyewitness details to single out any of the black TSG men?'

'Well,' Harry began, and the bloody telephone rang again.

'Superintendent Clark.' He turned sheepishly to Naylor. 'Harry, d'you mind?' Naylor trooped out again.

'Molly, hi.'

'Can you come to my place tonight?' she said immediately.

'Tonight? Oh, I don't really think . . .'

'There's something new and interesting I really think you should see.'

'Is there? What?'

'I can't talk.'

'Well, I suppose I should then. If you're sure I really should. I'll drop round tonight. What number Burleigh Road?'

He paused before calling Naylor in again. Was she tricking him? Who was playing with whom here?

Over at the TSG headquarters Cameron had worked himself up into such a frenzy that he had handed in a transfer request. He had been thinking it over at The Goose, and then at home, where he hadn't been able to touch the tea his mother cooked him. He just had to get out of the heat. Besides that, things would never be the same between him and Hartwell, not after what had happened on the night of the riot. He didn't want any part of that scene any more; the transfer request wasn't born solely of fear. Cameron wanted a change of air after the events at Bishopston. He had been badly shaken by the barbarity of his mate's behaviour.

The next morning he didn't say anything to Hartwell when they met as usual in the locker-room; he thought he'd wait until it was finalised, then there could be no argument about it. What Cameron would really like to have done was to have disappeared off the face of the earth. Instead he handed in the request, inside a sealed envelope, to Sergeant Richardson's assistant, whose labours were shared by a group of other TSG sergeants, at eleven o'clock.

At midday, Richardson summoned Cameron into his office. Richardson had the transfer request in his hand, and he narrowed his eyes menacingly at Cameron from behind his desk. Cameron stood in the middle of the room with his hands behind his back, looking frightened.

'Why?' asked the sergeant.

'Personal reasons, Sarge.'

'Personal domestic or personal job?'

'Just personal,' said Cameron, not giving anything away.

'Be straight with me, Cameron,' said Richardson. 'Be straight and I can be a powerful friend, but get on the wrong side of me. . .' He paused, allowing the threat to sink in. 'I know what's going on.'

'Do you, Sarge?'

'Yes. You are panicking. That yuppie superintendent has put the wind up you and you want to break cover. Not in my team, son – nobody breaks ranks.'

'I don't think you understand,' Cameron stammered.

'I watched it,' said Richardson emphatically. 'Stay calm, button your lip, stick by us and we'll stick by you. Understood?' Richardson was like a piece of flint. He didn't feel anything. But he would fight for his men, whatever the cost.

'Yes, Sergeant,' said Cameron, feeling wretched.

211

'And can I take it that this request is withdrawn?' he asked, holding it up.

Cameron just stared at him. Richardson obviously took this as assent, because he screwed up the transfer request form and dropped it into the wastepaper basket next to his desk. Then he nodded at Cameron, indicating that the interview was at an end, and Cameron left.

Richardson tipped back his chair and drummed on his desk with a ruler. He wasn't quite certain what he'd seen on the videos, actually. Someone had done for Page, that was for sure, and it looked as if it was Cameron, but it might not have been. Not such a big deal – Richardson had covered up for men in that kind of position hundreds of times. It was normal, wasn't it? Couldn't be avoided. He was confident that they could weather this one. And he thought he could probably have confidence in Cameron not cracking.

Richardson looked at his watch. It was twelve-thirty, and he stood up, took his jacket from a hook behind the door and headed down to the bar.

'You gave me the impression that it was something more important than a great new Indian restaurant you wanted to show me,' said Clark ironically as he sat on the floor in the flat Molly was looking after for her friend Sabine. When he had arrived at about eight-fifteen she had the menu out on the table. It had been delivered through the letterbox the day before, and she thought it looked promising; besides that, they delivered free. The pair of them had chosen and rung through an order, and Cope had opened a bottle of Chilean red:Errazuriz Panquehue. It was very good. It was a fun flat with bare brick walls, venetian blinds, large stripy sofas, woven Iranian rugs with geometric patterns and a glass table with an electric typewriter on it. It suited Molly. The television was on. Clark was

212

mildly annoyed, but not very; he was enjoying himself now that he was there, and he was absolutely certain that he wasn't going to stay late. She looked great, in a loose white sleeveless shirt and long cotton skirt. But he didn't really feel like making love.

'It is more important,' she said in reply, sitting down on the floor next to him. 'I wanted you to see this brilliant new film.' She had slipped a video into the machine, and she pressed the remote control unit as Clark took another forkful of prawn vindaloo.

'I hope it's not very long,' he said with his mouth full, 'as I have to go by ten.'

'No,' she said as the machine whirred into action. 'It's not very long.' She sipped her wine, and her eyes were shining.

The neon blue light of the screen lit their faces. It was the meat pie riot. It was new footage he hadn't seen before. It was very clear. Clark almost choked on his food. 'Where did you get —'

But she just said, 'Look.' He looked, and he saw Dunn, blazing. A few moments later, in one corner, as the camera followed the charge, he saw the Page family turn and run. Clark clearly saw Billy stumble, and then he saw the back of a TSG man laying into him with his baton as he climbed up the perimeter fence. Billy fell. It got less clear then, and when Cameron appeared it wasn't apparent if he was also hitting Billy. The first man ran off. His face couldn't be seen. Cameron turned to call for medical help. He was identifiable all right. He too shot off into the crowd.

'Where did you get this?' said Clark as he put his plate down and took the remote control unit from her.

'A friend,' she said flirtatiously, feeling powerful.

'I love you, you're a genius.'

'I know,' she said.

'That's what Neame was trying to hide. I've got him cold. Just when the second tape was becoming incriminating he over-recorded it with Ed the Duck.' This was wonderful – really wonderful. He couldn't wait to shove it up Deakin and Huxtable's noses.

'Ed the Duck?' she giggled.

Clark nodded, and Cope giggled some more. He laughed too, then winced. 'Oooh! Don't make me laugh!' he said, raising his hand to his split lip. She put one arm around him, resting the hand on his shoulder, and stroked his cheek sympathetically with the other hand. He was still transfixed by the video, but she whispered into his ear 'Bed?' and kissed him on the cheek just as the medic in the white crash helmet arrived and lifted the unconscious Billy's head.

He still didn't feel much like making love, but he now found himself under a curious moral obligation, as if it were a trade-off. Once she started to undress him he began to feel aroused, however, and it began to seem like rather a better idea. They staggered into the bedroom together and collapsed onto the king-sized bed with its Moroccan covers. Impotence was never a problem for Clark.

Later she lay on top of him, feeling satisfied – physically, if not emotionally. She was thinking about what they had just been doing to each other in bed. He wasn't. He looked across at the clock. It was ten-fifteen. Damn! Sue got home from work at ten-thirty, and he'd said he'd be there. Now he wouldn't be. He was pissed off at Cope and at himself.

She felt very, very vulnerable, but couldn't say so. She hated this bit. It was when she suddenly turned from the all-powerful to the all-weak, from holding all the cards to holding none at all. Every woman who has had an affair with a married man knows that feeling. 'I wish you'd stay,' she said, her hair falling onto his chest, although in her heart she knew he wouldn't.

'I can't,' he said, and he noticed that Sabine had glued small luminous stars on the ceiling. They were

214

made out of the kind of hydrocarbon which absorbs the light and then glows in the dark. It was quite effective. Typical Camden, he thought, and then he wondered if Kentish Town counted as Camden. Was it north Camden? Or south Tufnell Park? Or what?

'You could, if you wanted to. I do love you, you know.'

'I know,' he said, and he thought, fuck. 'You've let me sleep in your bed and sit on your lavatory. A rare honour,' he tried to lighten things up, referring back to the comment she had made on the first night they stayed at the Adelphi in Liverpool when he had asked her why they couldn't stay at her place.

'Unique,' she said, and paused, trying to phrase what she had to say. She shouldn't have bothered. 'If you love her, then you should go, but ... if you're just keeping up appearances you should stay here with me.'

He looked at her, and she stroked his chest.

'I should go,' he said cruelly, and he got out from underneath her, and started picking his clothes off the floor and putting them on, and she watched him, until he was quite dressed, and then he pecked her on the cheek and walked out of the door.

He made rather a poor fist of excuses to Sue, who was lying in bed reading when he got home, and he had intended to make love to her, as he knew that would put her in a good mood, but then he bloody well fell asleep, fool that he was. She didn't fall asleep though. She lay awake, thinking.

The next morning he had to dash out before eight as usual, and at the last moment he remembered that he had to confirm lunch with Jenny before she left for the station and before his round of meetings kicked off. Shit, life was getting complicated! From the foot of the stairs he called her number. He knew it by heart. Sue was in the shower.

'Hello, Jenny. I can do it today, one p.m. Where?'

215

She suggested their place on the river. 'No, that's a bad idea,' he said immediately. He had asked Sue how she had known that his affair had been with Jenny Dean, and she had told him the ghastly story of how she had driven down there that day and spied on them from under the willow tree. Clark never wanted to go there again. Besides, he wanted somewhere totally unromantic. 'How about Benny's?' he suggested. Benny's was a pleasant café-type Italian restaurant in Borough High Street, which was relatively convenient for both of them – and they don't come more unromantic than Borough High Street. 'Great. See you there. Bye bye.'

He put down the phone, and Sue appeared at the top of the stairs with her dressing-gown on, scrunching up her wet hair. 'I'm afraid I have to dash, darling,' he said, running up to kiss her. 'I shouldn't be late tonight. Bye darling.'

'Bye,' she said as he went out of the front door, and she heard him turn the key in the Sierra. She had heard the second half of the phone call. Didn't sound like a professional call, that was for sure. That cold chill she had experienced before came back, and slipped right down to her stomach. Sue had already begun to suspect that all wasn't so well between her and Tony after all. A brief quasi-honeymoon lull, and here they were again. Or was she mistaken? She walked slowly down the stairs to the phone, pulling her white towelling dressing-gown tightly around her. Then she picked up the receiver and pressed the redial button, gripping the telephone table with the other hand. She braced herself.

'Hello?' said a young woman's voice. Sue slammed the handset down, her knuckles white.

Naylor and Clark were watching the video Cope had procured in Clark's office later that morning. Of course, Naylor had asked where the hell it had come from – it was dynamite. 'Can't reveal my sources, Harry,' said Clark provocatively. He thought it was probably a good idea to keep one or two secrets from the team. Gave him a bit of distance, didn't it? That extra *je ne sais quoi* that made for successful leadership. It was wishful thinking. Naylor knew where it had come from, though that didn't mean he wasn't impressed. Despite his disapproval of his guv'nor's extra-curricular activities, Naylor did have respect for his professional capacities. When the pressure was on, he often observed that Clark came up with the goods. Clark was almost impervious to pressure, and this was a great quality in Naylor's eyes.

They had watched the crucial piece of the video seven or eight times, frame by frame, to see if Naylor could identify the TSG man who could be seen next to the fallen page. As Naylor had spoken to all the lads at the TSG he was familiar with their faces.

'I think it's a chap called Cameron,' said Naylor.

'Are you sure?' said Clark, who was sitting at his desk.

'Well . . . ' said Naylor, raising one hand parallel to the ground and wiggling it from side to side to show that he couldn't be a hundred per cent sure. This was delicate – very delicate, and he was anxious to prevent Clark racing ahead of himself.

'We'd better set up an ID parade this afternoon for Billy Page's dad,' continued Clark calmly, looking through some papers on his desk. As he was speaking, the door burst open and Deakin came in like a stormtrooper, a copy of that day's *Guardian* in his hand.

'Harry, do you mind?' he said.

Naylor was getting used to it.

'Look at this,' said Deakin, obviously furious, opening the newspaper at page seven and slamming it down on Clark's desk. The headline read, FACTORY

217

RIOT INQUIRY RUNS INTO TROUBLE, and underneath a large photograph of the action at the perimeter fence the story began, 'A row broke out yesterday when it was revealed that a vital videotape had been over-recorded with a children's programme. The tape, which contained scenes of the Bishopston riot . . .' The byline was Molly Cope's.

'Shit,' said Clark.

'Are you trying to kid me you knew nothing about this?' fumed Deakin.

'I didn't,' said Clark lamely.

' "Molly Cope" – doesn't that name mean anything to you?' snarled Deakin, stabbing at the byline with his finger several times. 'You had at least two meetings with her last week. And didn't you work intimately with her in Liverpool?' 'Intimately' was not a word Deakin often used.

'Yes sir.'

'Don't yes sir me, Clark. You're not just going over the top with this personal vendetta against Commander Neame, but I'm pretty sure you're going over the side with this trendy little lefty.'

'Sir . . .'

'Don't piss me about. I won't have you playing power games with your seniors and betters, d'you hear me?'

'Yes, sir.'

'Now tell me. Did you set this up?'

'Not exactly, sir.'

'Then what exactly, sir?' Deakin glared at him.

Clark started bluffing. He was in trouble here.

'It was a trade. I gave her the story in exchange for the TV news footage we needed. It clearly identifies one of the TSG men hitting Page.'

Deakin was momentarily taken aback by this revelation about the new film. Neame wasn't going to like it. He composed himself. 'I want a copy of that film and a report of your overall progress in my office by tomorrow, understood?'

'Understood, sir.'

Deakin did a bit more glaring and then stomped out. Clark looked at the newspaper piece. He was wild. It wasn't true about the trade-off – he hadn't intentionally given Cope the story. She had used information that had simply come out in the course of conversation. She had betrayed him.

Naylor came back in through the sliding door. Just as he was about to speak, Huxtable appeared at the other door. Naylor knew what was coming, so he nodded and turned on his heel without being asked, wagging the cigarette which was dangling between his fingers. Huxtable registered Naylor's enigmatic behaviour, then shut the door and turned to Clark. Please don't you start, thought Clark.

'Have you got a suspect?' asked Huxtable.

'I think so, sir.'

'Oh good. Well done.' That was a relief. Huxtable turned to leave, but before he did he glanced down at the incriminating *Guardian*. He studied it for a moment, then looked up at Clark, smiled a broad smile and gave him a conspiratorial wink. The difference in attitude between Deakin and his immediate boss was striking, and it gave Clark pause for thought. Huxtable left, and Naylor was back.

'Not surprisingly,' said Naylor, trying to get it out quickly before he was thrown out again, 'Commander Neame is being unhelpful about the parade.'

'Of course,' said Clark. 'Call the witnesses for two-thirty.' He was absolutely obdurate in his determination to ride roughshod over Neame and his obstructive behaviour. When Clark felt he was in the right, or when he had decided to go ahead anyway, even if he wasn't sure he was right, he didn't let anything stand in his way. It was one of his greatest strengths – and it was sometimes a great weakness, too.

'Right, Guv.' Naylor turned and headed off, then swivelled round and leaned on a filing cabinet. 'Oh yeah, and Commander Neame also indicated that he felt your inquiries were arrogant, aggressive and now openly racist.' He turned away, heading towards the sliding door.

'And what do you think?' asked Clark coolly, raising his voice to make Naylor turn around and face him.

'I think you need to be careful,' said Naylor as he went through the door into the adjacent office.

Clark thought. He had dealt with a nasty business with delicate racial implications several months previously, and he hadn't enjoyed it. A WPC had made a formal complaint against her sergeant, alleging sexual harrassment. The complainant was white, the sergeant black. Clark had experienced a lot of conflicting attitudes when he had interviewed at the nick where the incident was alleged to have taken place. To a certain extent it was the most difficult work going, hacking through the jungle of prejudices, positive discrimination and secretly harboured dislikes. This wasn't going to be easy, especially with Neame on his back.

20

When Clark arrived at Benny's it was two minutes to one: it must have been the only date he had ever had with Dean for which he wasn't late. The restaurant was crowded, and the only table left was by the window. He sat down, facing in, hung his jacket over the back of his chair, and when the waitress came he ordered a coffee. He felt reasonably relaxed, though he wondered to himself if Jenny was going to behave. He didn't have to wonder long, as she arrived on the dot of one and slid in opposite him, facing the street. She was simply dressed in a cream short-sleeved shirt and loose black trousers.

'Hi,' she said, and smiled. He knew then that it was going to be all right.

'Hello, Jenny,' he said. The waitress arrived, and Dean ordered a diet Coke.

'How's life at the station?'

'Fine. How was Liverpool?' They ploughed their way through the small talk, discussing work, a few mutual friends, Dean's sister, whom Clark had met – nothing controversial. It was awkward for the first few minutes, but after that they both felt reasonably relaxed and relieved, though a certain amount of tension hung in the air. It was only after they had eaten a plate of the day's pasta special that she said, 'How's Sue?' It was a natural question, born of genuine interest. She had liked Sue on the few occasions they had met at Mulberry Street socials. She didn't feel guilty towards her: she saw her as a fellow victim.

'Great,' said Clark. 'She knew about us.'

'How?'

'Don't know.' He did know, of course, but he didn't want to go through all that: he hated even thinking of that ghastly story about how she spied on them by the river, and anyway he couldn't be bothered to recount it. There was no need for Dean to know.

'I'm sorry,' said Dean, and she meant it. Her own pain had made her more sensitive to other people's.

'It's going to be all right,' said Clark, and she could tell that he really believed it. She didn't mind: she yearned for normalisation. The suffering she had been through had burned out any hope of a reconciliation. She couldn't have gone through any more of the tension involved, anyway. The first few months of her affair with Clark had been wonderful – he hadn't been able to keep away from her, and that had made her feel great. She hadn't minded the subterfuge and the broken appointments, the sitting alone in bars coming to terms with the fact that he wasn't going to turn up, the fact that she couldn't introduce him to any of her friends; she hadn't minded because he had always come through. He had made everything all right by being so wonderful. But once the spell had been broken, she had minded everything, and she had been through a lot.

'How about you?' he asked. Well, he had to, didn't he?

'I'm going to be all right, too,' she said simply. 'It's been painful, more painful than I could have imagined, but . . . ' she wasn't going to cry – she just didn't know what to say. He leaned across the table and took her hand.

'I'm really sorry,' he said, feeling that the moment

had come to deliver his set piece. 'I was, well, I suppose I was just totally unpleasant. I wanted you to think for certain that it was over. I think I even thought it would be easier if you hated me.'

'It wasn't,' she laughed lightly. It was amazing to her that he could have got it that badly wrong.

'I know, and I'm sorry. Have you got another man?'

She smiled in disbelief, looked away and shook her head. If the most handsome man in the world had come riding out of the sunset in her direction over the past weeks she wouldn't have noticed him. 'Men!' she exclaimed, only partly in exasperation. 'We're not like you, you know!'

'No, I'd noticed!' he said, feeling on a high. This meeting had worked. He felt righteous. 'So it's nobody I know?' he said, trying to make her laugh some more, and succeeding.

At that moment a car on the opposite side of the road outside pulled out sharply and accelerated away down the street, screeching slightly. The driver was weeping. It was Sue.

After overhearing the phone call at the foot of the stairs that morning she had steeled herself. It was the only way – she had to know. She had driven to Benny's on her way to the hospital to see who it was that he had called, who it was that he wanted so badly to have lunch with in the middle of a busy day. She had suspected that it was Dean, and it shocked her, because she had really believed him when he had said that the affair was over. Sue had wondered if he had started another dirty little liaison already, but that voice on the phone, when Sue had hit the redial button, certainly sounded like Dean.

They had made it very easy for her – she didn't have to get out of the car, or do anything – all she had to do was look in at the window. She just parked opposite, and there they were. She had watched for a few minutes, and she had seen her husband take Dean's hand, and watched them laughing in the way lovers do. It was like a replay of what she had observed under the willow tree, only this time it was worse, as this time she knew it meant something final. The extent of his duplicity made her sick to the bottom of her stomach, and great waves of misery and fear swept over her as she confronted the enormity of what she had to do and began to feel that familiar maw of pain closing over her again.

She wanted to lie down in the car and die, but she had to start work in half an hour. She contemplated phoning in sick, but that wasn't like her, and she already had her uniform on. She was afraid that if she didn't marshal all her energies to face the ward that day, she would never be able to do it again, so she drove off to the hospital, her face taut with anxiety, half dead with hurt and anguish.

Sue and Tony had met at a dinner party given by mutual friends: Clark had been working at the time with the husband, and Sue had trained as a nurse with the wife. It had been a very good dinner, with large quantities of wine consumed by everyone. Three other guests were present. Sue was engaged to an airline pilot at the time, and he was away on a trip. She had been her usual sparkling self, and Clark had felt attracted to her right away. He had recently emerged from a two-year relationship with the fashion editor of a women's magazine. She had wanted him to commit, and he hadn't been able to; he couldn't say why. He loved her, but there had been a doubt in his mind that he couldn't dispel, and seeing as there seemed to be no way forward he had reluctantly ended the relationship.

He and Sue had taken a taxi home together: he was living in Stockwell then, and she in nearby Camberwell Green, so it was natural that they should share a cab.

He had considered asking her if he could go home with her, but he liked her rather too much to risk blowing a relationship with a one-night stand – he had made that mistake before. Better to build up to it. He had asked instead if she'd have dinner with him the following night. He knew she was engaged, of course: her fiancé had been spoken of several times during the course of the dinner party.

Sue had said she was busy the next night, and smiled at him. She could see that he was the kind of man who was used to getting what he wanted, and she found it amusing to brush him off. She was the monogamous type, and in the three years she had known Richard it hadn't occurred to her to cheat on him. But she did think Clark had a dangerously beguiling smile.

A refusal was like catnip to Clark, of course. He asked if she'd have dinner with him another night. She had hesitated: it was the fatal moment. He had ended up cajoling her number out of her, and when the taxi dropped her off he clocked her address.

The next morning he sent her flowers, and called that evening. She had agreed to dinner later in the week, thinking – in the conscious part of her mind, at least – that there wasn't any harm in a straightforward dinner; Richard was on a two-week trip, so she had to fill her time somehow. And then something happened to her during that first date. She began to fall in love with him.

Within two months she had broken off her engagement and they were living together. It had come as a great shock to both of them; he had been incapable of taking that decision with a woman he had been going out with for two years, and she had wanted to do nothing else but marry Richard. Starry-eyed, they had both reached the conclusion that that was what true love was all about.

They were married a year later, in a small church in

her parents' village of Wonersh in Surrey. It had been a great day. Clark's niece and nephew had been bridesmaid and page, and Sue's nurse friend, the one at whose house they had met, was her matron of honour. The reception – for a hundred and twenty – had taken place in a marquee in Sue's parents' garden, and it had run straight on into a party with a jazz band in the evening. There were masses of policemen there, of course, and they all got drunk, though it didn't stop them making a spectacular job of decorating Clark's car.

She had let him arrange the honeymoon as a secret from her, and they had gone to the Canaries and had a blissful time. Sue thought of all that, during the long afternoon at the ward after she had stopped outside Benny's. It scrolled through her head like a film. After a few hours it felt as if it wasn't her life at all: it was somebody else's, and she was standing outside, on a higher plain, observing.

Clark felt perky when he got back to the yard, revved up for the ID parade. He arrived outside the parade room as Naylor was talking to Neame. Colin Page, an inspector and a sergeant were waiting to go into the small room in which they would scrutinise a row of men on the other side of a glass wall. The potential suspects hadn't yet been taken in.

Clark walked up to the small group assembled in the corridor, and Neame looked at him with contempt. Page had a plastic cup of coffee in his hand. 'Mr Page, hello,' said Clark. Page nodded. He was nervous. He was caught between a desperate desire to identify someone, and a nagging doubt about whether he really could. He had replayed the scene in his head so many times that he felt he couldn't remember anything any more. He was not the kind of man who would happily have nailed an innocent victim and he knew in his heart that it wasn't going to make Billy better. Billy was still in a coma.

'Sir,' said Clark, turning brightly to the sour-faced Neame, 'thank you for your co-operation with this ID parade.'

'My pleasure,' said Neame blandly. Clark passed on to the sergeant.

'Thank you, sergeant. Shall we get this going?' He turned to Naylor. 'I have a good feeling about this.'

The sergeant opened a door and they all filed into the small room, standing up expectantly in front of the glass. 'Into the room, face the glass,' they heard the sergeant say, and when a door opened on the other side a row of TSG men marched in and stood in a line facing them, an uncomfortable Cameron among them. A light was switched on. They were wearing full riot gear. Their helmets were on, their visors were down, and their shields were up in front of them. Clark was gobsmacked. He had never before seen a parade take place in which everyone wore helmets. Not only that: to a man, they were breathing deeply through their mouths, so that their visors were immediately steamed up. It was totally impossible to see even the ghost of a facial feature.

Colin Page looked around him, confused: did they expect him to pick out one of these, then? Not only was he being asked to do the impossible, but he was also aware of tensions and undercurrents among the people on his side of the glass. He didn't understand what was going on. Why had they brought him here, if they knew it was going to be such a joke? Were they setting him up? That nice man whom Dan had duffed up looked cross. Why didn't he ask the riot policemen to take their helmets off, then?

Clark looked down the room to Neame, who turned to stare coldly and proudly in his direction before leaving the room. It was clear to Clark that this was

Neame's doing. He had agreed to the ID parade, all right, but he had instructed his men to put on full riot kit, and to breathe through their mouths and steam up the already small windows onto their faces. Neame was still fighting hard, and he was fighting to win.

'Well?' said the inspector to the bewildered Colin Page.

'I think that's quite enough, thank you,' interjected Clark, who felt an awkward sense of reponsibility towards Page. 'Parade terminated.'

'I'm awfully sorry, Mr page,' Clark said outside in the corridor. 'I quite appreciate that we've dragged you in here on a wild goose chase. Er, we'll . . . be in touch. I'm confident that we'll have something to tell you soon. Er, Inspector Naylor will show you out.'

Naylor shot his boss a deadly glance, and shepherded Page away.

Later in the afternoon Clark and Naylor were discussing strategy in Clark's office, Clark having first unloaded a few expletives about Neame. They couldn't decide whether they had enough evidence to question Cameron directly. Naylor was concerned about the racist innuendo.

'I think we should bring him in anyway,' said Clark, his feet up on his desk, doodling with one hand and loosening his tie with the other. He was always less cautious than Naylor on such matters.

'Just on the evidence of the TV film?' said Naylor.

'Why not?' asked Clark, though he knew perfectly well why not.

'Well,' said Naylor darkly, also with his feet up, but only resting on the edge of the desk, 'it looks like him, but I wouldn't say it was a hundred per cent. And it's touchy.' He was smoking.

'Because he's black?' said Clark.

'Yeah. And because of Neame.' He paused. 'He's

228

after you. Better not make a mistake. I wonder if his bloody-mindedness may not be provoking you to push too hard.' It was a shrewd observation. 'If you do, he'll have your balls.'

'You were in Special Branch with him, weren't you?' asked Clark. This was also a shrewd move. Clark wanted to know where Naylor's allegiance lay. Was he sticking up for Neame as an old colleague? Was there a residual loyalty lurking under Naylor's impassive exterior? How seriously should Clark take his inspector's apprehensions?

'Yes,' said Naylor.

'How was he?' said Clark, playing a straight bat.

'Solid. Rock solid,' said Naylor gravely. 'Dealt very straight and completely loyal to his men.'

'Yeah, I can see that,' said Clark.

'Guv?' said Naylor, who had been thinking fast. There was something on his mind, and it was time to unburden it. 'Between these four walls?'

'Yes.' Clark had felt there were things he didn't know in this complex little web of relationships, and he was very glad that Naylor had decided to let him in on them – or on some of them, at least. It was about time.

Naylor spoke very slowly and deliberately. 'I was a sergeant, he was the chief super and guess who was the super?'

Clark thought. Of course! 'Deakin!' Naylor nodded. The penny dropped. Old loyalties never died in the force, especially if they had been richly reciprocated. They lay dormant until they were called upon when serendipity brought people together again. That was why Deakin had come down so hard on Clark over his confrontational behaviour towards Neame, and also why Deakin had indulged Neame's obstructive attitude to the Bishopston inquiry. Deakin was loath to criticise Neame's fierce protection of his men, because he himself, had been at the receiving end of it for a number of years – and he had appreciated it, at the time.

'So it's not been that easy for either of us,' said Naylor, glad to have unburdened himself. 'It's what he would have done for us, you see. Probably did, once or twice.'

'I do see,' said Clark. 'Thanks, Harry.'

'What for?'

'I suppose I'd expect your loyalty to be with them – old soldiers, and all that. I'm grateful that you've been straight with me.'

'You're my guv'nor.' That came from the heart.

'Oh Harry, don't, I think I'm going to cry.'

'Would you like me to leave?' quipped Naylor.

'Yes,' said Clark, his mind switching back to the job, 'and come back with Cameron. We'll give it a try. Agreed?'

'You're the boss, thank Christ!' said Naylor as he left.

Clark chuckled as he picked up the remote control unit and rewound the film.

As Naylor drove away from the TSG headquarters, where Richardson and Hartwell had watched him taking Cameron off with him and clocked this ominous development, Sue was walking through a ward carrying a cup of tea. She stopped at the foot of a small bed where a pale two-year-old girl was asleep. The girl had just had chemotherapy, and the tea was for her father, who was also asleep, on a sun-lounger next to the bed. Sue put the tea on the floor directly next to his head, and walked back through the ward into the sister's office, where overworked nurses bustled around, ignorant of her distress.

She sat down at a table next to a VDU and began flipping through a file. Telephones were ringing. She tried to write up her notes, but she couldn't concentrate. She felt like a robot, and couldn't think of anything except what she had seen through that window. What should she do? When? She closed the file and picked up the telephone.

At the Yard, Clark and Connell were drinking coffee in Clark's office, waiting for Naylor to get back with Cameron in tow. Connell was standing up. Her hair was piled back and clipped in a loose bun. Clark took advantage of the rare lull. 'I saw Jenny today,' he said quietly, his hands out in front of him on his desk. 'I think it's going to be OK.'

'Good,' said Connell. She was pleased and flattered that he had listened to her.

'Thanks,' said Clark, very delicately, and shot Connell a little smile.

'I hear Chief Superintendent Deakin is after you for the Cope woman now?' said Connell.

'What!' exclaimed Clark. 'Who says?'

'I think I read something in the *Police Gazette*,' she said. Clark sighed heavily and raised both hands to his face, cupping them around his nose. He had just dealt with one bloody headache, was he going to have to face another immediately? It was all getting too much. After a pause Connell continued, 'I'm afraid the walls here have big ears and even bigger mouths.'

Naylor's head appeared round the door, cutting this painful (for Clark) conversation short. 'I've put him in the interview room, Guv,' he said, referring to the hapless Cameron.

'No, change of plan, Harry – I want him here,' said Clark, who had decided to run the film through to Cameron and so needed him in the office, next to the screen. Clark's telephone rang, and Naylor left. 'Could you get that in the other office, please, Maureen? If it's not urgent, I'm not here.' Connell hurried out, and as Clark tidied his desk in came Naylor alongside Cameron, who was carrying his hat in his hand and

231

looking terrified.

'Hello, Colin,' said Clark benignly, as if they were holding a coffee morning in his office. He got up and shook Cameron's hand. 'Can we get you a tea or something?'

'No thanks, Superintendent,' said Cameron.

'OK,' said Clark. 'Take a seat.' Cameron sat down next to him, looking at him nervously.

'I'm very grateful to you for agreeing to come in to talk informally to us. I think there's something here you'll be able to help us clear up.' He hit the play button, and as they waited for the video to begin Connell came back into the room and walked up behind Clark, whispering in his ear, 'It was your wife, sir. I told her you were tied up.'

'That was rather tactless of you,' he said quietly in reply, never too pressurised to make a joke. 'Am I to ring her back?' Connell nodded, refusing to acknowledge the joke. But Clark's mind was back on the job before he had even registered Connell's answer.

The film began to roll. Everyone was concentrating on it. Cameron was visibly disturbed, though he struggled to retain a rigid exterior as he was aware that he was being watched. On the screen three TSG men were advancing cautiously, their shields up. Suddenly one of them burst into flames, and Cameron heard that gut-wrenching scream again. His stomach turned over. A few moments later, when they saw a TSG man who was almost certainly Cameron kneeling at the foot of the perimeter fence, looking down at the already unconscious Billy Page, Clark used the remote control unit to freeze the frame. Then he sat in silence and looked at Cameron, who looked at the screen, and then at Clark.

After a pause Clark said, 'Well?' Cameron shrugged as if to say, well what? and looked back at the screen. 'If you don't wish to speak to me, if you want a solicitor or a Fed Rep, or if you deny that that is you, I will arrest you.' Cameron was silent. 'When I sent Inspector Naylor over to collect you that was what I had in mind to do anyway. However, while he was gone I watched the film again. I'll show you what I saw.' He wound it back, and spoke as he replayed it on slow speed. After a minute he stopped it again.

'When we watched it before we all saw you, and another as yet unidentified officer, beating the shit out of a defenceless and unaggressive man. A man who is still comatose and critically, possibly terminally, ill in hospital.' Cameron was externally unmoved. 'And then I saw this,' Clark continued, and hit the play button. 'I saw a youth running away. A TSG man using his baton once, twice . . . and then I see you. Not, as we all thought, joining in, but restraining . . . there! The unidentified man runs off. You lift the victim and . . . we have a witness to this, you call for help . . . ' The medic wearing the white crash helmet loomed into view. 'Here comes our witness, his name is Dave . . . and there you go. Getting on with your job or leaving the scene of the crime?' And he stopped the film.

'Make no bones about it, Colin, a serious, unpleasant and vicious crime, with appalling consequences for the victim and his family. Cameron was clearly uncomfortable, looking over towards Clark with eyes like a rabbit caught in the headlights, but he was still silent.

'I'll tell you what,' said Clark, as if he had just had an idea (in reality it was all part of a strategy he had planned in advance), 'I'll give you a few minutes to think about it on your own. You can watch the tape again, if you like. You know the man responsible, and I'd like you to tell us his name.' He handed the remote control unit to the wretched young man, and left the office. Naylor followed him.

'Tea or coffee?' asked Connell. Cameron shook his head, and Connell too left the room, leaving him to wrestle with his conscience.

The three of them stood in a corridor, drinking coffee and smoking. Clark and Naylor were looking pleased with themselves. They thought Cameron was going to crack. 'He didn't deny it was him,' said Clark, leaning against a doorframe.

'No. That was beautifully done, boss,' said Naylor sincerely.

'The problem now is whether he's going to spill the beans. He's probably protecting his friends – have we any idea who his friends are?'

'Only one of them. The guy in hospital with the burns.'

'There's your motive. We're getting closer. We're getting very close.'

Cameron sat alone, watching the incriminating piece of film again. It was clearly him, and everything was as Clark said. Not a trace of evidence on Hartwell. He froze the video again on the frame of himself crouching by Page, and he shivered. Well, if it was a choice between being arrested and grassing on Hartwell, he had to grass, didn't he? Being arrested was a concept he could not even entertain; he thought he would rather have killed himself. But when he contemplated giving Hartwell's name to the CIB it seemed to him to be an even more revolting prospect; indeed, it was one which actually made him feel nauseous. In the police culture ingested by the likes of Cameron, there seemed to be little meaning in anything if you broke the highest rule of all.

No, he couldn't do it. He tried to face up to the consequences, and a sea of faces came forward to greet him. His mum, who had a photograph of him in uniform on the television, and his grandmother, whom he visited at the nursing home every Sunday morning. The football team, about to get promoted to the first division of their small league. Jeanette, the WPC he had been dating for the past month. The people in his street who watched him walk to the train station each morning on his way to work. He supposed he'd be unemployed – if he wasn't in jail, that is – and he imagined himself in that Job Centre in the high street, scanning the noticeboards for jobs that didn't exist like that layabout Jonathan in their street. His head throbbed. Never in his wildest dreams had he envisaged this.

Fifteen minutes later Clark and Naylor went back into the office, and they found Cameron sitting exactly as before, looking morose. Naylor had his jacket on, Clark was in shirt-sleeves. 'Well, Colin,' said Clark straight away from the doorway. 'Are you going to talk to us?'

'I'm afraid not, sir,' he said. It was a blow.

'Fair enough,' said Clark confidently, walking round to his desk and picking up his jacket from the back of his chair. 'Where d'you live?'

'Where do I live?' said Cameron, taken aback by the question.

Clark nodded.

'Greenwich.'

'I'll give you a lift home,' said Clark affably. 'You two tidy up and we'll meet here tomorrow morning. Goodnight.' He and Cameron went out. Naylor and Connell were left standing in the office looking at each other, and before they could speak the telephone rang. Connell picked it up.

'Oh, hello Mrs Clark . . . No, I'm afraid not. He's just left. He's on his way home.' She looked up at the clock. It was ten-thirty. 'Goodnight.'

Sue put the phone down. She was about to go home herself, but unlike her husband, she wasn't planning on remaining there long. She wanted to talk to him to tell him to stay away until she had packed and left. Or maybe she just wanted to tell him that she knew. Or maybe she simply wanted to hear his voice. She wasn't sure of her motive. She wasn't sure of anything. Why hadn't he bloody well called her back?

Clark strolled down the corridor, one hand in his pocket and the other swinging his briefcase. Cameron followed, his cap still in his hand. They waited for the lift in silence, but when they were in it and travelling down to the ground floor Clark spoke up. 'I understand your loyalty. It's drummed into all of us. The job wouldn't function without it. But this is different. Playground loyalty has no place when a dangerous and indisciplined fool is involved. The man's a liability.'

Cameron nodded, his head leaning back against the carpeted wall of the lift. It was an almost imperceptible nod, as if he were nodding to himself. Clark sighed and handed him a cigarette, which he took. 'Make no mistake, Colin,' Clark ploughed on, lighting both their cigarettes with a gold lighter, 'we'll go the distance. If you withold evidence it'll cost you your job.' He paused meaningfully. 'Is he really worth it?' Clark felt reasonably confident that Cameron was going to crack. He had made up his mind to keep going for as long as it took. After what Connell had told him about Deakin being on to him, virtually publicly, about the Cope affair, it was imperative for him personally to get a result on this case. Not just because of the Cope factor, either, of course. There was Neame, too.

'Can I speak to you off the record, sir?' said Cameron as the lift doors opened on the ground floor.

'Yes,' said Clark, hope rising like sap. They remained in the lift. Cameron began.

'It'll cost me my job either way. No one rats on a mate. It's been a long slow climb for me in the Met. It has been for all black coppers – you must know that.

236

We're thick, all our brothers sell dope, we're all screwing every WPC we can get our hands on, and now? We grass on our mates. Can't do it, boss, just can't do it.' His head was still pressed back against the wall.

Clark nodded and thought fast as he led the way through to the car park. Cameron's heartfelt words hadn't changed anything. Clark realised that he had to show him the limitations of the loyalty that the police force had inculcated into him. Talking to him wasn't going to do the trick, that was clear. He had to pull in something concrete now.

'Mind if we stop somewhere on the way?' he asked Cameron as they got into the Sierra.

As he slammed the door he thought, damn, I didn't call Sue. She didn't even know he was going to be late home. What had he said this morning? That he wouldn't be late. He felt mildly irritated – not at himself, but at the difficult situation his work had got him into. Now that he'd started with Cameron, he had to see it right through, and if he didn't hurry, he wouldn't be able to execute his newly formed plan. He pushed Sue out of his mind. He could deal with her tomorrow.

It wasn't going to be quite as easy as he envisaged. An hour later Sue was standing by the window of their bedroom, fully dressed. The curtains were open and the room was lit only by the streetlights. Scrutinising a telephone number she had written on a piece of paper, she walked over to the phone and dialled the number.

'Hello?' said Jenny Dean, who was lying face down on her bed, wearing a dressing-gown and reading a novel, a glass of white wine on the bedside table. It hadn't been difficult for Sue to find her number. She had looked it up in the phone book – she could remember Dean herself telling her where she lived when they met once. She had just moved into a new flat at the time – the first one she had owned herself –

and had recounted her grisly experiences on the move day to Sue.

Sue stood up next to the neatly packed suitcase on the bed, its lid open. 'It's Sue Clark,' she said, her voice tense. 'Tony's wife. I know he's with you and I don't want to speak to —'

'Mrs Clark!' said Dean, jerking upright on the bed, amazed at what she was hearing. 'He isn't —'

'It really doesn't matter what you say,' continued Sue, barely registering her own words, her hand on her forehead. 'I'm sick of all of you. You think you're the centre of the bloody universe but you're just a bunch of immature, self-centred, insensitive, irresponsible egotists. Just tell him that when he gets home, I'll be gone.'

She slammed the handset down and sat on the bed, and then she started to cry. In her own flat about five miles to the north, on the other side of the river, Dean sat on her bed, transfixed by this new development. She thought very hard, and then she decided what to do.

Clark had taken Cameron to St Mary's. It was way past visiting time, of course – it was half-past eleven by that stage – but Clark presented his ID to the nurse on duty at the desk at the end of the corridor. 'Billy Page,' said Clark softly. 'Can you tell me where he is?'

'Through there,' indicated the nurse, and the pair of them walked along to the door of Billy Page's room. The hospital was very different at night. It was quiet, and dimly lit, with muffled noises emanating from corners and nurses' footsteps echoing like in a museum after closing time. It was warm, and safe – there was something uterine about it. Cameron and Clark felt like the intruders that they were.

'Take a look,' said Clark, indicating that Cameron should move close to the window in the door. Cameron

238

saw that pale, unblemished face, the closed eyes, and he saw the ventilator, up and down, up and down, and the tube, and the green nozzle, and the band around the face, and all those bottles and switches. He heard the sinister bleeping.

'Hasn't woken up since you crouched down next to him at the foot of the fence,' said Clark. 'Come on.' And he hustled Cameron further along the corridor, until they reached the swing doors near Dunn. Clark knew where they were, because he had visited Dunn himself. They went through, and Cameron went up and stood next to his friend.

'Dunny!' Dunn couldn't have been sleeping very soundly, if at all, as almost immediately he opened his slit eyes and looked up.

'Hello, Colin,' he said. He didn't seem at all surprised to see him there at that time of night. He had only a very dim awareness of the passage of time. There wasn't much that would have surprised Dunn during that period. He was still in deep shock. Being engulfed in flames is one of the most profound physical traumas a human being can experience, and when the damage is deliberately incurred by another person, the psychological implications are devastating.

'Hello, Dunny,' said Cameron. 'This is Superintendent Clark of the CIB.' Clark lingered by the door.

'Hello, sir,' said Dunn, his weak voice indicating concern and bewilderment.

'Hello,' said Clark gently. 'I think you two should have a little chat. I'm going to make a phone call. And he left through the swing doors.

Dunn shut his eyes. It hurt him to keep them open for long. 'What's the story, Col?' he mumbled. Colin drew up a chair and ran his hands through his hair. He leaned over and spoke into his friend's ear. 'It's a heavy number, Dunny. They've got the video film of what went down at Bishopston.' There was a silence.

'Dunny, I'm not sure if you can cope with this, but I want to tell you something. That geezer that Ian did for you – it was the wrong man. I'm sure of it. Ian just went for the first poor bastard he could lay his hands on. You know what he's like.' Cameron looked at his friend's blistered, disfigured face. He'd be hideously scarred for life, that was for sure. Colin saw years ahead, visiting his mate in this hospital as he underwent skin graft after skin graft.

'Can he be identified on the video?' Dunn asked. Cameron was glad to see that Dunn was able to follow what he was telling him and realise the implications. At least they were going to be able to talk it through.

'No. They can identify me, but they can see that it wasn't me who clocked the poor fucker. Now they want me to spill it, and grass on Ian. I've said I won't, of course.' Another silence passed between them, this time more heavily loaded. 'I'll lose my job, of course, Graham, for not speaking up. But it's not that that worries me. I just can't understand why Ian did that. Even if he was sure he had the right bloke, why didn't he nick him? He's a vicious bastard, Graham; I know I shouldn't say it about a mate, but I can't help it. The lad he got that night is still in a coma – probably'll never wake up again. I've whopped enough around the head in my time, just like you have. There can't be many coppers who can put their hands on their heart and say they haven't. But that? The man's a liability.

'I've always known that he went a bit beyond the limit, but I suppose I've pushed it out of my mind – didn't want to recognise something that didn't fit in with our nice little system. And he's been loyal to us – it was loyalty that made him beat the shit out of that poor innocent at Bishopston. Do you remember that afternoon we were down at St George's football ground after the local derby, and we chased those drunk supporters down that alley? Don't you

240.

remember, Dunny, that look in his eyes as he was laying the boot in? He's a liability – a man like him shouldn't be in the force. He's exactly the kind of dude who gets us a bad name.'

Cameron wiped the back of his neck with his handkerchief. He was beginning to see things more clearly. But he felt he needed Dunn's sanction before he could grass on Ian Hartwell. After all, the physical suffering was Dunn's and he must have been feeling the need for revenge, any revenge, even if it happened to be against the wrong person; it was presumably an important part of the healing process. It would be a harsh moral judgement to say that it was a lack of moral fibre which made Cameron need Dunn's support before he could proceed.

Dunn was thinking. His mind had sharpened, now that it had something to grip on, and he was very touched by his friend's moral ordeal. He, Dunn, knew very well what Cameron was going to go through if he grassed on Ian. But there was no doubt in Dunn's mind. He knew what Hartwell was capable of, and he didn't like it. He extended one big boxing glove towards Cameron, feeling for his arm. Cameron moved his hand towards him, and when the bandages were touching the clenched hand, Dunn opened his red eyes and looked across at Cameron.

'We've got to do it, mate. We'll do it together. This is the big one. I'm with you.' And he made a feeble little punch in the air. Cameron lowered his head and rested it on the bedclothes, and all he felt, for one long moment, was a wonderful sensation of relief, as if the burden of days had been lifted from him.

241

21

Clark really did have a call to make, though it wasn't to Sue. She would be asleep, and anyway, he wasn't thinking about her. No, it was Molly Cope who was on his mind. But he wasn't thinking what he'd like to be doing to her on a deep-pile carpet in front of a raging fire, as he often had before. He was thinking that she had punched too far below the belt by using that story about the Bishopston inquiry running into trouble and the TSG video being spiked by a kid's programme. It had turned him against her – terminally so, and he wanted to vent his spleen and make himself clear.

She was lying on the sofa at Sabine's when he called, reading a book. The lights were dim, except for an anglepoise trained on her book, and she had put her favourite Mozart sonata on the CD player. Cope was feeling pleased with herself. She had just put a deposit on a flat, and was moving in the following week, the day before Sabine got back. The flat was perfect: a large studio in Elephant and Castle, south of the river (but only just), and it was conveniently situated for work and most other things. The rent was reasonable, and Molly had made a list of what she was going to buy for it and how she was going to arrange it, and she had worked out when she was going to move the rest of her things down from Liverpool. She was halfway through a book about labour relations in the seventies, as the news editor had asked her to prepare a general background piece on Bishopston. Work was going exceptionally well. She had got a story in almost every day since she started, and they had all gone down a storm – even the editor had sent her a note congratulating her on a 'dynamic debut'. Yes, life was looking good.

She had positioned the phone at her side in case anyone rang – well, in case he rang, actually. She was thinking about him when it did ring. 'Hello?' she answered.

'Hello,' he said curtly. 'It's me. I don't want to talk for long, I just wanted to tell you that what you did today could have cost me my job and —'

She wasn't too worried about the serious tone of his voice. 'I'm sorry Tony,' she said, thrilling just to hear him speak. 'I just thought —'

'Don't talk, just listen,' he snapped. 'My job is more important to me than anything except Sue. So I won't be seeing you again.'

'I see,' she said, feeling as if she had been hit over the head with a hot, wet towel.

'Is that all you're going to say?' he said, wanting at the very least to hear her apologies.

'You told me to shut up and listen, and you know me,' she said obliquely, scrambling around to think of a suitably caustic retort and not succeeding.

'I'm not sure I do,' he said honestly.

'And I'm not sure I know you,' she let fly. 'I thought you had more balls. You know we belong. You should dump your corrupt little job and your empty sham of a marriage and live.'

'Thanks for the advice,' he said, stung, even though he didn't care about her and knew she was talking from a position of humiliation. 'I have to go now.'

'Why, can't you take it?'

'No, it's not that, I'm . . . I haven't got any change.'

243

The line went dead. It seemed appropriate that their relationship should end on such a farcical note. There had been something farcical about it from the beginning. 'Goodbye,' said Clark into the empty corridor. Bitch, he thought.

She held the receiver to her ear for a few seconds, listening to the dialling tone. She couldn't believe it; no, she couldn't. She got up nervously and paced about, running her fingers through her hair. How could he be denying that feeling between them? Cope had never felt anything that powerful before, in any area of her life, and she couldn't understand that anyone could throw it away. It was a common mistake: she felt love, he felt lust, and she had transferred her own emotions onto him. She had projected her own emotional make-up onto a married man – a happily married man, in his own terms. There was only ever one person of the two of them who was going to lose out, and that was Molly Cope. But she hadn't seen it. She might have been one hell of a reporter, but she couldn't see the disaster heading towards her until she was mown down by it.

Now for the next ordeal, thought Clark as he walked back to Dunn's ward. What exactly was he going to do if Cameron was still insisting on keeping his mouth shut? To his discomfiture, he realised that he didn't know. He pushed open the swing doors and looked at the pair of them.

'Well?' There was a silence. Clark thought, this isn't going to work.

'We'll co-operate,' said Dunn.

'Thank you. Thank you very much.' He closed his eyes momentarily. He had done it.

'I'll get a cab home, Superintendent,' said Cameron. He needed to absorb a bit more reassurance before he left Dunn, and he didn't particularly want another interrogation by Clark as they drove to Greenwich. He had made his decision, but he needed some time to prepare himself for the nightmare which was to follow.

Clark was pleased, as it was late enough already, and he couldn't be sure Sue was asleep. 'OK, Colin, if you're sure. Goodnight lads,' and he left.

He loosened his tie as he drove home. Shit, was he looking forward to springing this one on Neame. Signed testimonies by two of his own men that a third had done Page! Neame's career would never recover. Deakin would regret setting so much store by old loyalties, and Clark felt sure that in future he'd trust his own instincts more. Naylor and Connell would be impressed, and the team would be strengthened. And Huxtable? Huxtable would feel vidicated for leaving Clark on the case despite the stiff opposition, and he would remember that Clark had come through when the heat was on. Yes, it was a great triumph, and as Clark swung the Sierra into his quiet street in south Clapham he decided to wake Sue up and tell her. He needed to share his elation, and he knew she'd be thrilled for him. It was a doubly good day because he felt as if he had finally sorted out his women troubles, too. He had got rid of Cope once and for all, and he was sure that he'd never see her again. She had too much pride to come crawling. And he was happy about the way the Jenny drama had resolved itself; he could look her in the eye, if they met at police functions, and he didn't think she was going to go round slagging him off or causing trouble now that he had staged his little contrition number.

Besides, he reflected, if he did wake Sue up to tell her about the bust he was poised to make, it also meant that in the atmosphere of celebration his lateness would be forgotten. They could go out for a special dinner the next night to celebrate: he would suggest it.

Now, where would she like to go?

He was pondering this weighty matter when he pulled into their drive. He didn't notice a car parked on the opposite side of the road with a young woman at the wheel. It was Dean. She had decided to be there when he discovered Sue had left him. It seemed like the right thing to do. Sue had involved her, hadn't she, by calling her? Driving to south Clapham wasn't a conscious move by Dean to ingratiate herself with Tony, and her heart hadn't leaped for joy when Sue had announced that she was leaving him. But she felt that her life was intertwined with Clark's now for better or worse, and it seemed natural that she should be there for him. You don't stop loving someone just because the relationship doesn't work out.

She watched him walk up the path, unlock the door and go inside. She saw the hall light being switched on, and she heard him calling 'Sue?' and then, more urgently, 'Sue!' and then she got out of the car and walked to the bottom of his small front garden. Clark flew out of the house, in his desperation calling his wife's name in the empty street. He looked around, as if he might see her standing there, under a tree or next to a lamp-post. His mind was in such turmoil that he wasn't surprised to see Dean there, wearing the same red coat that she had been carrying over her arm that night when he discovered her at the bottom of the stairs at the Shaftesbury. His mind emptied of everything except one single yell of pain: his wife had left him.

'She's gone,' he said to Dean in a dull voice.

'I know,' she said, and she put her arm around him, for comfort.

BETWEEN THE LINES

THE CHILL FACTOR

Tom McGregor

Nobody's above the law. And even in the police force, nobody's above suspicion . . .

A policeman's lot is not a happy one – especially if you're Detective Superintendent Tony Clark. Tough, dynamic and highly professional, he's also pretty unpopular. For like all his colleagues, he's there to tackle criminals. But unlike them, his targets are criminals who have another, highly respectable job. They're policemen . . .

With his deputy Harry Naylor and Sergeant Maureen Connell, Clark is used to corruption in high places. But this time the stakes are higher. Much higher. For suddenly an ongoing case, a catastrophe in his already complex personal life, a prostitute, a murder and a blackmailing porn-merchant become linked by one thread. And at the end of that thread is one of the most powerful men in the police force. A man who has covered his tracks so well that he reckons he's untouchable. Fireproof. Invincible. But he's reckoned without Tony Clark . . .

THE LAST DETECTIVE

Peter Lovesey

Detective Superintendent Peter Diamond is the last
detective: 'not some lad out of police school with a degree
in computer studies' but a genuine gumshoe, given to
doorstopping and deduction. So when the naked body of
a woman is found floating in the weeds in a lake near
Bath with no-one willing to identify her, no marks and no
murder weapon, his sleuthing abilities are tested to the
limit.

Struggling with a jigsaw of truant choirboys, teddy bears,
a black Mercedes and Jane Austen memorabilia, he
alienates his superiors, forensic scientists – and many of his
suspects. He even persists when 'the men in white coats'
decide they have enough evidence to make a conviction.
It's just as well: for despite disastrous personal
consequences, and by following the real clues hidden
amongst Bath's historic buildings and intertwined with its
literary past, the last detective exposes the uncomfortable
truth . . .

'Admirably unpredictable (Lovesey keeps you guessing
until the very end) and entertaining all the way – Philip
Oakes, *Literary Review*

'Lively . . . Articulate' – *Sunday Times*

☐	Between the Lines: The Chill Factor	Tom McGregor	£4.50
☐	The Last Detective	Peter Lovesey	£4.99
☐	Breach of Promise	Roy Hart	£3.99
☐	Orchestrated Death	Cynthia Harrod-Eagles	£4.50

Warner Books now offers an exciting range of quality titles by both established and new authors. All of the books in this series are available from:

Little, Brown and Company (UK) Limited,
P.O. Box 11,
Falmouth,
Cornwall TR10 9EN.

Alternatively you may fax your order to the above address. Fax No. 0326 376423.

Payments can be made as follows: cheque, postal order (payable to Little, Brown and Company) or by credit cards, Visa/Access. Do not send cash or currency. UK customers and B.F.P.O. please allow £1.00 for postage and packing for the first book, plus 50p for the second book, plus 30p for each additional book up to a maximum charge of £3.00 (7 books plus).

Overseas customers including Ireland, please allow £2.00 for the first book plus £1.00 for the second book, plus 50p for each additional book.

NAME (Block Letters) ....

....

ADDRESS ....

....

....

☐ I enclose my remittance for _____

☐ I wish to pay by Access/Visa Card

Number ⬚⬚⬚⬚⬚⬚⬚⬚⬚⬚⬚⬚⬚⬚⬚⬚

Card Expiry Date ⬚⬚⬚⬚